Bello:

hidden talent rediscovered

Bello is a digital-only imprint of Pan Macmillan,
established to breathe new life into previously published,
classic books.

At Bello we believe in the timeless power of the imagination,
of a good story, narrative and entertainment, and we want to
use digital technology to ensure that many more readers
can enjoy these books into the future.

We publish in ebook and print-on-demand formats
to bring these wonderful books to new audiences.

www.panmacmillan.co.uk/bello

Richmal Crompton

Richmal Crompton (1890–1969) is best known for her thirty-eight books featuring William Brown, which were published between 1922 and 1970. Born in Lancashire, Crompton won a scholarship to Royal Holloway in London, where she trained as a schoolteacher, graduating in 1914, before turning to writing full-time. Alongside the *William* novels, Crompton wrote forty-one novels for adults, as well as nine collections of short stories.

Richmal Crompton

THE HOLIDAY

First published 1933 by Macmillan

This edition published 2015 by Bello
an imprint of Pan Macmillan
20 New Wharf Road, London N1 9RR
Basingstoke and Oxford
Associated companies throughout the world

www.panmacmillan.co.uk/bello

ISBN 978-1-5098-1012-3 EPUB
ISBN 978-1-5098-1010-9 HB
ISBN 978-1-5098-1011-6 PB

A CIP catalogue record for this book is available from the British Library.

Typeset by Ellipsis Digital Limited, Glasgow

Visit **www.panmacmillan.com** to read more about all our books
and to buy them. You will also find features, author interviews and
news of any author events, and you can sign up for e-newsletters
so that you're always first to hear about our new releases.

Chapter One

THE grandfather clock in the hall gave a preparatory wheeze, then struck one.

Rachel sat up in bed and listened. She had never been awake at one o'clock in the morning before, and the thought of it made her feel proud and important and yet somehow guilty.

Mother and father had come up some time ago. She had heard their footsteps on the stairs, then their voices in the next room. . . . Once they had both laughed, but stopped abruptly, as if mother had said, "Hush! We mustn't wake the children."

Their voices had become lower, sleepier, and finally died away altogether, leaving Rachel with an odd sensation of loneliness and fear. The house, abandoned to silence and darkness, seemed suddenly to have become strange and hostile. She saw the darkness as a tall man with black trailing draperies, creeping through the rooms trying to find someone still awake. . . .

The stairs creaked sharply, and she burrowed her head under the bedclothes in a sudden access of terror. When she looked out the room was full of moonlight. It was as if she had been rescued from an ogre's clutches by a prince in shining armour.

The stairs creaked again as the darkness crept down them, conquered. All her fear had vanished now. She slipped out of bed very quietly and, going over to the window, held aside the blind to look at the moon. Its wistful, anxious face peered down at her. He wasn't a prince in shining armour, after all. He was, as he had always been, an unhappy, lonely little old man. The familiar wave of pity and compunction swept over her.

"Don't be so unhappy," she whispered. "I'll think of you. . . . I'll be your friend."

His face seemed to flicker into a grateful smile, then a cloud swept over it, and the room was plunged again into darkness, but it was a friendly darkness now. The black man lurked downstairs, not daring to come up to the room from which he had been driven.

Rachel turned away from the window and stopped for a moment by Thea's bed. She could just see the dark, tumbled curls on the pillow and the outline of one smooth rosy cheek. She went to her own bed and sat on it, her arms clasped round her knees, thinking of Thea, pretending that she was Thea. Rachel loved Thea so much that it was impossible for her to feel jealous, but sometimes she liked to shut her eyes and pretend that she was Thea and not herself. She shut her eyes now and saw herself with dark curls and a rosy, dimpled face, sitting at the piano and moving her fingers firmly and lightly over the keys. Everyone said how extraordinarily well Thea played the piano considering that she was only thirteen. Thirteen. . . . It was for that, after all, that Rachel envied her most. To have an age for the first time in the family. . . . By the time thirteen reached Rachel—eighteen months later—it would be spoilt and familiarised by Thea's long use of it, like the frocks that came down to Rachel when Thea had outgrown them. Then it had to descend to Susan, and after that to Jane.

The calendar on the mantelpiece looked like a dim white square. Rachel could just see the figures of the year 1901 and the large red circle that Thea had drawn round to-morrow, Wednesday July 31st—the day the Holiday began. That, of course, was why she could not sleep—because she was so excited about the Holiday. They were to set off directly after breakfast. Over the back of the chair by her bed hung the new sailor suit—blue drill with a white stripe—that had been made specially for the Holiday and that she had never yet worn except for the trying-on. All last week mother and Nurse had been busy making the sailor suits. They had made one for each of them—even for five-year-old Peter, though Nurse often said that she'd rather make a dozen skirts than a pair of knickers. For once Rachel was to have a new dress all to herself, not one that Thea had outgrown.

Suddenly the clock struck two, and again that sense of mingled guilt and pride swept over her. Everyone in the whole world was asleep by now—except, of course, the robbers and policemen. . . .

Again her thoughts went to the Holiday. It was to be a different place this year—a place that they had never been to before. A locum, of course, because they always went to a locum. A vicarage right in the country, with a large garden. . . . Their own home was a vicarage, too, but it wasn't in the country. It was just outside Manchester, hemmed in by little shops and houses, overshadowed by towering mills. Rachel rather liked the mill chimneys, they stood so tall and straight and waved their plumes of smoke in the air with such gallant light-heartedness, but mother and Nurse and all sensible grown-up people hated them. "You can't keep a curtain clean from week's end to week's end," they said.

And it was the mill chimneys, too, that made it impossible to grow any flowers in the small, shut-in vicarage garden. Only stunted grass and sooty laurel bushes would grow there. The chimneys poisoned the air, people said, but Rachel felt that they didn't know that they were poisoning the air. They were so busy making patterns in the sky with their feathery tails of smoke that they had no time to look down and see what was happening to the gardens and window curtains so far beneath them.

And to-morrow the Holiday would begin. No—Rachel sat up with a little tremor of delight at the thought—to-day. It was to-day already. But there was a long time before one could get up. Five hours at least. Five hours—she did a quick sum in her head—three hundred minutes. Her delight faded, and suddenly the thought of the long night began to oppress her as if it were something horrible, unbearable, like the Eternity of which one never dared to think. "For ever and ever. Amen. . . ." She wouldn't think of it. She'd try to go to sleep. She lay down and closed her eyes, screwing up her face tightly with the intensity of her effort. . . . Strange pictures began to flicker to and fro inside her eyelids.

A ring of women danced round hand in hand on the grass. . . .

A man ran out with a dagger and killed one. ... She fell down, and the others went on dancing round and round. ... He ran out with a dagger and killed another. ... There was always the same number of women dancing round, and, though the man kept running out to kill one each time, yet they never lay on the grass for more than a second. They didn't ever jump up—they just disappeared. ...

Suddenly Thea awoke with a little gasping cry and sat up in bed.

"Rachel!"

"Yes?"

"I've had a horrid dream. I'm so frightened. Come into bed with me."

Rachel slipped from her bed and got in beside Thea, putting her arms around her and holding her tightly.

"It's all right," she said. "It's all right, Thea. Don't be frightened."

"I was falling through water," said Thea, "on and on and on ..."

"Never mind," Rachel comforted her again. "It's all right now."

Thea's plump, solid little body was still trembling slightly.

"It doesn't sound anything, but it's *horrible*—falling on and on and on through water. ... Tell me a story, Rachel, to stop me thinking about it."

"What sort of a story?"

"Anything. ..."

Thea often had bad dreams, and always when she awoke from them she roused Rachel, so that Rachel could come into her bed and tell her a story to take her mind from the lingering horror that they left in their train. Rachel felt a warm thrill of pride in the fact that Thea, so self-sufficient and independent in the day-time, needed her and depended on her at these times.

"Would you like one about the Civil Wars?"

The period of the Civil Wars was their favourite historical period. Both, of course, were ardent Royalists, and Rachel had invented a group of characters round whom she wove innumerable adventures, occasionally introducing King Charles or Cromwell in person, always as hero and villain respectively. She had various other stock characters, too, whose histories she could continue whenever demand was made for them—a knight whose brother had stolen his castle from him, a girl kidnapped by gipsies, a princess who had been put under a spell by a witch.

The last one was Rachel's favourite, but Thea disliked fairy tales, and so Rachel, who tried in everything to model herself on Thea, made great efforts to overcome her secret affection for them.

"It was a hateful dream, Rachel."

Already the tremor of fear was fading from Thea's voice and was being replaced by a faint note of superiority. "You've no idea what it's like because you never have bad dreams. ... Yes, tell me one about the Civil Wars."

Rachel began her story and grew herself so much interested in it that she felt almost regretful when Thea's deep, regular breathing told her that she was asleep. She wondered whether to stay in Thea's bed or to go back to her own, but while she was wondering she too fell asleep.

When she awoke in the morning all was bustle and commotion. Nurse was washing Peter and Jane in the bathroom. Susan had already washed, and mother was calling to Thea and Rachel to get up quickly as the bathroom was now empty. The neighbouring church bell was sending out its wistful, urgent notes. ... "Come ... *do* come ... *please* come ..." Then it stopped abruptly as if in sudden despair, and the grandfather clock downstairs in the hall struck seven in its ordinary daytime voice. Father, of course, would be taking the service in church, perhaps with only one or two, other people, because it was so hard to get people to come to week-day services. Once there had only been a robin there. It had perched on the choir stalls quite near father and had trilled and sung all through the service. Father had been very much pleased about that. ... While Rachel was sitting on her bed thinking about the robin, mother came in. Her fair hair was massed in neat coils at the back of her head. Her brown serge skirt just touched the floor all round and was trimmed by rows of brown braid reaching almost to the knees. Her white blouse had a soft double frill that fell from the high collar, secured by a cameo brooch, to her trim waist. A gold chain held the watch that was tucked away out of sight behind the leather belt.

"*Do* hurry up, Rachel," she said. "We shall never catch the train if you're going to dawdle about like this."

There was a faint edge of irritation in her voice, and Rachel remembered that, however much everyone had been looking forward to the Holiday, they were always rather cross on the actual morning of setting out for it. Nurse, of course, was never cross, but then she was never jolly either. Not like Elsie, who had looked after them before Nurse came and who had been always jolly and exciting.

Mother gave a quick, unsmiling glance round the room and went out. Rachel drew on one long black stocking and began to look for the other. Suddenly Thea threw it across to her.

"I *wish* you'd keep your things in your own part of the room," she said severely.

Thea was scrupulously tidy, and Rachel's untidiness in the bedroom always annoyed her. Rachel's thoughts had gone back to the story she had been telling Thea last night, and she sat, holding the stocking in her hand, staring dreamily into space.

"It was Sir Rupert's uncle who'd told him about the secret passage, Thea," she said. "I forgot to tell you that."

"Oh, *that* old tale!" said Thea impatiently. "I'd forgotten all about it. . . .

"I'm going to wash now," she went on, snatching up her towel, "so you'll have to wait till I've finished."

Rachel roused herself again from her dreams. A completely new and thrilling story about Sir Rupert had suggested itself to her, but she resolutely thrust it aside and began to put on her stays and fasten the tape suspenders to her stockings. She was fumbling with the buttonholes of her knickers when Thea reappeared.

"You're going to be the last," said Thea in an aloof, superior voice. Thea was always especially aloof and superior on the mornings after she had had a bad dream and had awakened Rachel for comfort in the night. It was as if she didn't want Rachel to consider herself too important.

Rachel washed, undid her plaits, and began to brush out her

hair. Thea's hair had a natural curl, but Rachel's was, as Nurse always said, "straight as paper." On ordinary nights it was plaited in two tight plaits and sometimes damped. For special occasions it was rolled up in curling rags that formed tight, hard little knobs all round her head and made sleep difficult if not impossible. When loosened from its plaits and brushed out, it hung in tight, uneven ridges down her back. She took a handful of hair from the front on both sides, brushed them together, and tied them securely on to the top of her head with her black hair-ribbon, carefully smoothing out the bows. She rather wished that there had been a new hair-ribbon to go with the new sailor suit. This one was fraying in the middle, as hair-ribbons so quickly did. She slipped the skirt over her head and buttoned up its petticoat bodice behind. She couldn't reach the middle button from either the top or the bottom, so she left it unbuttoned. One generally had to leave the middle button unbuttoned when things did up behind. Next the tapes of the front, with its embroidered anchor, had to be tied round her chest under her arms. Then came the collar whose tapes had to be tied in the same way. Then the blouse, then the black tie. There ought, of course, to have been a whistle on a cord to go into the pocket. Rachel regretted the absence of the whistle, though she felt that it was childish of her to want one. She was ready now all but her boots. The sailor suit really was rather thrilling in spite of the missing whistle. She stood in the middle of the hearth-rug and pretended that she was a real sailor shipwrecked on a raft. She shaded her eyes, looking round the horizon for a sail. . . .

The door opened, and mother came in again.

"Do hurry, darling. Everyone else is dressed. I wish you wouldn't dawdle like this. Put on your boots, then bring me your night things."

She spoke kindly, but there was a tense little frown between her eyes as if she were saying to herself: "It's terribly annoying, but I mustn't let myself get cross."

Feeling very much abashed, Rachel put on her boots and began to button them up. It was always worse when people tried not to be cross than when they really were cross.

Then she went to the night nursery, where mother and Nurse were finishing the packing. Susan was asking mother to pack Lena, the old rag doll that she had had since she was a baby. Susan was six, and Thea said that it was time she stopped playing with dolls, but Susan said she was never going to stop playing with them.

"Oh, *darling*," said mother, still frowning and trying hard to be patient. "I said only four dolls, and you brought me four dolls to pack yesterday. You said you were going to leave Lena behind."

"Yes, but she doesn't *want* to be left behind," said Susan breathlessly. "I had a sort of feeling in the night as if she was trying to tell me that she wanted to come."

Her small face was pale and anxious, her lips unsteady. It was clear that the whole holiday would be spoilt for Susan if Lena didn't come.

"Oh, well," said mother, relenting, "but you must carry her. There isn't an *inch* more room in the box."

Susan drew a deep sigh of relief and hugged Lena to her with a fiercely protective gesture.

Then Peter and Jane wanted to peep at their toy boxes to make sure that they were still at the bottom of the trunk where Nurse had packed them yesterday. Mother had given each of them a cardboard box and said that they could take any toys that would go into them. Peter had filled his with tin soldiers, cannons, a box of coloured chalks, and a small toy monkey most of whose stuffing had come out; Jane with a collection of her "treasures"—ribbons from chocolate boxes and a queer assortment of odds and ends from her doll's house. Peter had not packed his most precious possession, a small, battered cloth owl, called Owly. Instead he had put him into his pocket with his head sticking out so that he could see all that happened during the journey. He wore a luggage label round his neck that Peter had begged from mother, and Rachel had written his name, "Owly Cotteril," in large letters. Having seen that his toy box was still at the bottom of the trunk, Peter suddenly became excited and demanded to take the goldfish, Napoleon, with him.

"I'll carry it carefully," he shouted, "I won't spill it."

"Nonsense, Peter," said mother, "of course you can't take the goldfish."

For a moment it looked as if Peter were going to fly into one of his tempers, tempers in which he would scream till he was black in the face. Jane watched him anxiously. She adored Peter, and suffered far more than he did when he was in disgrace. But he only pouted and said, "I don't care. . . . I expect there'll be rivers there, and I'll catch hundreds of goldfish."

Then father came back from church, and the atmosphere at once became less tense and electric. He was as excited as any of them at the thought of the Holiday, though he was not setting out for it till later in the day. He always walked to the Holiday. He loved long walks, and his parish work gave him little opportunity for them. It would take him three days to reach the Holiday this time.

The bell rang, and they ran downstairs to the study. Blackie, the cat, was parading the hall restlessly, with tail erect, as if he knew that something unusual was afoot. He mewed softly and rubbed himself against mother's skirt as she passed him.

Susan picked him up and kissed him.

"*Poor* Blackie!" she said. "Won't he be lonely!"

"He'll have Cook, and Cook's his favourite," said mother.

He ran into the study when Susan put him down, but Thea carried him out ignominiously by the scruff of his neck and dropped him into the hall.

"You *know* you aren't allowed to come in to prayers, Blackie," she said severely.

Blackie always tried to come in to family prayers. Sometimes he succeeded, and would jump on the chairs at which they were kneeling, and rub himself against their faces till they began to giggle, and then mother would get up and put him out.

"Almighty God," prayed father, "Who fillest all things with Thy presence and art a God afar off as well as near at hand, we humbly beseech Thee to give Thy holy Angels charge concerning these Thy servants now setting forth on their journey. . . ."

Rachel thrilled at the familiar words that always ushered in the

Holiday. She seemed to feel an actual stir in the room—a soft, faint flutter of wings as the angels came to take charge of them. . . .

They said the Lord's Prayer together very quickly, Peter shouting it as he always shouted when he was excited.

"The Lord defend you with His providence and heavenly grace. May His fatherly hand ever be over you, and His Holy Spirit ever be with you, through Jesus Christ our Lord . . . Amen."

They were on their feet again, scrambling eagerly into the dining-room for breakfast. Maria, the housemaid, brought in the porridge and a plate of boiled eggs. She wore her apron over her best dress of navy blue serge, because she was coming with them on the Holiday. Only Cook was being left at the Vicarage.

Maria had at first been delighted by the idea of accompanying them, but, since hearing of it, she had begun to "walk out" with the man who drove the butcher's cart, and now she was overcome with grief at the thought of leaving him for four weeks. She had frizzed her hair luxuriantly for the occasion, but that was the only sign of festivity about her. She was red-eyed and sniffed lugubriously as she set down the eggs and porridge.

After breakfast father carried the trunks down to the hall, and mother came to count them and make sure that everything was there. She looked very neat in the bolero serge jacket that showed her slender waist and the long, graceful sweep of her skirt. She stood in front of the mirror in the hall, putting in the pins that fastened her hat to the thick coils of hair at the back of her head. . . .

"I wish you weren't walking, darling," she said. "I feel so anxious about you."

Father smiled down at her from his lanky height.

"I shall be all right. It will do me all the good in the world."

"It won't. You're tired out. I've never, seen you look so tired. You're in no state to start a three days' walk."

"Nonsense!" he said. "There's no tonic like a long walk."

"Well, promise that you'll come on by train if you find it too much for you."

"Of course," he said. "Don't worry about me. You've got enough to see to . . ."

"I shall be miserable till you come."

She went upstairs to help get Jane and Peter ready.

Maria came down, wearing a shapeless navy blue coat over her dress and a small black straw hat, under which her frizzed fringe stuck out unevenly. She stood by the pile of trunks, an expression of ludicrous misery on her plain sallow face, drawing on black cotton gloves.

Nurse came out of the kitchen, carrying the bag of provisions that they would need for the journey. The strings of her straw bonnet were tied in a symmetrical bow just beneath her chin. There was something very businesslike and severe in the cut of her coat and skirt, the coat shaped closely to her ample waist. Nurse was to be with them for the first week, and then was to go away for her own holiday to a married sister's.

"Now, Maria," she said sharply, "look alive and take this bag. Don't stand there mooning like that."

Maria sniffed, took the bag, and stood holding it listlessly.

"And you might have darned your gloves while you were about it," went on Nurse, whose keen eye had detected glimmers of white at the ends of the black fingers.

The meaning of the "while you were about it" was fully conveyed by a disapproving glance at the frizzed fringe.

Maria tossed her head and sniffed again—a sniff in which despair was mingled with defiance.

"The cabs are coming," shouted Peter excitedly from the landing window.

Over the children came a sudden rush of exultation, followed by as sudden a compunction. They were leaving everything behind them for four long weeks—Blackie, Napoleon, all their beloved toys and treasures. . . . There seemed to be something unbearably pathetic about the rooms that would be silent and empty for so long. Even Cook, standing arms akimbo at the kitchen door, looked lonely and desolate. They ran all over the house, saying good-bye to their possessions, snatching Blackie from one pair of arms to another to be hugged and kissed till he managed at last to escape by an agile twist from Jane's arms, hanging over Napoleon's bowl and throwing in reckless handfuls of ants' eggs. . . . Susan clasped Belinda, her sixth-best doll, whom she was leaving 'at home,' in an agonised farewell embrace. Rachel, having said good-bye to everything, ran out to watch father and the cabman hoist the luggage on to the two cabs that rocked and swayed alarmingly during the process. One of the horses stood in the shafts dispiritedly, with drooping head. The other kept looking round at her, with a humorous, rather wistful expression, as if he knew all about the Holiday and wished he were coming too. She tried to stroke him, but he jerked his head away with a rattle of his harness. His coat was dusty and left sticky black marks on her fingers.

"Come along, children!"

They packed themselves into the cabs—mother and father, who was coming to the station to see them off, and Rachel and Thea in one, Nurse and Susan and Maria and Jane in the other. Peter sat on the box of the first cab with the cabman.

Cook stood at the door with Blackie in her arms, and they all leant out of the windows waving to her till the cabs turned the corner of the street.

Chapter Two

THEY tumbled excitedly out of the wagonette that had brought them from the station, and stood at the Vicarage door looking around them. Beneath their excitement was something solemn. . . . Here they were at last. This was the Holiday. This house and garden would be the subject of conversation and games for all the next year. Their eyes darted over it keenly, almost anxiously. Was it going to surpass all previous holidays, as the ideal holiday should do? So far as their memories went back, every holiday had been better than the last.

Barwick Vicarage was a long, low house, built of stone and covered with climbing roses. There was something vaguely ecclesiastical about its architecture. The front door was of oak, with a big iron handle. The windows, long and low like the house, had pointed arches between their mullions.

The drive had led from the road through a rough paddock that was separated from the garden by a hedge. In front of the house was a lawn with a copper beech at its farther end, and beyond that an orchard.

"Now come in, all of you," Nurse was saying in her brisk voice. "A good wash is what you want."

They clattered into the house, sniffing enquiringly like puppies. A nice smell . . . a smell of old leather, tobacco smoke, wood fires, and roses, a smell that ever afterwards was to mean that particular Holiday to the children.

The trunks had been carried upstairs, and already the clothes were being unpacked and put away in drawers by mother and Maria, while Nurse helped the children to get clean and tidy.

Susan was ready first. Her small face shining with cleanliness, her hair well brushed back and tied on one side, wearing a clean, stiffly starched white pinafore, she slipped downstairs and out of the side door into the garden. She carried the battered Lena tenderly in her arms. She still felt self-reproachful for having thought of leaving her behind. Quietly, purposefully, she began to explore the garden, choosing all her little places. Here her dolls would have their tea parties, this corner would be her house, this her palace when she was pretending to be a princess, the space between the yew hedge and the wall her secret hiding-place. She would tell no one about that. . . .

Just near the doorway in the wall that led into the kitchen garden she found the stump of a cut-down tree. It was like a little table with a smooth flat top. Fairy feasts were held there. . . . She could see them—fairies with gossamer wings, and tiny green-clad elves, drinking dew from acorn cups. She must get up very, very early and find them one morning. . . . The garden was full of traces of fairies—little dancing-floors of moss, little magic circles of toadstools, little sleeping-holes in the tree-trunks. Susan set her small mouth determinedly. She *must* see a fairy this Holiday. There were no fairies at home because of the mill chimneys. There were only fairies in the country. She had tried hard to find one when they'd been away for the Holiday last year, but she hadn't been able to. She mustn't let another Holiday go by without finding one. They were all around her, of course, even now, peeping at her behind leaves, gazing down at her from the branches . . . but they were so quick. They disappeared just as you turned to look at them. No, she *mustn't* let this Holiday go without seeing one, because after you were ten you couldn't see them any more. Rachel had told her so. That left only four Holidays after this. . . .

An old man came down the path, wearing an apron of sacking and carrying a spade. Breathlessly she accosted him, pointing to the round, smooth surface of the tree-stump.

"Have you ever found little acorn cups all round here early in the morning?" she said.

He was a very old man, and his face seemed to be made up of innumerable tiny lines. When he smiled the tiny lines suddenly changed their directions and pointed in different ways.

"No, missie, I've never seen it. A fairy feast, I reckon, you're thinking on?"

She nodded and clasped Lena more tightly to her, quivering with eagerness from head to foot, and standing on tiptoe as she always did when she was excited.

"Yes . . . if you find one, please will you leave it just as it is and come and tell me?"

The criss-cross lines again seemed to shoot in all directions over his face.

"Yes, missie . . . I'll do that."

"Thank you."

He went into the kitchen garden and began to dig. She lingered for a moment, watching him. A robin, who stood on long, thin legs about a foot from the old man's spade, looked up at her with bright, friendly eyes as if he would have liked to talk to her. He could tell her about the fairies, of course, if only she could understand him. But she couldn't, so it wasn't any use staying there.

She turned away and went to the orchard. Here and there tall white daisies still grew in the long grass. She chose as her own a tree that had bright red apples on it, like the decoration of a Christmas tree, then went indoors to fetch the other dolls, Hetty and Grace and Louise and Victoria. She carried them out to the orchard and arranged them in a circle, Hetty and Grace leaning against the apple-tree trunk, Louise and Victoria and Lena propped up against the long grass. They stared blankly in front of them, but she knew that, as soon as she was out of sight and hearing, the fairies would come to them and they would all talk together in tiny voices. She went away to the end of the orchard, then began to creep back again, slowly, cautiously, hiding in the long grass, trying to come upon them unawares. But they had heard her. They were all sitting motionless, staring silently in front of them again when she reached them. In the middle of the group, however, was a large rosy apple. Susan knew really that it had dropped from the tree above, but she pretended that the elves had brought it to her for a present. She imagined little green men drawing it across the grass by ropes of gossamer, heard their voices, like the drones of insects, "Give it to Susan when she comes back. . . ." Perhaps they had all danced in a circle—Hetty and Grace and Louise and Victoria and Lena and the little green men; and then suddenly they had heard her coming, and immediately the elves had vanished, and the dolls had resumed their blank expressions and stiff, motionless attitudes.

She was just going to take a bite out of the apple when she noticed a tiny round hole in the skin. A caterpillar. . . . The round hole was his front door. Susan imagined his small green head peeping out of the hole while he looked up at the sky to see whether it was going to be a fine day or not. Inside the apple was his home. . . . She bit into it carefully so as not to hurt him. Her bite laid bare the whole of his little brown passage-hall. How surprised he must be! She imagined enormous teeth suddenly biting into their hall at home. There he was, right in the core, in his little dining-room. She picked him out very carefully and put him on a blade of grass. He seemed to look about him in a startled way, as if he were saying, "Well, I never!" then suddenly overbalanced and disappeared from view. Susan imagined him at the bottom of the long blade of grass surrounded by the insects who lived there, telling them his adventures. "And a giant came and bit my house all to pieces. . . ." They crowded round him to listen.

Rachel came out into the garden. She too had washed her hands and face and tidied her hair and put on a pinafore over her sailor suit.

She wandered down the path with the herbaceous border on one side and the yew hedge on the other, passed the door that led to the kitchen garden, and reached the orchard. She could see Susan in the distance sitting with her dolls eating an apple, but she didn't go to her. Susan was such a baby, always talking about dolls and fairies. . . .

At the end of the orchard she came to the hedge that separated it from the paddock, and in the hedge was a little gate leading into a spinney that ran down one side of the paddock to the road. She opened the gate and entered.

It was a tiny wood, but the trees in it were quite big—oaks and beeches and tall firs. The roots of one of the trees stood right out of the earth, forming a little armchair. She sat in it and leant back. It was very comfortable. She would tell Thea about it, but no one else. She and Thea would come and sit here. It would be their secret place. Looking up, she saw the green branches swaying gently against the sky, and the sight filled her with an aching rapture. She became aware of the immense quiet around her. The sunshine fell in shafts through the trees, making pools of light on the ivy that covered the ground.

She picked a piece of ivy and examined its shining greenness with delight. There was ivy at home, but it wasn't like this. It wore a faint veil of griminess that killed its colour. That was because of the mill chimneys, of course. . . .

Everything around was so clean and bright and happy that quite suddenly it seemed to Rachel that there was nothing in the whole world to be afraid of. Usually she was afraid of a lot of things. She was afraid chiefly of not growing up good. Miss Kingsley, the head mistress of the school to which she and Thea went, used to talk a lot about that. She used to say that every little thing you said or did or thought went to the making of a good or bad habit, and it was your habits that made your character. She said that you were making your own character every day, minute by minute. She said that bad people hadn't wanted to be bad and hadn't meant to be bad and probably hadn't known they were growing bad. They'd just got bad by not being particular about forming good habits when they were children. Sometimes Rachel would lie awake at night terrified that she was growing bad. Often she wished that she had died when she was a baby, because babies always went to heaven. Once she and Thea had discussed at what age the baby automatically lost the chance of going straight to heaven and had decided that it was when it began to walk. Rachel herself had secretly come to the conclusion that fifteen was the age at which your habits had hardened so completely into a good or bad character that you couldn't change. She was going to try very hard to be good till she was fifteen, and then—well, if she wasn't good by the time she was fifteen it wouldn't be much use trying any more She knew that she was more inclined to be bad than good at present. Often she had a torturing suspicion that if she had lived when Jesus was on earth she would have been one of the people who didn't believe in Him. She believed in Him now, of course, but would she have believed then? The thought worried her terribly, sometimes making her feel as if she had actually helped to crucify Him. Then there were other things. . . . Leprosy, for instance. Ever since a visiting clergyman, who had come to appeal for money for a leper colony, had described leprosy in his sermon, she had lived in secret horror of it. At first she had examined herself every night for the little white spot that meant it was beginning, but now she only did it once a week or so. Some things were even worse than that. Once she had found a report of the Society for Prevention of Cruelty to Children, and she had read page after page before, hearing footsteps and knowing that she was not supposed to read the book, she had hastily thrust it back into the shelves. What she read made her feel sick and had turned life into a nightmare for days afterwards. Moreover, there had come to her a monstrous thought—suppose that her own happy home life was only a dream and that at any moment she might wake up from it and find herself in reality the child of parents who starved and beat her, as the parents in the book starved and beat their children. . . .

Then there were the horrors that one didn't understand. They lived in a dark cupboard in one's mind, which one opened as seldom as possible. Elsie . . . Elsie, whom they had all loved so, was somehow connected with the horror that one didn't understand. She had left them suddenly and without farewells. She had been crying as she got into the cab that had come to take her to the station. Father was away, but mother's face had been set in lines of stern disgust. Neither father nor mother ever mentioned her afterwards. Once Thea had said, "Why did Elsie go away?" And mother had replied, "She wasn't a good girl."

"Did she steal something?"

"No, Thea. It was something you're too young to know about. Don't ask any more questions. And don't talk about her to the younger ones. I want them to forget her."

"I'm going to find out what it was," Thea had said to Rachel that night, "and then I'll tell you."

But Rachel's mind had swerved away from the subject with instinctive horror. "Please, God," she had prayed, "don't let Thea find out ... don't let me know."

But to-day as she sat in the green shade, her eyes fixed dreamily on the tree-tops that swayed in the breeze against the blue sky, all the fear and horror seemed to have vanished from life.

Thea had changed into her best frock—a white voile dress with rows of ruching at the waist and yoke.

"May I change, mother?" she had called carelessly. "I got my sailor suit so crumpled in the train."

She was afraid that mother would know she hadn't got the sailor suit crumpled and say she mustn't change it because it was only clean on that morning, but mother, who was still busy with the unpacking, had answered "Yes, dear," absently, hardly hearing what she had said.

She knew, of course, that even if she changed she ought to put on another cotton frock, but she longed to put on the white voile dress, because it made her feel grown-up and elegant, like someone in a picture or a book. She changed into it quickly and guiltily, tied her hair at the back of her head, not on the top, which she considered childish though mother was always telling her it was neater, arranged her curls over her shoulders, and, waiting till no one was about the hall so that she couldn't be sent back to take off the voile frock and put on a cotton one instead, slipped downstairs and out of the front door.

The garden didn't interest her much, and she soon found her way down to the paddock where people passing along the road could see her. There she pretended to be busied in picking the white field daisies, but in reality she was a passer-by, watching herself from the road—a girl in a white dress with dark curls falling over her shoulders, picking flowers in a field. It was just like the sort of picture that you saw hung on the wall in people's drawing-rooms. She was saying, "She must be one of the locum's children. How pretty she looks in that white frock with her curls falling over her shoulders like that! . . ."

Nurse gave a last tug to Jane's curls with the comb, parted them at the side, deftly tied up a handful with a pink ribbon, slipped on a clean pinafore, and took her downstairs to the side door.

"Now go into the garden and play by yourself," she said. "You're, a big girl now, you know. You're four. I'll send Peter out as soon as I've got him ready."

Jane trotted happily down the path and turned a corner into another path. . . . On one side was a tall green hedge, on the other flowers, beginning small near the path, then going taller and taller as they went away till they were as high as the hedge. This led to a sort of field, where the grass was almost as tall as Jane herself. It was all strange and rather terrifying. Her heart beating more quickly, she turned and began hastily to retrace her steps. As she went everything around her seemed to grow still stranger and more terrifying. The flowers seemed to be frowning at her angrily. The tall hedge towered above her. She began to run. Reaching the opening that led to the kitchen garden, she plunged into it and ran along a brick path, her small face crumpling up in terror. There was a high wall on one side of her with pears and peaches growing on it. Suddenly she realised that this was not the way she had come. She was lost. . . . Horror and desolation swept over her. She began to cry—loud, gulping, heart-broken sobs.

"What's the matter, missie?"

An old man had appeared suddenly, a bent, wrinkled old man just like the wizard in the fairy stories that Susan told her. He put out his hand towards her as if he were going to turn her into something. Her terror deepened to panic, and she turned and fled from him, screaming.

Nurse came running out of the side door and down the path.

"What*ever*'s the matter?" she said.

"I'm lost!" sobbed Jane. "I'm lost!"

"Nonsense!" said Nurse, "of course you're not lost."

She picked her up, but Jane struggled away from her, still sobbing.

"Elsie," she sobbed, "want Elsie. . . ."

Her shrill screams had floated over the garden to the other children. "Elsie . . . want Elsie."

Susan, who had finished her apple and was engaged now in planting the seeds in a little circle round the apple tree, suddenly stopped and stared unseeingly in front of her, thinking about Elsie and the warm, cosy, hugger-mugger days when Elsie had presided over the nursery. They had been exciting days of forbidden treats, of secret, lawless expeditions. . . . Ice-cream from the ice-cream cart that patrolled the back streets ("Don't tell your mother I gave it you"); visits to an aunt of Elsie's who lived in a dirty little house with a lot of dirty but fascinating children, one of whom could walk on his hands with his feet straight up in the air, another of whom could emit piercing whistles by putting a finger into each corner of his mouth ("Now don't tell your mother I took you here . . ."); walks accompanied by a soldier with a red jacket and red stripes down his trousers, who twirled a cane and told them stories about the time he had fought black men who wore no clothes and threw spears ("Now don't tell your mother we met him"). Elsie was always jolly and exciting and good-tempered. She let them all come into her bed in the morning and sit on her while she made earthquakes and switchbacks for them with her knees. She let them ride round the nursery on her back, pretending that she was a camel and they were travelling over the desert. She spent money on them generously, buying toys and sweets for the younger ones, brooches and necklaces for Thea.

"I do wish she *wouldn't*," mother said irritably when she found out. She took away the necklace that Elsie had given Thea, and once she threw into the fire a packet of very green sweets that she had bought for Susan. Elsie used to buy them sticks of rock or ice-cream sandwiches, too, to eat on their walks, though they were not supposed to eat between meals ("It won't do you any harm, but don't tell your mother"). She had a sweet, rather husky voice, and used to sing to them the old folk-songs she had heard in her native village, of which their favourite was "Randall, my son." She was a wonderful comforter. Even Thea was not ashamed of sitting on her knee to be comforted when she was in trouble.

But they all knew that mother disapproved of her. She didn't keep them clean, and she didn't keep the nursery clean. She never looked really clean herself. She was a poor needlewoman and slap-dash in everything she did. So she had gone, and Nurse had come—Nurse who was so just and calm and remote and who kept them and the nursery so immaculately clean and tidy, Nurse who had never kissed any of them, even Jane, because she "didn't hold with mawling children about." . . .

Susan sighed, then returned to her apple-planting.

Jane's shrill cry had reached Rachel in the spinney. "Elsie . . . want Elsie."

Elsie. . . . The horror that lay at the heart of life seemed to creep back again through the wood, dispelling the brightness of the sunshine, clouding the blue of her sky, dimming the radiant greenness around her. She saw again that look of stern disgust on mother's face. . . . Elsie. . . . Then quite suddenly a frog jumped on to the little patch of moss just by her foot, and squatted there, looking at her boldly. She could see his tiny throat moving tremulously. His skin shone like golden satin against the green moss on which he sat. He seemed to blink at her in humorous friendliness. The horror crept away, and happiness flooded her soul again. . . .

Thea heard Jane's cry and stood for a moment listening. Elsie . . . I *will* find out what it was, she said to herself. It's something to do with what Dulcie Masters told some of the girls at school. There was a dreadful row when Miss Kingsley got to know about it, and she asked Mrs. Masters to take Dulcie away. . . . Thea had tried to find out what it was, but the girls whom Dulcie had told wouldn't talk about it, because Miss Kingsley had said that they would be expelled if they did. Lily Beverly was one of them. She'd try to get it out of Lily next term. . . .

Suddenly she saw that a little group of village children had gathered in the road at the gate and was watching her. She shook the curls over her shoulder again and went on picking the field daisies, pretending not to see the children, but keeping always where they could watch her. As she picked she sang carelessly to herself in a sweet, clear little voice. . . .

Miriam Cotteril had come out into the garden at the sound of Jane's cries, but now, seeing that Nurse had already reached her and that nothing serious was the matter, she turned back to the house. Jane's cry for "Elsie" had irritated her. . . . Absurd that the child hadn't yet forgotten the girl. The very thought of her coming straight from that man, whoever he was, to her children made her even now feel hot and breathless with anger. She had never liked her. The children had looked dirty and untidy all the time that she had had them. She had been furious when she found that she let them all get into bed with her in the mornings. And once she had caught her cleaning Jane's face by rubbing it with a handkerchief that she had moistened with her own tongue. A born slut—and stupid, too. Almost mentally deficient. She would never have kept her so long if she had not been so busy with the Missionary Exhibition that she literally hadn't a minute to look for anyone else. Then she discovered that the girl was going to have a baby, and all the pent-up exasperation of months found outlet in the angry disgust with which she dismissed her. Dismissed her on the spot. Had her out of the house within an hour of making the discovery. The children's affection for her, their persistent memory of her, filled her with a quite disproportionate feeling of vexation.

She went into the study and sat down to rest for a moment on an armchair by the fireplace. The journey had been tiring, and there was something depressing about the strange house and garden. The housekeeping was going to be a problem. There were no provision shops in the village. A fish cart came once a week from Harborough, the market town five miles away, and a butcher's cart twice a week. The house was old-fashioned and inconvenient. She'd been prepared for oil lamps, of course, but not for having to pump into the cistern every drop of water that they used. To crown everything, Maria was being awkward, crying and saying that she didn't like the country and wanted to go home. Her heart sank as she looked forward to the holiday. It wasn't going to be much rest for her. . . .

She imagined herself arriving at a large hotel . . . waiters . . . other people to watch . . . no responsibilities . . . beautifully cooked meals of which one knew nothing till one saw the menu. . . . She'd always secretly longed for a holiday like that. . . . She was so tired of these country vicarages without gas or water and with no shops within reach. And, of course, they couldn't pick and choose even among country vicarages. Five children made it difficult. So many vicars didn't want a locum with children at all. . . .

Her thoughts went to Timothy and grew heavier. To-day had been hot, and the sky promised that to-morrow would be still hotter. He was tired and overworked and out of condition. He flung himself into everything with so much vigour. He wore himself out. He did two men's work and would never admit that he was tired. Though he would not have acknowledged it, the airlessness and dinginess of his slum parish frayed and irked his spirit continually, for he had been brought up in the country and loved it with a deep, inarticulate passion. He looked forward all the year to this month's holiday. If only he would take it more easily. . . . She saw in imagination his thin, tired face with its faint smile—gentle, eager, patient—and was conscious suddenly of that something of peace and joy that seemed always to hover near him however weary or dispirited he was. Her heart went out to him in a rush of love and compunction. She felt ashamed of her frequent moods of discontent, of her unconquerable dislike of parish work, of her impatience with the shifts and restraints of poverty.

Where was he now? Tramping along the hot, dusty road, perhaps . . . or perhaps he had already put up at some cheap, uncomfortable inn. He hated spending money on himself. . . . She longed to hold his tired head to her breast.

Peter came into the room and stood staring at her solemnly.

"Well, Peter . . ."

He smiled at her. He had a radiantly sweet smile.

"Did you hear Jane crying?" he said. "She thought she was lost, and she was only in the garden. Wasn't she silly?"

"Yes, wasn't she!"

He took her hand.

"Come out with me. . . . Let's go and see what there is in the garden. I think it's a lovely Holiday, don't you?"

Her depression left her as suddenly as it had come, and she went out into the garden with him.

Upstairs Maria was snivelling despondently as she helped Nurse put the children's things away into the chest of drawers. It would have been her night out at home. She and George would have gone to the first house at the Hipp., then had a fish-and-chip supper, and then roamed the streets, with their familiar glaring lights and cheerful noise and pungent smells. When she came in and went to bed she would lie awake thinking of him and listening to the friendly clanging of the trams outside in the street. The street light always shone into her room, and she never drew the curtain because she liked it. The silence of the summer evening here seemed terrible and unnatural. And the night was going to be worse still—pitch dark without a street lamp to be seen anywhere. She went over to the window and, looking out, gave a sudden gulp.

"What's the matter?" said Nurse.

"It's all them trees an' things," snivelled Maria. "They fair gives me the creeps."

Chapter Three

PETER and Jane were making countries on the lawn. For some time they had worked silently and apart. Then Peter said: "I've finished my country, Jane. Have you finished yours?"

"Nearly, Peter," replied Jane earnestly.

"You must finish it quickly," said Peter, "or I'll send my soldiers to conquer it."

"No, please don't, Peter . . . it's finished now."

"All right . . . I'll show you mine first, and then you show me yours."

Jane got up and went over to Peter's country.

Cook had been clearing out a cupboard and had given them an armful of empty cardboard boxes. One of them was placed on end like a sentry-box, and in it stood the battered and shapeless Owly, still wearing his luggage label now scrawled over with mysterious hieroglyphics in coloured chalks.

"He's the king," explained Peter, "he's the king over all my country. He's such a very high-up person that he's always the king of any country he's in. The box is his palace and the label's his crest, to show that he's a high-up person."

Near the box stood a little company of tin soldiers behind a row of cannons. Peter had had the tin soldiers a long time, and many arms and legs were missing as well as most of the paint.

"That's his army," went on Peter proudly. "It's the best army in the world. And here—" he turned to the stones forming the rockery that edged the lawn near the house, where his toy monkey was perched despondently with sagging head—"here are the wild Indians. They live on the rocks. You can only see one, but there are hundreds more. And then over there," he swept his arm vaguely towards the path that ran along the top of the rockery, and the bushes beyond, "there the preheristoric animals live."

Peter had once seen pictures of prehistoric animals, and they had made a deep impression on him. He always referred to them as "preheristoric" animals.

"They often come down over the rocks," he went on, "into Owly's kingdom. That's why some of his soldiers haven't got arms and legs. They've been bitten off by preheristoric animals. They live on people, you know, Jane, do preheristoric animals. And when they can't get people they live on air. And they play at rolling down the rocks."

Jane gazed wide-eyed at Peter's country. It was thrilling and rather terrifying. She glanced apprehensively at the bush that might conceal a preheristoric animal and automatically backed a few paces.

"Now come and look at my country, Peter," she said.

He came across to her corner of the lawn. Jane heaved a sigh of relief when she found herself back in her own country. Cardboard boxes formed little houses furnished with chairs and tables made of chestnuts with pins for legs that Susan had once given her. In front of each house the grass had been marked off into gardens by fences made of spent matches of which she had found a collection in a vase in the study. Little chestnut chairs stood in some of the gardens, under tiny trees made by hawthorn twigs stuck into the ground.

"Look, Peter, there's a linen cupboard in this house," she said proudly, and showed him a matchbox with a piece of rag inside, "and there's a study in this one."

The study was a little cardboard box furnished with a chestnut table and chair and an enormous note-book propped against the wall, with a pencil by the side of it.

Peter examined everything with interest, then smiled a tolerant, amused smile.

"You haven't any soldiers or any cannons, Jane," he said. "What are you going to do if an enemy attacks your country?"

"There aren't any enemies near my country," said Jane firmly.

"But they might come," he persisted. "The preheristoric animals might come. They aren't very far away, and they're *very* fierce. What would you do then without any soldiers? They'd knock down your houses and eat your people."

Dismay descended upon Jane, and her small round face puckered up suddenly.

Peter relented.

"It's all right, Jane," he said. "If any enemy comes to you, I'll send you all my soldiers and cannons, so it will be all right. Now I must go back to my country, because I think the preheristoric animals are coming down in a minute."

He went back, and they played silently for some moments in their separate corners of the lawn. Then Jane said:

"Peter, I've made a feast. May I invite Owly to it?"

"No, please don't invite him," said Peter. "He's so polite that if you invite him he'll come, but he doesn't want to."

Jane set her small lips stubbornly.

"I want him to come, so I'm going to invite him."

"Well, I won't tell him you've invited him," said Peter, "so he won't come."

"*I'll* tell him."

"He can't hear you. He can't hear anyone but me."

"It's a nice feast, Peter," she pleaded. "Do let him come."

"He doesn't want to."

"Oh, *Peter*!"

"Well, I'll come and look at it," said Peter, again relenting.

He came across to her corner of the lawn. She had made a table of the smallest cardboard box and placed the chestnut chairs around it. On the middle of the table was the sugar-basin from her dolls' tea-set, filled with small daisy-heads. Nasturtium leaves were ranged round the table for plates.

She watched his face anxiously.

"Will you fetch him in a cart if I let him come?" said Peter at last.

"Yes."

"Can he have a chair to himself?"

"Yes."

"And a table to himself?"

"Yes."

"And will you call him 'Your Majesty' when you speak to him?"

"Yes."

"What is there to eat?"

"It's daisies really, but he can pretend it's anything he wants."

"He doesn't eat daisies. He eats turkey and plum pudding. High-up people always eat turkey and plum pudding."

"Then it can be turkey and plum pudding. May he come, Peter?"

"Yes. I'll tell him that he's coming, and you send a cart for him."

At that minute Nurse appeared from the house.

"I want you indoors a minute, Peter, to try on your new blouse."

"I can't come," said Peter firmly. "Owly's going to a feast."

"Come along, Peter. Be a good boy."

But Peter was now as eager for Owly to attend the feast as a moment ago he had been reluctant.

"I *won't* come," he said stormily. "Go away. I don't want you. Owly's going to a feast in a cart."

Jane had already begun to decorate one of the cardboard boxes with leaves and to fix little ribbons to it to pull it with. She looked from one to the other, distressed.

"Now be a good boy, Peter," said Nurse.

She took hold of his hand and began to draw him away. Immediately he flew into a temper, screaming and kicking and growing purple in the face. Nurse bundled him up, still screaming, under her arm and carried him indoors. The screams continued from indoors, and there came the sounds of loud thuds. Nurse had shut him into his bedroom, and he was kicking at the door.

Jane cried desolately for a few minutes into her pinafore, still crouching over the little decorated box. When she raised her eyes, Owly, perched awry against the wall of his palace, seemed to be watching her in grim disapproval.

She addressed him apologetically, still gulping.

29

"I *know* he has to be punished when he's naughty so that he'll grow up a good man, but I can't help crying when he is."

The screams from upstairs had ceased, and Jane dried her eyes and wandered across the lawn to the orchard. There wasn't any fun in playing with her country now that Peter wasn't there to play with his. At the end of the orchard she found the wooden gate, and, hearing Rachel's voice, she opened it and entered the spinney. There she walked down the path that wound in and out of the trees till she came upon Thea and Rachel. Thea was sitting on the roots of a tree that made a little armchair, and Rachel was lying on the ground on her back, her hands under her head. By them were two bottles of lemonade, bought at the village shop.

"He *knew*," Rachel was saying, "that there was a secret hiding-place there, but he didn't know where it was, so he began to press all round the panelling to try to find the spring. He hadn't a minute to lose because——"

Thea took up her bottle of lemonade and raised it to her lips, then saw Jane and lowered it quickly.

"Go away, Jane," she said severely. "We don't want you hanging about. And you mustn't come here again. It's our place."

Jane trailed disconsolately back to the orchard and found Susan at the farther end of it. Susan had made a little swing from the lowest branch of an apple tree with a piece of cord and was swinging Lena in it slowly to and fro. The other dolls sat round on the grass waiting their turns.

"May I play with you, Susan?" said Jane.

But Susan said:

"No. I don't want anyone to play with me. I want to play alone."

Jane returned to her deserted country and suddenly saw Peter coming out with Nurse. His eyes were red, but he was smiling radiantly. Peter's rages always left him as suddenly as they came.

"I'm good now," he announced importantly to Jane.

"Yes, you *were* a naughty boy," said Nurse.

Peter was the only one of the children who gave her any trouble, but, though she never showed it, he was her favourite. She tried to be detached and impartial and scientific. "It doesn't do to get really fond of them," she would say. "You have to give them up as soon as they're school age and go on somewhere else, so the less you let yourself care about them the better." But occasionally a child would worm its way through her armour, as Peter had done.

"Lift me up high," he said to her.

"No, not when you've been such a naughty boy as that."

"But I'm good now . . ." he said indignantly.

She swung him up suddenly in her strong arms, holding him high above her head, and from that point of vantage he raised a shrill scream of "Daddy!"

They all came running—Thea and Rachel from the spinney, Susan from the orchard, mother from the house—down the drive to the gate where the black dusty figure had just appeared. They clung about him, all talking excitedly at the same time. After kissing mother, he picked up Jane, carried her a few yards, then put her down quickly. He was smiling, but his face looked thin and grey, his clothes were covered with dust, and he wore a large rhubarb leaf under his hat.

"Daddy's got a funny hat on," shouted Peter delightedly, thinking that he was playing a trick to amuse them.

"Oh, my dear, how tired you look!" said mother. "I've been so anxious about you in this dreadful heat."

"It's been a bit hot," he admitted, "but I've enjoyed it, and it's done me all the good in the world."

"You're limping. . . ."

"I've got a blister on my foot, but that's nothing. No, it's been a fine walk. Out in the air all day . . . and there's no exercise like walking. . . ."

She made a little gesture of impatience.

"It's been too much for you . . . anyone could see that."

They walked up to the house together arm in arm, the children clinging round them.

In the study he sank wearily into a chair.

"I came the last bit by train," he said. "The heat made my head feel rather strange, so I thought I'd better. Do you know," he smiled,

"I couldn't remember the name of the place, so I got the booking clerk to read out the names of all stations on the line to see which sounded familiar. And a woman in a cottage garden I passed gave me the rhubarb leaf. It made a wonderful difference. She gave me a drink of buttermilk, too. People really are extraordinarily kind."

The children all began to chatter again, but Miriam turned them out, then came to sit by him, taking his hand in hers.

"How I wish you wouldn't knock yourself up like this."

"My dear, I'm not knocked up. I've enjoyed it. Now tell me, do you like the place?"

"The children love it."

"And you?"

"Oh, it's very nice. . . . All the water has to be pumped. Cook does it, of course, but it means that every drop is precious. The cistern's small, and she doesn't like to have to fill it more than once a day. It's harder work than you'd think."

"I'll do it now I've come. I shall enjoy the exercise."

"I should hate making you do it a second time, even more than Cook. There's no gas, of course, and Maria's very stupid about the lamps. It's really less trouble to clean them myself. She's being very difficult altogether. She keeps crying and saying she wants to go home. Sometimes I think I'll send her away and manage without her."

He held her hand in both his.

"You mustn't do that," he said. "It would be too much for you. What's the cook like?"

"She's all right. And nice to the children, which is a great thing. But the housekeeping's difficult. There's only a small general shop, and one has to think out meals for days ahead."

She had made up her mind not to grumble to him, but, though she hated herself for doing it, somehow she couldn't stop. Ever since the first night she'd had that nagging sense of resentment at her heart. And Maria was being so unspeakably irritating. . . .

"Of course," she went on, "the children keep me pretty busy as usual. I've hardly had time to sit down since we got here."

"I was thinking on the way," he said, "suppose we ask your

cousin if she'd care to come over and help with the children. It would be a holiday for her."

"Bridget?"

"Yes. She came a few years ago, didn't she?"

"Of course. It was quite a success, too. She's awfully good with children. I expect she'd love it. That's a good idea, Timothy. I'll write to-morrow." The thought of Bridget's coming cheered her. She could go for walks and expeditions with the children. It would be an enormous help.

"People have been very kind," she went on. "They've all called to ask if they could help in any way."

"I'm glad."

He raised her hand and pressed it to his lips for a moment, then rose.

"Well . . . I suppose I'd better go and have a bath."

After tea he looked less tired, and they strolled round the garden together. The gardener touched his hat respectfully to the new locum, and Timothy stopped to speak to him.

"Do you come from the village?"

"No, sir, I come over from Hinchley."

"Where's that?"

"Upon the moors, sir. About three miles off."

"How do you get here?"

"I walk, sir. I'm used to walkin'. I like it."

Timothy smiled.

"I like walking, too."

"Hinchley?" said Miriam as they walked on. "Wasn't that where that girl Elsie came from? *Surely* it couldn't be from near here!"

"I don't know . . . poor girl!" he said compassionately. Miriam set her lips. It was all very well for him to say "poor girl" like that. He was a priest, and she supposed that in a way it was his duty to take that attitude. But, if once ordinary people began to countenance what the girl had done, it would be fatal. Decent people had to band themselves together against it. She said nothing, however. He had been away from home when she packed Elsie off, and they had come as near to an estrangement as they ever came over the matter on his return. He had been angry at her summary dismissal of the girl and at the contempt with which she had referred to her. She had cried beneath his rare anger, and he had comforted her, feeling bitterly remorseful at sight of her tears. They had made up the short, sharp quarrel, and had in future avoided all reference to the episode that had caused it. Now he looked down and, seeing the tight lines of her mouth, smiled.

"My dear," he said, "you must make allowance for her bringing-up. The girl probably never had a chance."

"I know," she said. "All the same——"

She stopped and, after a pause, he said:

"It's a beautiful garden. And not too orderly, I'm glad to see, for the children to play in."

"Oh, they love it," she said.

But somehow the reference to Elsie had jarred the atmosphere. She felt secretly hurt and offended. To minimise what Elsie had done seemed in some way to minimise her own value in his eyes.

He looked down at her and drew her arm through his.

"It's good to be with you again," he said.

She laid her head against his arm, and suddenly love for him surged over her in a flood, drowning all her depression and weariness of spirit.

"Oh, it's good to have you back," she replied. They returned to the house, and he began to examine the books in his study and arrange the room as he liked it, moving the desk into the window and clearing an array of useless knick-knacks from it.

The case of books that he had sent from home stood upon the floor, and he began to unpack them, emptying a shelf in one of the bookcases to receive them. He was studying the early fathers and writing an account of their lives and doctrines for popular reading. One volume had already been published. His annual month's holiday was the only time he had for the work, so it did not progress very quickly. He was, however, in no hurry to finish it. He was a born student, and returned each holiday with eager zest to the reading for which his normal life as a slum parish priest left him little time. In the intervals of his work on the early fathers he would refresh his memory of the classics—reading the Homer and Plato, the Horace and Virgil and Cicero that he had always loved. Occasionally as a relaxation he would re-read a play of Shakespeare or a novel of Dickens or Scott, but he was wholly ignorant of modern literature. Whether it was the result of this or not, he had rather an old-fashioned, stilted manner of speech, especially when among strangers.

She watched him now as he set out on the desk the books that he would need to-morrow. His expression was dreamy and abstracted. Already he was planning his work and had forgotten that she was there. Her depression returned like a tide that has ebbed, only to flow back with greater force. Beneath her calm, rather cold exterior she was passionately possessive, and he had always eluded her. He had never belonged to her, as she had wanted him to belong to her. She had in the early days of her married life suffered acutely because of this. Now she had resigned herself to it, but beneath the resignation was a faint smouldering sense of grievance that sometimes flamed up into an anger that bewildered him because he could not understand it. Nor could she explain it. It was not that she thought he did not love her. She knew that he loved her. But—she didn't come first with him, as he came first with her and as she had always wanted to come first with him. His work came before her. It sometimes seemed that the claims of any ragamuffin in the parish were prior to hers.

At times she looked forward to their old age when he should have retired and his work would no longer stand between them. They would live together in the country. She would share his life fully at last. But—she glanced now at his thin worn face and sighed. He would have killed himself with overwork long before he reached retiring age.

"Why not have a real holiday for a change?" she said suddenly.

"A real holiday?"

She swept her arm round the desk.

"All this . . . it's hard work."

He smiled at her.

'A change of work's as good as play, my dear. Far better in fact. . . ."

The door opened, and Rachel slipped into the room, carrying a rose that she put into Timothy's buttonhole.

"That's to celebrate you coming to the Holiday," she said.

"Thank you, my dear," said Timothy.

"May I help you unpack the books?"

"That would be very nice of you."

She knelt on the floor by the case of books, her straight hair with its tight, uneven ridges falling over her shoulders, handing up the books to him one by one.

Miriam watched them from the sofa.

Suddenly the door opened again, and Maria entered.

"Mr. Moyle's here, please, sir," she said.

She said it in the tone of exaggerated misery and despair that she had used ever since she left Manchester.

"He's the organist," said Miriam. "He called yesterday to ask when you'd be here. Show him in, Maria."

The man who entered looked younger at first sight than he probably was. He was tall and good-looking in rather a theatrical style, with fine eyes, a well-modelled mouth and chin, and dark curly hair. He greeted them in an easy, assured manner and sat down on the armchair by the fireplace.

Rachel had joined Miriam on the sofa as soon as he entered. She was always painfully shy with strangers, and unconsciously she pressed close to Miriam as if for protection. Miriam, slipping her arm round the child, was aware of a feeling of warm happiness and comfort. Her failure to possess her husband had made her turn to her children as if for something that she had not been able to find in him. She loved to feel their dependence on her. It terrified her when they seemed self-sufficient and independent, when they turned away from her as if they did not need her.

Mr. Moyle spoke to Rachel, and she answered shyly, almost in a whisper. She was bitterly ashamed of her shyness. Thea laughed at her for it, and even Susan could chatter away quite happily to strangers. Only Rachel was held in this paralysing grip. Often when she was alone she practised not being shy, and then it was fairly easy. She could talk to imaginary strangers almost as if she were Thea herself, but as soon as she met a real stranger again it was as bad as ever.

Miriam was talking to the visitor about music.

"You play, I suppose?" he was saying.

"I used to," said Miriam, "but I have so little time nowadays. Thea plays rather nicely. She's our eldest girl. I suppose that one's own geese are always swans, but she really seems to me to have talent."

"I'd like to hear her," he said.

"I wonder—I suppose you give organ lessons?" said Miriam.

"Yes."

She turned to Timothy.

"You were saying you'd like Thea to learn the organ."

He leant forward, interested.

"Yes . . . I'd like it very much."

"Suppose you hear her play now and see what you think of her," said Miriam to Mr. Moyle. "There's a piano in the drawing-room. Rachel, tell Thea to come."

They went across to the drawing-room, and Rachel ran upstairs to look for Thea. She found her in her bedroom. Thea had seen Mr. Moyle arriving and had gone upstairs to do her hair again. She had come to the conclusion that she looked childish with her hair over her shoulders and had done it in quite a different way, tying all of it right back at the nape of her neck, so that its waves fell softly about her ears and one curl still came forward over her shoulder.

"They want you to come and play to Mr. Moyle," said Rachel. "He's the organist, you know, and they want you to learn the organ."

"Where are they?"

"They've gone into the drawing-room. Oh, Thea, aren't you *terrified*?"

"Of *course* not. You are silly, Rachel. What is there to be terrified of?"

She went downstairs and stood for a minute outside the drawing-room door, rubbing her cheeks and biting her lips to bring the colour into them, then opened the door and went in. She felt that her entrance into the room was somehow rather impressive. She wasn't only herself entering the room. She was also Mr. Moyle watching her enter the room. As Mr. Moyle she was thinking: So that's the eldest girl; she's prettier than the others. . . .

"This is Thea," said mother.

Thea walked across the room to Mr. Moyle and said "How-do-you-do" in a grown-up way of which she was secretly very proud.

"How-do-you-do," he said. "And how old is Thea?"

"I'm thirteen," she said.

"You look older than that," he said.

"Do I?" she said, and flushed with pleasure.

"Your music's here, isn't it, dear?" said mother. "Play the Grieg piece."

Thea sat down at the piano and began to play. She knew the piece well and could play it by heart. She was glad that the side where Mr. Moyle sat was the side on which she had drawn a curl over her shoulder. Once she shot him a quick glance then looked back at the music again because he was watching her in a funny, interested way, as if he were thinking about her and not listening to the music. There was something rather exciting about the way he was watching her, as if she were grown-up and not a little girl. It made her heart beat more quickly, though she didn't know why.

When she stopped and turned to him, however, he was looking at her in just an ordinary way.

"Very good indeed," he said, "excellent"; and to father, "I'd like to give her organ lessons. I think she'd be a very apt pupil."

"It's exceedingly kind of you," said father, speaking in the old-fashioned manner that always irritated Thea.

She often wished she had a father like Lily Beverly's father. He was very well dressed and up-to-date and talked slang and took Lily about to theatres and parties. She loved father, of course, but he was such miles behind the times, and his clothes were always so shabby. He'd looked ghastly when he arrived this afternoon. Just like an old tramp, with his suit all dusty and wearing that awful rhubarb leaf. She imagined Lily Beverly's seeing him like that, and the thought sent little shudders up and down her spine. And he was so terribly particular, too. Lily's father only laughed when they told him about ragging little Miss Forster, the deaf drawing mistress, and getting half tickets on the railway though they were over twelve. But father—well, one simply daren't tell him things like that. One was always having to pretend that one was better than one was. He wasn't often angry, but when he was it was terrible. Like the end of the world.

Her eyes roved approvingly up and down Mr. Moyle's figure. He was very well dressed and very nice looking. She wished suddenly that she was properly grown-up. She wasn't a child exactly. You couldn't call thirteen a child. And yet—well, you couldn't call it properly grown-up either.

"I'm glad she's fond of music," father was saying; "it's a great joy to oneself and to everyone around one." He smiled half deprecatingly as he went on. "Horace Walpole said, 'Had I children my utmost endeavour would be to make them musicians.' "

Thea set her teeth. There he was again with those awful quotations.

. . .

"Your usual terms, of course," he said. "And now shall we go back to the study and talk over the services?"

As he passed Thea, he put his hand on her shoulder and smiled down at her.

"Thank you for your playing, my dear," he said. "I enjoyed it very much."

The pride and affection in his voice made her suddenly feel a beast. And yet something in her hardened, resenting being made to feel a beast. Father was always making one feel a beast.

Rachel peeped in at the door.

"Has he gone?"

"He's in the study with father," said mother. "Why didn't you come back, Rachel, and listen to Thea playing?"

"Because she was shy," said Thea scornfully.

Miriam put her arm round Rachel and, smiling, held her closely to her.

"What a little silly!"

After supper, when Peter and Jane had gone to bed, Timothy read *The Swiss Family Robinson* aloud in the drawing-room. He enjoyed reading to them in the evenings, but at home there was little time for it, as the various parish organisations took him out every night.

Miriam sat embroidering a dress for Jane. She wasn't listening to the story. Her heart was full of a great content. Timothy had arrived safely. Her family was complete. Sitting there with them all around her, she had an illusory sense of being shut in with them in some guarded place where nothing from outside could touch them.

Susan sat forward on a footstool, her eyes fixed intently upon Timothy. A delicious anxiety held her taut and rigid. There *mustn't* be any enemies on the island. Wouldn't it be *dreadful* if they found enemies on the island or if there wasn't any food and they had to starve! How *brave* they were! She wouldn't have been so brave as that. She'd have sat down and cried. She hoped that they'd find a lamp with a gene, like Aladdin, or that a fairy would appear and give them three wishes each. But she was beginning to be afraid that it wasn't that sort of story. Still—it was a lovely story.

Rachel sat gazing dreamily into space. Father reading to them like this in the evening made it completely and absolutely and satisfyingly the Holiday. Somehow it hadn't seemed quite the Holiday till now. . . .

Thea lay back in an armchair in the shadow. As he shook hands with her, he had looked at her again in that funny exciting way in which no one had ever looked at her before. And he had held her hand just a little more tightly than people generally did when they shook hands. She felt thrilled and excited. The curl had fallen down her back with the others. She put up a hand carelessly and drew it forward on to her shoulder again.

Chapter Four

THE day after father had arrived seemed the first day of the Holiday, the other three days merely a kind of prelude to it.

He got up early as usual, had a walk before breakfast, and after breakfast went across to the church for matins. They were going to have lessons when he came back. Always on the Holiday they had half an hour's lessons after breakfast. Thea and Rachel did sums, Susan wrote a copy, and Peter did strokes and pothooks. Father had taught all three of them to write and read in the Holidays before they went to school.

"Would you like to try a real copy to-day, Peter?" he said at breakfast.

"Yes, please," said Peter pleasantly but without much interest.

Jane's small face became tense with anxiety.

"Me too," she pleaded. "*Please*, me too."

"You're too little, darling," said mother. "Peter's a big boy."

"I'm a big girl," said Jane, and the corners of her mouth turned down ominously.

"She might as well if she wants to," said father. "It can't do her any harm."

"I'm a *very* big girl," said Jane earnestly.

But she was still afraid of being left out, and waited in his study till he came back from church in case he forgot to call her with the others.

"Anyone there?" said mother when he returned.

"Two," he said. "It's a nice little church. You've been into it, of course?"

"Yes. I liked it. It's very old, isn't it?"

"Yes. Part of it's Early English. It's been well restored. I must get Moyle to tell me what he knows about it."

"Is the bell all right?"

On nearly all the Holidays the verger was not available on week-days, and father had to ring the bell himself for daily matins and evensong.

"Yes, quite. Not like last year's."

They both laughed.

The bell at last year's Holiday used to swing father right off his feet. He never learnt to manage it during all the four weeks he was there. When the verger rang it on Sunday, it had an odd choky sound as if it were giggling at the memory of father's week-day efforts.

"Who were the two in church?"

"An old lady who was quite deaf and a middle-aged one. She spoke to me. Said that she lived at Meadow Cottage. That's near the shop, isn't it?"

"Yes. She's Miss Pilkington. She lives with an invalid sister. She called, but we'd gone for a walk. The deaf one is old Mrs. Carew."

He took off his cassock and sent Jane to tell the others to come in for lessons. She returned herself first of all, running eagerly in front of the others. As she sat down at the desk with Peter she felt more proud and happy than she had ever felt in her life before. She was a Big Girl. She was Having Lessons. . . .

Father drew a row of slanting lines for her at the top of a page in an exercise-book and gave her a pencil.

"Make a row like that, Jane," he said. "Try not to let them go beneath the big line. And, when you can do those nicely, you can start pothooks. This is a pothook."

He drew a wonderful little curly creature at which Jane gazed in breathless admiration. Then he gave her a pencil.

"Do the strokes first. I'll come and see how you are getting on in a minute."

Jane gazed at the line of even, slanting lines that he had made and worshipped them in her heart. There was something almost unbearably beautiful about them. The thought of doing another row just like them sent quivers of ecstasy through her small body. She took up the pencil.

Thea and Rachel finished their sums and ran out into the garden. Father leant over Susan, who was doing her copy.

"Don't hold the pen so tightly, Susie," he said, "it won't fly out of your hand. I'll give you a sovereign if it flies out of your hand. Now, that's a promise. Thin upstrokes, thick downstrokes . . . that's right. Two fingers on the holder, remember, and the pen pointing over your shoulder like this, not away from you . . . nice round curves like the pothooks."

Father's own writing, even when he was only making rough notes for a sermon, was just like the copy-book's. He loved the regular flowing lines of "copperplate" writing and took a real delight in penmanship.

"That's right, Susie. That's the best you've ever done. I couldn't have made a better B than that myself. And remember, I'll give you a sovereign if the pen flies out of your hand. Now, run along."

"A pick-a-back," she pleaded.

He bent down so that she could climb on to his back and carried her out into the garden.

Peter slipped from his chair and followed them. He had made two or three large capital A's under the copy-book ones, then he had tired of the process and had drawn a frog, which he had licked all over, explaining to Jane, "I'm making it wet, Jane, because frogs are always wet."

Jane didn't hear him. She didn't even know that she was left alone in the room. She worked with desperate eagerness, her pink tongue protruding from her small tense mouth, her fat little fingers clenched round the pencil till they were white and shaking. At last she reached the end of the row of strokes. She drew a deep breath and leant back to look at them. . . . They weren't straight, they weren't even, they leant against each other drunkenly in huddled groups, they plunged wildly beneath the line, they soared erratically to the line above, no two were the same size or at the same angle. She gazed from them to the copy, and horror dawned slowly upon her. She'd thought all the time that she was making a beautiful row just like father's, but hers was ugly, horrible. A bitter sense of failure, failure complete and irrevocable, possessed her. She laid her head down upon the exercise-book and sobbed aloud.

They found her like that a few minutes later, her uneven row of strokes made sodden by her tears. They couldn't understand why she was crying. They tried to comfort her, but nothing could take from her that bitter sense of failure.

Then father called them to a game of rounders in the small clear space at the end of the orchard where there were no trees.

Susan was the last to come. She had been kneeling down under her tree in the orchard and praying: "Please, God, do a miracle and make it fly out of my hand, so that I can have the sovereign. Please, God, may it fly out to-morrow. . . ."

Father's playing with them was, of course, part of the Holiday, He had no time for it at home, but he enjoyed it so much that the children too enjoyed it far more than they enjoyed an ordinary game. Even Thea forgot to pretend that she was grown-up and ran about and screamed just like a little girl.

Mother came out to watch them, and father made her join in the game, and she won a rounder her first turn, picking up her long skirts and running swiftly round the course. When she had made a second rounder she sank down on to the grass, laughing and panting, her thick fair hair uncoiling from its large bun. They all left the game and gathered round her, winding the long golden coils and pinning them up unskilfully with much laughter and scuffling.

Gradually Jane and Peter and Susan were ousted in the scuffle, and Thea and Rachel began to take down the whole structure and build it up again seriously and carefully. Father was sitting on the grass by mother with Jane on his knee. Peter had thrown himself down with his head in mother's lap. Susan was searching in the grass for hairpins.

Suddenly to Rachel it was as if she were detached from the group, watching it from a great distance. Though she seemed so far away from it, every detail was clear and vivid—the tiny fallen apples on the grass, the coils of mother's hair gleaming in the sunshine, father's eyes screwed up as he smiled at Jane, mother's hand moving tenderly over Peter's curls, Susan's small solemn face bent downwards in her search. . . .

I'm going to remember it all my life, she said to herself.

Suddenly they saw Maria coming to them across the grass. Mother stood up and, putting both hands to her hair, said: "Oh, bother! someone's called."

"Miss Pilkington, m'm," said Maria. "She's in the garding; she wouldn't come into the house."

Maria's fringe, uncurled, hung lankly about her eyes beneath the large starched cap, bearing silent witness to her martyrdom. As she announced the caller she cringed in exaggerated panic from a wasp that was buzzing round her.

"This place'll be the death of me, m'm," she added plaintively.

"Surely you've seen wasps in the town, Maria," said Miriam tartly as she smoothed back her hair and straightened her skirt and blouse.

"Yes, but not great savage creatures like these here," said Maria, who was now dodging and ducking as though a whole swarm of wasps was attacking her.

"Bring my hairpins, darling," said Miriam to Susan. "I only hope I've got enough in to keep it up."

They went to the seat under the copper beech, where Miss Pilkington was awaiting her. The visitor was thin and middle-aged and vivacious. She had sharp features and bright, interested, friendly eyes. She was dressed in rather a youthful fashion in a large fly-away black hat and a flounced dress of pale blue muslin with a "V" neck that just showed her collar-bone. As if to compensate for the daringness of this, she wore a length of black tulle wound tightly round her throat and tied in an enormous bow under one ear. A lace scarf lay elegantly over her elbows, and she carried a blue flounced parasol. She greeted Miriam eagerly.

"You're Mrs. Cotteril, aren't you? I'm Miss Pilkington, Miss Caroline Pilkington. I called before, but you were out. I *knew* you wouldn't want to go into the house on a beautiful morning like this, so I do hope you don't mind my staying outside here. It's *quite* an informal call."

Miriam sat down with her, and Susan, deeply interested in the visitor, hovered near.

"Is this your little girl? What's your name, my pet?"

"Susan."

"Well, Susan, I want you *all* to come to tea with me this afternoon." She turned to Miriam with a quick bird-like gesture. "Will you? It's a very unconventional invitation, I'm afraid. Bella's always scolding me for being so unconventional. Bella's my elder sister. She never goes out because she's an invalid, but she's so intensely interested in everything and she *adores* children. You *will* come, won't you?"

"I'm sorry," said Miriam, "but I had a note from Mrs. Lindsay asking us to go to the Hall this afternoon."

"Then come to-morrow. Oh, to-morrow's Sunday. Then come on Tuesday. I won't say Monday, because Monday's our *very* busy day. On Mondays we do the newspapers of the week before. We cut out the items, and paste them in our scrap-book under the appropriate headings. Foreign news, you know, royalty, and so on. It makes a most interesting record. Bella's an invalid, and reading tires her, so I read the paper aloud to her every morning. So depressing nowadays, isn't it, with this terrible war dragging on like this after we all thought Pretoria would finish it? I hear that Kruger says that they won't surrender till their liberty's guaranteed. Did you ever hear such impertinence? I feel quite sure that it would have been ended by now if the Queen had lived. Things will never be the same again without her." She glanced at Susan and lowered her voice. "The new King's gay, you know, *very* gay."

But Susan heard in spite of the lowered voice and she saw the new King quite plainly. He was holding up his robes and dancing gaily round and round his throne, his crown merrily askew.

"And have you read this morning's news," went on Miss Caroline, hardly stopping to draw breath, "about the Empress Frederick? It's dropsy, I believe, and cancer as well. I'm afraid the end is near. Our dear Princess Royal. The Prince's favourite daughter, you know.

I always admired the Prince so much, didn't you? I saw him once when I was a child. Such a handsome man and so good. . . . Times are changing and not for the better, I'm afraid. So *vulgar* these motor-cars and telephones, don't you think? I've never seen a motor-car yet, and I hope I never will."

She paused at length to draw breath.

"You did say Tuesday, didn't you?" said Miriam, feeling almost as breathless as her visitor.

"Yes, Tuesday. Bella will be so disappointed that you can't come to-day. She *adores* children, you know. She wants to show them the little indoor garden that we've made in the conservatory. I *know* they'd love it. You're going to the Lindsays this afternoon, then? We see very little of them in the village. Mrs. Lindsay hardly ever goes out of the grounds. The child's——" She touched her forehead and nodded significantly. "So terribly sad for them."

She rose, gathering the lace scarf about her.

"Well, I must go now. And I'll tell Bella you'll come on Tuesday with the children. Good-bye."

She put up her blue flounced parasol with a click, shook hands with Miriam, kissed Susan, and fluttered off down the drive, turning round frequently to nod and smile.

Chapter Five

THEY walked slowly down the road that led from the Vicarage to the Hall—Thea and Rachel in front, Miriam and Timothy some distance after them. Susan was lagging behind last of all, so that she could trail her toes in the dust, as she loved to do, without being seen.

Miriam wore a green silk dress with a white feather boa and a large straw hat, which was tilted at the side to show the smooth golden waves of her hair, but dipped over her brow in front, throwing a becoming shadow on to her eyes. A gold locket, containing photographs of Peter and Jane as babies, hung on a short gold chain round her neck. She carried a parasol in one white-gloved hand, the other held up the train of the long flounced skirt. The three little girls wore white muslin dresses, with coral necklaces, frilled sun-hats of white organdie, white cotton gloves, long black stockings, and black button boots.

The hedges on either side were gay with traveller's joy and star-like blooms of wild convolvulus. There were long sprays of blackberry, too, some just in flower, others clusters of green berries, already stained here and there with purple. On the other side of the hedge they could see the drift of poppies that bordered the corn-field.

At the gate that led through the park to the Hall, Thea and Rachel stood to wait for the others. Thea watched Miriam admiringly. She longed to be grown-up so that she could hold her skirts up like that as she walked. There was something so unspeakably thrilling about it. Elsie used to let her put on her skirts, fastening them high under her arms, and sweep about holding them up. It wasn't quite as easy as it looked, of course. Lily Beverly's eldest sister had come out last year, and Lily said that it took a lot of practice to hold them up properly. One had to admit that mother did it very well. . . .

They all turned to look at Susan. Her shoes were white with dust, her hat hung down her back by its elastic.

"Oh, *Susan!*" said Miriam reproachfully.

Timothy gathered grass from the roadside to wipe the dust from her shoes, and Miriam tidied her hair and put her hat on.

"The elastic's too tight," complained Susan. "It hurts my neck."

Susan hadn't wanted to come with them. She had wanted to stay with Lena, who was giving a party in the orchard.

"You said it was too loose yesterday," said Miriam patiently, "so I put a tuck in it."

"It's too tight now," said Susan. "It's digging right into my neck."

"Oh, *dear!*" said Miriam, and unpicked the tuck with her teeth.

"It's too loose again now," said Susan, thinking without much real hope that perhaps they'd let her go home if her elastic was too loose or too tight.

"Rubbish!" said Miriam and, taking her by the hand, drew her with her up the long beech avenue that formed the drive.

The Hall was a seventeenth-century manor-house built of red brick in the E shape of the period and half covered by Virginia creeper. Stone steps flanked by wrought-iron balustrades led up to an exquisitely pedimented front door.

Susan's spirits rose as soon as she saw it, and she felt glad that she had come, after all.

It's like a palace, she said to herself. It's *just* the sort of place a princess might live in.

They were ushered into a large drawing-room, and sat together on an enormous sofa like a small shipwrecked party clinging to a raft.

Timothy's thoughts were already far away, planning his book. He had begun his reading for it this morning. It was to treat of the Latin Apologists of the third century—Tertullian, Minucius

Felix, Cyprian, Arnobius, Lactantius. To have time to study and to write was to him as is food to a starving man.

Miriam was thinking: It's going to be dreadful. They're going to patronise me. . . . Oh, well, it will soon be over, and the children look sweet.

Thea was throwing bright interested glances round the room. They must be very rich. A butler had opened the door. They had a carriage, of course. Perhaps two. It must be lovely to be as rich as that. She'd never marry for money, because it was wrong, but she hoped that she'd fall in love with a very rich man, who was nice as well, and they'd get married and keep two carriages and a butler.

Rachel was practising not being shy. Silently she was saying, "Yes, we live just outside Manchester. We love coming to the country for a holiday." She was always trying to say grown-up things like that to people, but she never could. She knew now that really she wouldn't be able to say it. She'd only be able to say "Yes" and "No" when they asked her questions. . . . There was something terrifying about the strange and magnificent drawing-room. It gave her a feeling of comfort to be sitting between father and mother. She stole sidelong glances up at them. How pretty mother looked in her green silk dress and the hat that turned up at the sides to show the soft golden waves of her hair, and how nice father looked with his kind, rather tired face. A wave of pride in them swept over her. She slipped her hand into father's, and, without looking at her or speaking to her, he pressed it in his.

Susan was thinking: It's just like a palace inside too. This is the throne-room, and that big chair over there is the throne. That statue in the corner holding the lamp is a genie. It comes to life when you rub the lamp. That dog sitting on the path just outside the window isn't a real dog. It's a witch in disguise trying to get into the palace to put a spell on the princess. But it can't get in because that bear rug by the fire isn't a real bear rug at all. It's a dragon in disguise guarding the princess, and the witch can't come in as long as it's here.

Then the door opened, and Mrs. Lindsay entered. She was small and vague and lost-looking, and somehow like a child, although her face was lined and her brown hair streaked with grey. She came forward shyly, apologetically.

"I'm so sorry you've had to walk. I didn't realise it was so hot. I ought to have sent the carriage for you."

Miriam said that it was quite all right, and that they'd enjoyed the walk, and that it would have been ridiculous to drive that short distance.

The little lady seemed immensely relieved to hear this.

"My husband's in the garden," she said. "Would you like to go out? It's quite shady there . . . or perhaps you'd like to stay indoors and rest a little first."

She spoke in a nervous, hesitating way as if she were half afraid of them and desperately anxious to please, and yet she still gave that impression of remoteness, like someone who was walking in her sleep. Rachel, looking at her suddenly, saw how pretty she must have been before her hair was streaked with grey, and that look of strained anxiety came to her face.

"I think we'd love to come out into the garden," Miriam was saying, and there was an unconscious note of reassurance in her voice, as if she were trying to set a shy child at its ease.

They followed her through the French window, down the stone steps guarded by a pair of stone lions, and on to the lawn. There was a group of basket chairs under a cedar tree, and from one of them a man rose and came forward to greet the visitors. He was tall, thin, and good-looking, though there was the same elusive suggestion of premature age about him as there was about his wife.

They sat down in the basket chairs, and Timothy, looking about him, said:

"How beautiful your trees are! Isn't it Pope who says: 'A tree is a nobler object than a prince in his coronation robes'?"

Rachel knew that he was thinking of their own parish, where the summer was airless and malodorous and oppressive, with no shade, no breeze, only a furnace-like heat that burnt and suffocated. Thea thought impatiently: Another of those dreadful quotations!

What will they think of him? And his suit looks so shabby in the sunshine. Almost green. I wish he'd get a new one.

"I'll fetch my little girl," said Mrs. Lindsay, standing up, and at once her husband said to Timothy:

"I wonder if you'd care to look round the green-houses?"

When they had gone, Mrs. Lindsay went into the house and soon came back with her arm round a girl almost as tall as herself. The girl walked awkwardly with shambling, unsteady footsteps. Her head drooped forward, and as she came nearer they saw that her mouth hung open in a meaningless smile, and that her blue eyes were fixed vacantly in front of her. There was something repellent about the large heavy-featured face, but the hair that framed it was beautiful—long and thick and wavy and the colour of spun gold. It hung loose down her back, and, like everything else about her, its floss-like silkiness bore witness to scrupulous and loving care. She wore a white silk dress daintily embroidered and trimmed with knots of pale blue ribbon.

Her vacant smile grew broader when she saw the visitors, and she began to make inarticulate excited noises. The mother settled her in an armchair and introduced her to the visitors.

"This is Agnes," she said. "Say 'how-do-you-do,' darling."

The girl made an unintelligible sound, and began to wave her arms about with clumsy, flail-like gestures. Mrs. Lindsay hung over her chair, coaxing, interpreting, reassuring, and occasionally wiping away the saliva that dribbled from the loose mouth.

"Don't get excited, darling. It's all right. Mother's not going away again. This is Mrs. Cotteril, this is Thea, this is Rachel, and this is Susan. They're coming to have tea with us." Then, aside to Miriam: "She loves visitors coming. . . . Yes, darling . . . pretty . . . she's trying to say pretty. . . . Look!" She took a string of large coloured wooden beads—of the kind generally used in kindergartens—from her work-bag, which lay by her chair on the grass. "Show the lady. Which is red?"

The girl, beaming widely, made a grab at the red beads.

"And count two for mother. . . . Show the lady two. . . . Two. . . ."

Fumbling and grinning, the girl divided two beads from the others on the string.

The mother raised her flushed worn face and looked at Miriam.

"The doctor says that she does get on ... of course, she's slow ... but she *does* get on. Three, darling, show the lady three. ... Three."

But the girl had tired of it and flung the whole string on to the ground. At that moment Mr. Lindsay and Timothy returned. As soon as the father's eyes fell upon his daughter his face seemed to harden and he looked away quickly.

"We're just going to the stables, Mrs. Cotteril," he said to Miriam. "Would you care to come?"

"I'd like to very much," said Miriam, rising with alacrity.

She was glad to escape, though she hated leaving the children there. Really, they oughtn't to bring the girl out before visitors like this. It was too painful.

The girl seemed to have taken a fancy to Thea. She was holding out her arms to her and making short excited noises.

"I think it's your necklace, dear," said the mother. "She wants to look at it. May she?"

Thea went across to her, and the girl laid her hands on the coral string, shouting excitedly.

"Quietly, darling! You don't mind, do you, dear? ... She likes the colour."

Thea unclasped the necklace and put it into the girl's hands.

"I'd love her to have it to keep if she'd like it," she said prettily.

"Oh, my dear, of course not," said the mother. "Just look at it, and then give it back to Thea, darling. ... It's Thea's. Give it back to Thea. ..."

The girl clung to it, and, when the mother tried gently to take it from her fingers, grew angry, drawing the heavy brows together and snarling.

"*Please* let her keep it," said Thea. "I'd love her to."

"It's so good of you," said Mrs. Lindsay, standing up and moving a strand of her brown hair from across her tired unhappy eyes. "If she may keep it just till you go. ..."

Left in possession of her treasure, the girl smiled and began again to gabble quickly and unintelligibly.

"She's pleased," said Mrs. Lindsay. "You see, she understands quite well."

"Can she walk far?" said Thea.

"Oh, yes . . . and much better than she used to walk. She needs someone there to help her, but she gets along quite fast now, leaning on my arm. We never go out of the grounds, of course."

"Of course not," said Thea in an understanding, sympathetic way.

She felt delightfully grown-up. She was talking to Mrs. Lindsay almost as if she were mother, and Mrs. Lindsay was talking back to her in the same way.

"She can tell the different colours quite well now," Mrs. Lindsay was saying. "All the doctors say that she's getting on. Of course, it's bound to be slow."

"Of course," said Thea again.

She hoped that Rachel, who was listening, realised how grown-up she could be when she tried. She didn't want Rachel to think that, just because she liked listening to her stories, she too was only a little girl. There was a tremendous difference between eleven and thirteen.

"Talk to her, dear," went on Mrs. Lindsay. "She'd love it."

Thea, smiling, bent towards the girl. "Do you like the necklace, Agnes?" she said.

The girl smiled and jabbered with delight.

"She couldn't walk at all till a few years ago," put in Mrs. Liadsay. "We tried every treatment."

"Really?" said Thea.

She felt more and more excitingly grown-up every minute.

The butler and two maids brought out tea, and the others returned from the stables and sat down in the basket chairs around the table. Mrs. Lindsay began to pour out the tea, but at sight of the food Agnes had grown so excited that she handed the tea-pot to her husband in order to sit by her and quiet her. Her husband took it without looking at either her or his daughter.

He was talking to Timothy about the harvest.

"This hot, dry weather," he was saying, "has ruined both the hay and the root crops, and the failure of the oat harvest, of course, is a really serious matter to horse-keepers. With all the shipment of forage to South Africa, the price at home is going to be extortionate. The wheat looks well enough, but the threshing machine will probably prove that it isn't. It can't be, after this long drought. These are bad days for the farmers all round. Some people say that labour-saving machinery will improve the situation, but I very much doubt it."

Miriam watched Mrs. Lindsay and her daughter in silence. She felt hotly indignant. She wouldn't have brought the children if she'd known the girl was as bad as this. Thea was being rather sweet, helping Mrs. Lindsay, picking up the string of beads to distract the girl's attention. . . . Looking from Thea to the other girl, she was conscious of a rush of pride and happiness. Money didn't matter, after all. She'd rather have Timothy and Thea and Rachel and Susan and Peter and Jane than all the money in the world.

Rachel was struggling with a nightmare feeling of panic. Here was something else to live in that dark cupboard of horrors that one's memory held, something that would creep out at unexpected moments, clouding the brightness of the sun, poisoning all the joy of life. That dreadful loose face, those shambling limbs, those hoarse animal noises. And that was not all. There was an odd sense of strain in the atmosphere that she couldn't understand. She sensed it dimly but unmistakably like a hound picking up a faint scent. It was something to do with Agnes's father and mother, something to do with the way they never looked at each other if they could help it, with the way they spoke to each other like people in a play saying words that they'd learnt by heart because they had to, not like people talking together ordinarily.

Susan's eyes never left the girl opposite. As soon as she saw her, the long, shining golden hair had reminded her of the picture of the princess on the front page of her fairy-tale book. And yet the face wasn't like a princess's. It was more like the face of the beast in Beauty and the Beast. And almost at once the explanation struck her. The witch *had* got into the palace, after all, in spite of the dragon and the genie, but she hadn't been able to put the princess altogether under a spell. She'd changed her face, but she hadn't been able to change her hair—the long thick hair that shone like gold and reached right down to her waist.

And one day a prince would come. He'd walk through the tall iron gates, up the winding drive, past the stone lions and into the house. And all he'd have to do would be to kiss the princess, and at once she'd change back into herself, becoming straight, slender, and beautiful. Only the golden hair wouldn't change, because it had never been under the spell.

Mrs. Lindsay was feeding the girl, bending over her, soothing, coaxing, eating nothing herself. Suddenly Agnes became excited again, shouting, and throwing her food about in all directions.

The father rose with an abrupt movement.

"Hadn't she better go in, Frances?"

He spoke with schooled gentleness, but his lips were set and tight.

"Yes . . . perhaps."

"I'll take her."

But his wife said "No, Roger" with a quick, odd intensity and began to help the big shambling figure of the girl out of the chair. He made no further attempt to assist them. Thea rose and, taking the work-bag from Mrs. Lindsay's arm with a "Let me carry this," followed them indoors.

Soon Mrs. Lindsay and Thea reappeared, and round Thea's neck instead of the corals was a string of seed pearls.

"I do hope you don't mind," said Mrs. Lindsay nervously to Miriam. "Thea kindly lent her corals to Agnes, and now I can't get Agnes to give them up. I hope you'll let her accept this necklace instead. I never wear it, and Agnes can't wear necklaces. She breaks them, and in any case she only likes coloured things. *Do* let me give it her."

At first Miriam refused, then—Thea drew a sigh of relief—began to waver.

"She's been so *kind* to Agnes," persisted the little lady fervently, "I should like her to have something to remember us by."

"It's very good of you," said Miriam, yielding finally with obvious reluctance.

It appeared that Agnes's mother could not stay in the garden with them.

"I'm so sorry, but I'm sure you'll understand. She's got a little over-excited, and she's so upset if I leave her at all. She won't let anyone do anything for her but me. . . . You *do* understand, don't you?"

Miriam said that it was time for them to go in any case, and they set off again down the drive and along the road. The sun was verging to the west and flooding the countryside with a golden haze. Farm labourers coming home from work touched their caps and gave them a friendly greeting. Thea hoped that they all noticed that she was wearing a string of seed pearls while Rachel and Susan only wore corals.

When they reached home Miriam changed her dress, then went to help Maria set the table for supper. Maria was showing her general resentment against the Holiday by refusing to learn the ways of the new household, so that Miriam had to help her in everything she did. Cook was pleasant and efficient, but between her province and that of the housemaid there was in her eyes an impassable gulf, and she declined with polite firmness to help Maria in any of her duties.

"I dunno where the knives are, m'm," said Maria gloomily as Miriam entered.

"The knife-basket's in that cupboard," said Miriam shortly. "I've told you so every time you've set the table."

Maria took out the knife-basket and laid the cutlery on to the table, assisted by Miriam.

"I never see'd such an ill-favoured set of men as the set round here, m'm," she said; "not one you'd want to look at in the whole lot of 'em."

Miriam smiled, despite herself.

"Well . . . you'll soon be going back to George," she said.

Maria abandoned herself to yet deeper gloom.

"I only hope I lives to see him again, m'm," she said. "The things that happen here with all these hanimals about you'd never believe. Cook's uncle knew a man what died of having his arm broke by a gander, and her own uncle was gorged by a bull."

"You mean gored," said Miriam, "and you shouldn't listen to Cook's tales. You ought to be glad of a nice quiet holiday in the country."

"Quiet!" sniffed Maria. "I can't sleep at night for the noise that there ivy makes moanin' an' groanin' just outside the window. Like someone bein' murdered alive."

"Maria, how can you be so silly! If you can sleep at home with trams clanging all night and the shop people shouting till nearly midnight, you can sleep here."

"I can't, m'm," said Maria with gloomy persistence. "There's somethin' nacheral about trams an' shoutin' an' shops, but this here ivy an' dark an' suchlike—it's unnacheral. It fair turns my stomach."

In the study Timothy had taken Susan on his knee. The others, he was sure, would understand and pity, but Susan was too young to understand without explanation.

"You must feel very, very sorry for her," he was saying, "because she can't think and walk and talk as you can. God wants us all to do our best to take care of people like that for Him and to be kinder to them than we are to anyone else. And you must thank God that He's sent you into the world strong and well."

Susan gazed at him solemnly with wide, uncomprehending eyes. He couldn't know, of course, that to Susan Agnes had stepped straight out of a fairy tale.

Chapter Six

THE children stood before the counter of the shop, helping Susan to spend her penny. The penny was a reward for letting mother pull a loose tooth out that morning.

"Get bull's-eyes," Peter kept shouting excitedly. "Get a pen'oth of bull's-eyes."

But Jane had seen a sugar pig in the window, and she was giving soft little tugs at Susan's frock and saying, "The sugar pig, Susan, the sugar pig," in a gentle, insistent whisper over and over again.

"Let her get what she likes," said Rachel, but she couldn't help adding: "Why don't you get liquorice ribbons, Susan? They're awfully nice."

Thea stood in the door-way, grown-up and aloof, trying to look as if she were in charge of the children instead of one of them.

"Do stop shouting, Peter," she said severely. "Don't listen to him, Susan. What about pear-drops? You like pear-drops, don't you?"

Susan looked tense and desperate, as though the responsibility of the choice weighed almost too heavily upon her spirit. She held her penny tightly in one hand, and gazed with large solemn eyes at the bottles of sweets on the counter.

"Toasted squares," shouted Peter, who was growing more excited every moment. "Look, Susan, there's some toasted squares."

"Oh, Peter, *do* be quiet," said Thea.

"The sugar pig, Susan," repeated Jane's small beseeching whisper. "Susan, the sugar pig."

Miss Thrupp had laid her large doll in its cradle to attend to tham. Now she took it up again and stood, holding it in her arms and smiling at the children over its flaxen head.

At first it had seemed strange to them to see Miss Thrupp standing at the door of her shop or sitting behind the counter nursing the doll. It was almost as big as a baby and was dressed in a long embroidered robe and a shawl. She undressed and dressed it every night and morning, and would often stand rocking it in her arms and crooning a lullaby to it. Everyone in the village seemed to take it as a matter of course, and the Cotteril children, too, had now grown quite accustomed to the sight. Once Susan, passing the shop as Miss Thrupp stood in the doorway with the doll in her arms, had found courage to say, "Please, may I look at your——" she was just going to say "doll," when some instinct prompted her to substitute "baby," and Miss Thrupp had smiled and drawn back the shawl from the pink-and-white china face and let Susan hold the bundle of beautifully laundered cambric in her arms for a few moments.

"She's a lovely baby, isn't she?" she had said as she took it back into her own arms.

Susan had replied "Yes," and then, feeling suddenly shy, had hurried on down the road.

"Make up your mind quickly, Susan," said Thea. "We can't wait all day. Why not have mixed fruit-drops? There are all sorts of different tastes in mixed fruit-drops."

"Toasted squares," yelled Peter.

"The sugar pig," whispered Jane.

Rachel lifted a shining length of liquorice ribbon from its box suggestively.

"Yes, I'll have mixed fruit-drops," said Susan, yielding automatically to Thea's suggestion.

She put down her penny, clutched it back. "No, no . . . I won't . . . I'll have toasted squares . . . no, liquorice ribbon . . ." She was flushed and quivering with excitement. "No, I won't. . . ." Her eyes fell suddenly upon a collection of tiny metal objects jumbled together in a box. On the top of them was a metal lantern about half an inch high with little red panes of glass.

"How much is that?" she said breathlessly.

"A penny, missie," said Miss. Thrupp.

"I'll have that," said Susan, pushing the penny across the counter and seizing the little metal lantern as tightly as if she thought that the other children were going to snatch it from her.

They went out of the shop and down the road again. Thea and Rachel walked in front, aloof, superior. Peter walked with Susan, shouting, "Why didn't you buy the toasted squares, Susan? Why didn't you buy the bull's-eyes? Why didn't you buy a ha'p'oth of each? I'd have done that. I'd have bought a ha'p'oth of bull's-eyes and a ha'p'oth of toasted squares." His raised voice bore witness to the depth of his feelings on the subject. Jane stayed behind outside the shop window, her vague button of a nose flattened against it, gazing wistfully at the sugar pig. Thea turned round and called, "Come along, Jane," and Jane obediently ran till she had caught up with Peter and Susan. Then Peter and Jane went on together, and Susan fell behind to walk by herself. She held the little lantern tightly in her hand. She felt half ashamed and wholly in disgrace. There was clearly implied reproach in the way the others left her to herself. If she had bought sweets she would have handed them round, of course. They would all be walking along the road together in a friendly group, eating them.

She opened her hand to peep at the little lantern, and a wave of delight swept over her. A tiny handle . . . tiny panes of red glass. . . . She walked very slowly, worshipping it. The others were a long way in front. . . . She was passing Meadow Cottage, where Miss Caroline Pilkington lived with her invalid sister. They were going to tea there this afternoon. She stole a glance at the windows. She would have liked to see Miss Caroline nodding and waving to her, but there was no one there. . . . The others were quite out of sight now. She was passing a fair-sized house, set a little way back from the road, called The Moorings. Again she threw a cautious glance upwards (you mustn't stare into people's windows, but you could let your eyes just pass them on the way to something else). A stout, handsome woman with elaborately dressed hair and very red cheeks stood at the window, nodding and beckoning. Suddenly she disappeared, then the front door opened, and she came hurrying down to the gate.

"You're Susan, aren't you?" she said. She had a husky, breathless voice and a tremulous, appealing smile that somehow went oddly with the majestic coiffure. "I know all about you, you see. There's Thea and Rachel and you and Peter and Jane. That's right, isn't it? And my name's Mrs. Seacome. I meant to call on your mother yesterday, but I wasn't well. Come in, and I'll show you my parrot."

She took Susan's hand and led her up the narrow path to the house. A rather grim-looking old servant was in the hall. She threw a quick glance at her mistress and said, "Don't you think you'd better go an' lie down, m'm?"

"Don't be absurd, Harriet," said Mrs. Seacome gaily. "This is Susan. She's come to see Polly, haven't you, darling? This way, Susan. . . . Polly lives in the dining-room. . . . And there are some sugar biscuits here, too. Do you like sugar biscuits, Susan? But of course you do. All little girls like sugar biscuits."

It was rather bewildering to be suddenly sitting on a chair in a strange house eating sugar biscuits and listening to a real parrot. But it was very nice. The parrot whistled "Ta-ra-ra-boom-de-ay" and "Soldiers of the Queen" and "Good-bye, Dolly, I must leave you," and made strange pops and catcalls, and laughed and cried at the same time. Susan didn't much like his doing the last, she didn't know why. Also, though she loved the parrot, the way Mrs. Seacome watched her made her feel vaguely uncomfortable. Mrs. Seacome looked at her all the time, never at the parrot, and it gave Susan the strange, suffocating feeling that she always had when people kissed and hugged her too much. And that was odd, because Mrs. Seacome hadn't even kissed her. Suddenly the parrot called out, "Hello, mummie," in a clear, child's voice, and at once the old woman came in and threw a cloth over him.

Susan remembered suddenly that she oughtn't to have come in alone. The others wouldn't know where she was, and Thea would be cross.

"I must go home now," she said.

"Put some sugar biscuits in your pocket to take with you," said Mrs. Seacome breathlessly, filling the tiny pocket in the blue sailor suit. "Oh, what a little pocket! I'll tell you what. I'll put some in a bag for you. Get me a bag, Harriet. Quickly, quickly!" The hands that poured the biscuits from the biscuit-box into the bag trembled so violently that several of them rolled on to the floor. Looking up into her new friend's face, Susan saw that her eyes were hot and flushed and that, though she was smiling, there were lines on it as if she had cried a lot.

"You'll come and see me again, darling, won't you? And bring the others. . . . Do you like dolls?"

"Yes," said Susan.

"How many have you got?"

"Ten," said Susan, warming to the subject. "Before we came away Nurse was teaching me to make dolls' clothes. I made a dress for Belinda out of an old blouse of mother's."

"Oh, darling, I've got lots of pieces of stuff you'd like, then. Bring me the 'pieces' bag, Harriet. . . . Do be quick. And some paper. Look, darling." The bag was emptied on to the table, and the unsteady fingers were picking out bits of lace and silk and satin and brocade. Susan's eyes shone with pleasure.

"Oh, thank you!"

"And I've got lots more, so come back for some whenever you like. Here they are."

Susan stood in the hall, the parcel of sugar biscuits under one arm, the parcel of "pieces" under the other. As though to reward the lady for her kindness, she opened her hand to disclose her treasure.

"Look!" she said.

The lady's delight over the little lantern was gratifying.

"How lovely! Where did you get it?"

"At the shop. It was a penny."

The lady's trembling hand fumbled in her skirts and brought out a purse. She took a long time to open it, then brought out a great, round five-shilling piece.

"I want you to have that, to buy something nice for yourself."

Susan looked at it regretfully.

"I'm sorry," she said, "but mother doesn't let us take money from people."

The lady seemed deeply distressed by this.

"Oh, *dear*! Well, you must come round again soon for some more pieces and biscuits, won't you? And tell your mother I hope to call on her tomorrow."

She took her visitor to the door and stood there waving till she had disappeared. Susan ran down the road after the others. It had been thrilling and exciting, but somehow she was glad to get away. The house was quite bright and sunny, but she felt as if it had been cold and dark. The lady hadn't kissed or hugged her, and yet she felt as if she had done both till she had been half choked.

Rachel had been sent back to meet Susan and tell her to hurry, but Rachel herself was dawdling dreamily along the road, quite forgetting her errand. She was thinking how strange and terrifying it was that each step she took, each breath she drew, each word she uttered, slipped behind her immediately and became the Past. You couldn't stay still for a second. Why, only a moment ago she'd been *going* to walk along that bit of the road, and now it was all over for ever and belonged to the Past. Why, even that thought about it was over now and belonged to the Past. . . . It was terrifying and mysterious. . . . The Holiday was slipping by, minute by minute, day by day, and you couldn't stop it, however hard you tried. Five days of it belonged to the Past already. It was the sixth day now, and every second brought it nearer to the seventh, and soon the seventh would come to an end, then the eighth, then the ninth, till the whole Holiday would have slipped by into the Past and they'd be at home again. . . . If only one could *stop* it just for a few days. . . . But you couldn't even think of days without thinking of minutes and hours passing by. . . . It *was* mysterious. . . . The first Sunday of the Holiday was over, and there were only three more. Rachel liked all Sundays, but the first Sunday of the Holiday was the nicest Sunday of the year. It had been warm and sunny, and the side door of the little church had been left open, so that from where she sat she could see a thrush hopping about in the grass by the church door looking for worms. Once she had quivered with sudden excitement, thinking that he was coming right in. It had been

Rachel's turn to sit next to mother, with Jane on the other side. They preserved their turns for sitting next to mother in church very zealously.

Mother had on her green silk dress, and Rachel leant her cheek against its soft coolness and slipped her hand into mother's during the sermon, Peter, who wore his white sailor suit with long trousers, was fidgety and dropped his penny and scuffled his feet so that once father turned right round to look at him. Jane was very good, sleeping as usual all through both lessons and the litany and the sermon. The sermon wasn't as long as father's sermons sometimes were. Father always began to preach just as if he were talking in an ordinary way, and then suddenly something seemed to take hold of him and the words poured out quickly as if they were saying themselves, and he couldn't have kept them back even if he'd tried.

In the afternoon he went to Sunday School, and Thea went with him to take the infants' class, and mother read aloud to the others in the garden from the Sunday book. They had begun that particular Sunday book three weeks ago. It was called *The Gospel in Caesar's Household*, and was so exciting that they could hardly bear to wait till the next Sunday to learn what happened.

Then father and Thea came back, and father said that Thea had managed splendidly, and that he was very proud of her, and Thea began to be most annoyingly grown-up, till she realised that mother had been reading the Sunday book, and then she wanted to know what had happened to Pompilia and begged Rachel quite humbly to tell her.

After tea father sat on the lawn with Jane and Peter and told them about David and Goliath, and the others came round to listen too, because father always made the Bible stories so real that they became quite new and exciting stories that you'd never heard before. Even Thea sat where she could listen, though she pretended to be drawing the copper beech on her sketching block.

Before they went to bed mother played hymns and they chose one each in turns. Cook had gone to church, but Maria came in as usual to sing hymns with them. Peter chose "Dare to be a Daniel," and Jane, "Gentle Jesus, meek and mild," and Susan, "Do no sinful action," and Rachel, "All things bright and beautiful," and Thea, "Art thou weary, art thou languid," because she thought that it was a specially grown-up hymn. Maria chose "Within the churchyard side by side," but mother wouldn't let her have it, so instead she chose "Abide with me," and sniffed luxuriously all through it.

Here Rachel's reverie was broken by the sight of Susan, coming towards her down the road with a paper bag under each arm.

"Hello!" called Susan.

"Where have you been?" said Rachel.

"I went into a lady's house," said Susan. "She asked me to. She's given me some sugar biscuits, and I'm going to divide them equally."

She had decided that to divide the sugar biscuits equally would partly atone for having bought the lantern instead of sweets.

Miss Caroline had asked them all to come to tea, but father had a wedding, and Peter and Jane were considered too young to go out to tea. They were apt to get over-excited, and then Peter shouted and Jane cried.

Miss Caroline was at the door to receive them. She wore a rusty, old-fashioned black silk dress, with a long train and heavy whaleboned bodice freely trimmed with jet. An enormous jet brooch held the collar together, and a jet chain dangled from her neck. Her greying hair was drawn into a bun on the top of her head, but little wisps of it escaped on all sides and hung round her ears and neck. There was about her a subdued air, which failed, however, quite to quench her native eagerness.

"She's gone," she greeted Miriam in a whisper. "Have you seen to-day's papers? She's gone."

"Who?" said Miriam, mystified. "Oh, the Empress Frederick."

"Yes." She ushered them into the tiny sitting-room. "One really hardly feels like *festivity*, does one? But after all, life must go on, and it's no use brooding over things by oneself. ... The dear Emperor gave up all his plans to be at her bedside. ... I saw him at Queen Victoria's funeral—not *really*, of course, but in the *Illustrated London News*—and I thought him so handsome. I've never been able to understand how gentlemen train their moustaches to grow *up*—considering the force of gravity, I mean—but I always think it's *so* becoming. . . . My sister doesn't get up till tea-time. She's an invalid, you know, and *so* brave. . . . I'm sure the children would like to see the little indoor garden that we've made in the conservatory. My sister never goes out, and it's such a joy to her. Come along, children. . . ."

The "conservatory" was a small greenhouse opening off the dining-room. The staging had been covered with slate and soil, and on this had been arranged the "indoor garden." It was in reality a miniature countryside—microscopic ponds and fields and rocks and fences with toy animals (not always in exact proportion) dotted here and there. There was a winding lane with a horse and cart going along it. . . . But its greatest glory was a waterfall that rippled down the rocks and fell into a little lake. Miss Caroline first filled a hidden tank with a jug of water, then pulled a string and—the little waterfall gurgled and rippled down its rocky bed.

"Dr. Flemming made that," said Miss Pilkington. "And he brought most of the rocks. I plant snowdrops here and crocuses here and scillas here, and in the spring it's a perfect picture."

The children hung over it, entranced, and Miss Caroline and Miriam returned to the drawing-room. It was a charming little room, panelled in cream-painted wood. At the open window fine net curtains billowed out in the breeze over the deep chintz-covered window-seat. A bowl of roses stood on a mahogany pie-crust table in the middle of the room. In one corner was a cabinet full of old china, and in another the sunlight caught the polished surface of a Queen Anne bureau. Miss Caroline's quick bird-like gaze flashed round the room. "Now where would you be *most* comfortable, Mrs. Cotteril?" Her visitor's comfort seemed an overwhelming responsibility to her. Her anxious glance seemed to try every chair in the room and find it wanting. At last she chose a winged chair with polished claw feet peeping from its chintz cover, and settled Miriam into it solicitously, drawing up a footstool of faded embroidery for her feet. Then she took her seat on a small upright chair, poised on the very edge as if ready at any minute to leap to her feet in answer to a summons.

She smoothed out her old-fashioned black dress and flashed her bright eager smile at Miriam.

"I'm afraid I never wear black in the ordinary way," she said. "I do so love colour. I had this when my dear mother died and wore it last this spring when the dear Queen died. I was thinking that I'd have to take it out and air it, but, of course, I needn't now that the dear Empress has died. I keep it for bereavements, and when no bereavement occurs for a year or so I take it out and hang it in the sunshine for a day to keep it fresh. . . . But now, dear Mrs. Cotteril, let's talk of something more cheerful. I suppose that you've met all our little community. You went to the Hall?"

"Yes, on Saturday."

"They're so nice, aren't they? but, of course, Mrs. Lindsay never goes out now. They say Agnes is worse. . . . *And* Mrs. Seacome . . . have you met her?"

"Not yet. She called Susan in this morning and gave her some biscuits."

"She lost her husband and children—four little girls—in a yachting accident three years ago, just before she came to live here. She was devoted to them. The parrot still imitates their voices. I don't know how she can bear it. I'd have got rid of him at once. . . . It was a *dreadful* tragedy, of course, and I suppose that really one can hardly blame her for——" She broke off abruptly. "But I mustn't gossip. How do you like the Vicarage? A dear old house, isn't it? I went to my first party there as a child. I shall never forget it. It was Christmas, and the vicar dressed up as Father Christmas, and I thought he was Guy Fawkes and screamed so much that I had to be taken home. I suppose you find housekeeping difficult after living in a town? Miss Thrupp always seems to have everything but just the thing one wants, doesn't she?"

"Yes. . . . How odd of her always to nurse that doll."

"I suppose it does seem odd," said Miss Caroline thoughtfully. "Of course, we've all grown so accustomed to it now. She's had it about two years. . . . It's a very strange story. She was becoming so unbalanced that everyone—even Dr. Flemming—thought she'd have to be put away. Then Dr. Flemming won this doll in a raffle at the Sale of Work, and he gave it to Miss Thrupp. We thought it was so strange of him to give it to her instead of to a child. . . . But the stranger thing was that Miss Thrupp seemed at once to grow normal in the ordinary way, though, of course, she's quite abnormal about the doll. She undresses it every night, you know, and puts on its nightdress and has it in bed with her. . . . And she nurses it all day, as you've seen. But except for that she's quite pleasant and capable, while before she was most neurotic and queer-tempered. Mrs. Rothwell says that she ought to be certified even now, but, of course, Dr. Flemming would never allow it. You've not met the Rothwells, have you? He's the vicar's churchwarden, but they've not come back from their holidays yet. Two children. I don't think you'll——" Again she broke off abruptly. "But I mustn't gossip." She rose with a jingle of jet ornaments. "I do hope you'll excuse me while I go and help my sister dress. . . . The dear children are still quite happy in the conservatory."

She fluttered out of the room, and Miriam joined the three children. Thea and Rachel were filling the tank and turning on the waterfall over and over again. Susan was watching, her eyes bright with ecstasy.

"We've not got very wet, mother," said Thea, "and it's such fun."

Miriam stayed with them till Miss Bella Pilkington, swathed in shawls and supported by her sister, came down to the drawing-room.

Miss Caroline was flushed and panting as she supported her sister's heavy frame. She introduced them breathlessly.

"Now I'm going to leave my sister to entertain you, Mrs. Cotteril, while I see about tea. We have a clever little maid, but she's not *very* experienced yet. . . . My sister will show you our news scrap-books. They're such a pleasure and interest to her. I read the paper to her all through every morning, and then we cut out the items and paste them in."

She drew up a table, put on to it a large pile of scrap-books, and fluttered away again.

Miss Bella Pilkington was as stout and lethargic as her sister was thin and mercurial. Small petulant eyes were sunk deeply in the flabby flesh of her cheeks, which seemed to have pushed the mouth together from either side, till it was merely a peevish little button. Miriam tried to talk to her, but she answered in monosyllables, refusing even a pretence of interest in her guests. Miriam at last confined herself to the scrap-books, turning over page after page of newspaper cuttings neatly pasted in under their appropriate headings. Soon Miss Caroline entered, flushed and smiling.

"Tea will be ready in a few moments now. . . . Let me show you the scrap-books, Mrs. Cotteril . . . The foreign news is in that one, the domestic news in that, fashion in that, and—*here* is the Royal news."

It was obvious that Miss Caroline's deepest interest was centred in the Royal news. Every possible item dealing with the Royal family was there, with innumerable illustrations cut out of the *Graphic* or the *Illustrated London News*.

"I never tire of looking at these old pictures of the dear Queen and her children," she said. "They're so touching. I can *cry* over them." As if in proof of this her voice grew tremulous and her eyes misty as she turned the pages one by one. "Such a splendid mother. . . . And now," her face glowed with enthusiasm, "here's this wonderful Empire tour of the dear Duke and Duchess. I almost wish I'd got a fresh book entirely for that. They reached Port Louis yesterday, you know, and had a most magnificent reception. So cheering, and one needs something cheering among all the other sad news—this dreadful war and the dear Empress's death. These news records are such a great interest and pleasure to my sister."

Her sister's behaviour certainly did not support this view. She looked at them peevishly and without interest, complaining first that there was a draught, then that the room was stuffy, then that she wanted a footstool, then, when one had been brought, that she didn't want a footstool, then that her shawl was too thin, then that she didn't want a shawl at all. Miss Caroline flew about, waiting on her, soothing her, reassuring her. "So trying for her," she whispered to Miriam, "and she's so brave."

A gong in the hall announced tea, and they all went into the sunny little dining-room, where eggshell china and Georgian silver were spread upon a polished mahogany table.

Miss Bella Pilkington, though she ate largely, seemed to grow more and more fractious as the meal went on, and Miriam and the children took their leave soon afterwards.

The children chattered about the "garden" all the way home.

"Just like a little magic waterfall," said Susan.

"There was nothing *magic* about it," said Thea scornfully. "It was just a tap that let the water out of a tank ... but it *was* interesting."

"It was lovely," said Rachel, "but it makes another day of the Holiday nearly gone."

When they reached home they found that a letter had come for Miriam by the evening's post. She opened and read it.

"Aunt Bridget's coming on Thursday," she announced. "Won't that be nice!"

Chapter Seven

THEA was having her organ lesson, and Rachel was "blowing" for her. The handle of the bellows was like a pump handle. You worked it up and down ... up and down. Near it a little bobbin dangled against the wall at the end of a string and went down when the bellows were full and up when they were empty. On the wall was a line drawn in chalk, and when the little bobbin went above the chalked line it meant that there was no air in the organ, and the emptiness made a loud moan.

At first Rachel had found enough interest and excitement in watching the little bobbin jumping up and down, in letting him get almost on his danger-line, then working the bellows hard and fast to send him down again. As he drew near his danger-line, he always seemed to grow very excited, dancing about as if trying to warn her: "Quick, quick! Wake up! I'm nearly there."

But after a time the antics of the little bobbin man ceased to amuse her, and now she always brought a book with her to read.

She had found the *Idylls of the King* on a bookshelf in the study, and since finding it she had lived in a new and glamorous world, with Gareth and Lynette, Geraint and Enid, Merlin and Vivien, Lancelot and Elaine. The stories about Lancelot and Guinevere touched the borders of that region of horror from which she always shrank, but even so they held a strange alluring loveliness. She told the stories to Thea, and Thea liked them too, but Thea could not really know how beautiful they were because she wouldn't read them or let Rachel read them to her. She didn't like poetry; she only wanted to hear them told as an ordinary story in Rachel's own words.

Rachel turned over a page of the book that was propped up on the top of the chair where she could both read it and work the bellows. Occasionally she raised her eyes to the little bobbin and, seeing him near the danger-line, would quicken her pace, which was apt to become very slow and dreamy as she grew absorbed in the book. She must be specially careful not to let the air out to-day because it was a lesson. She could hear Mr. Moyle's voice teaching Thea, though she couldn't see them. It was much worse to let the air out when it was a lesson than when it was just a practice.

> Then rose the dumb old servitor, and the dead,
> Oar'd by the dumb, went upward with the flood—
> In her right hand the lily, in her left
> The letter—all her bright hair streaming down—
> And all the coverlid was cloth of gold
> Drawn to her waist, and she herself in white
> All but her face, and that clear-featured face
> Was lovely, for she did not seem as dead,
> But fast asleep, and lay as tho' she smiled.

A lump rose into Rachel's throat, and her arm ceased to work the handle. She raised her tear-filled eyes from the book and fixed them unseeingly on the rich colours of the window where Jesus walked on the sea.

A loud moan from the empty organ bellows rang through the little church.

"Oh, *Rachel*!" said Thea's voice from the organ recess.

"I'm awfully sorry," said Rachel, forgetting all about Elaine and pumping so hard that the book fell down from its precarious position on the ledge of the chair.

"It doesn't really matter," came reassuringly in Mr. Moyle's pleasant voice, "it's time we stopped now anyway."

But he did not make any move to get up from the organ bench. He was looking at Thea, noticing the dark velvety eyes with their sweeping lashes, the flawless skin, the soft brown hair that fell in curls about her shoulder. She was only a child, but a child on the threshold of womanhood, seductively fresh and innocent. He was an adept at flirting, and he could flirt as discreetly and expertly with a child of thirteen as with a woman of thirty. He stood up and leant over her shoulder, one hand on the bench behind her, the other pointing to the book.

"You'll practise that bit well, won't you? It's rather difficult."

His cheek almost touched her hair. Though his hand rested on the bench behind her, his arm seemed to encircle her closely. She could smell the mixture of tweed and tobacco and soap that in after life stirred always a faint elusive chord of memory, long after she had forgotten Gilbert Moyle.

"Just that bit," he said pointing again; "the rest you've got very well."

He spoke in his ordinary lesson voice, but his cheek, as if by accident, now actually touched her hair, and she could feel the pressure of his arm along her back.

A strange feeling of excitement swept over her.

"Yes, I'll practise that bit specially," she said, and to her surprise her voice sounded breathless and unlike her own voice.

He sat down on the bench by her, and, taking one of her curls in his hand, drew it out, letting it fly back again into its coils.

"That was never made in a curl-paper," he said, smiling at her.

He had taken his arm away, but his eyes as he smiled at her and his voice (it wasn't his lesson voice any more) still sent that strange thrill of excitement through her.

"Will you give me one before you go away?" he went on.

His voice was suppliant; his smiling eyes pleaded, and a sudden heady sense of power seized the child. She tossed her curls, and her bright eyes danced at him.

"Why should I?" she said.

"Because——" He leant nearer, then suddenly saw Rachel standing behind them, waiting for Thea. Rachel had been standing there for several moments. She had listened with a bewilderment that had gradually changed to anger—an anger mixed with a terrifying feeling of loneliness that she didn't understand. She felt somehow as if

Thea had deliberately turned from her, betraying their friendship. It wasn't just that she was pretending to be grown-up. Rachel was used to that and didn't mind it. The state of being grown-up was familiar and normal. It awaited both of them equally, inevitably. As Thea emerged from childhood, discarding pinafores, tying her hair back at the nape of her neck, lengthening her skirts, Rachel could think: I shall do that too when I'm as old as Thea. But this was different. Thea had gone somewhere where Rachel could never follow her. She had turned into someone quite different, so that she was no longer Thea. It was a sudden parting of the ways they had trodden together from babyhood. Rachel couldn't have put this into words. She did not even understand it. She could not have told what it was she had seen or heard that had made her feel so angry and frightened.

"I'll bring the book of exercises to the Vicarage this evening," he said. "Sorry we've kept you, Rachel. I'm going to stay here and practise for half an hour. Good-bye."

They walked together in silence out of the church and down the road to the gate that led into the paddock.

"What's the matter, Rachel?" said Thea.

"Nothing," said Rachel.

That black sense of desolation was still heavy upon her. She still felt as if Thea had gone right away and left her. Nothing could ever make up for that. Life would be unbearable without Thea.

"Did you read some more *Idylls of the King*?"

"Yes."

"Tell me one, Rachel. Let's go into the spinney to our place."

They turned to cross the paddock to the spinney.

"You will tell me one of the stories, won't you, Rachel?"

"No, I can't," said Rachel. "I don't really know it well enough."

She couldn't tell Thea stories with this heavy blackness of loneliness upon her. Besides, stories belonged to the old life before Thea had left her.

Thea was silent. Something in her knew what it was that had hurt Rachel, though she couldn't have put it into words any more than Rachel could. It was connected with that moment when Mr.

Moyle had leant over her and had smiled at her and asked for one of her curls in that odd un-lessony voice; connected, too, with the strange exhilarating excitement that had seized her. But that memory was unreal and dreamlike. It didn't belong to ordinary life as Rachel belonged to it. She often pretended to despise Rachel, but life would be impossible without her ready, loving friendship.

They had reached the oak tree with the gnarled protruding roots.

They sat down, and there was silence.

They avoided each other's eyes.

"*Do* tell me a story, Rachel," said Thea at last.

Rachel's head was turned away. She pulled up little bits of moss from the roots of the tree and laid them in a heap.

Suddenly a memory returned to Thea, driving everything else from her mind.

"Oh, Rachel!" she said excitedly, "I've got something to tell you. Do listen. You know I went for a walk with father this morning."

Rachel turned to her, infected despite herself by Thea's excitement.

"Yes."

"Well, we passed a cow in a farmyard, and it looked just as if its inside was hanging out, and I said to father, 'What's happened to it?' and he said, 'It's had a calf,' and I said, 'Do calves come from inside cows?' and he said, 'Yes,' and I said, 'Do babies come from inside people?' and he said, 'Yes.' So *that's* what it is."

She looked at Rachel triumphantly.

Rachel considered this statement dispassionately. She compared it with her mental pictures of her own birth—mother turning the clothes back as usual one morning and finding to her joy and surprise a tiny baby there, sent by God in the night. That seemed reasonable, normal; the other monstrous, impossible.

"But, Thea," she objected, "how *could* they? How could they *possibly?*"

Something of Thea's triumph left her.

"I don't know," she said, "but that's what he said."

"But how *could* they?"

"I don't know," said Thea again.

Rachel considered the information once more, and finally dismissed it from the realms of possibility.

"You know father's always thinking of other things," she said, "and says, 'Yes' or 'No' without knowing what you've asked him. He probably didn't even hear what you'd said."

"Yes, I suppose that was it," said Thea despondently.

She'd felt so pleased to have got at last to the heart of the mystery.

"Well, there is *something* anyway," she said, "and I'm going to find out."

"Why don't you ask mother?"

"I did once, and she said she'd tell me when I was old enough to know. I'm not going to ask her again. I'm going to find out. . . . I remember Peter and Jane being born, of course, but Aunt Mary had asked us to go to stay with her, do you remember? and the babies just weren't there when we went away and were there when we came back, so that doesn't help at all. Lily Beverly knows. I'm going to get her to tell me. I'll tell you when I find out."

"All right," said Rachel.

Somehow to-day the forbidden subject had lost its horror. She didn't shrink from it. She felt almost grateful to it. It had brought Thea back to her, made her again just another little girl, not an inhabitant of a strange, incomprehensible world that Rachel could never enter.

"*Do* tell me a tale, Rachel," pleaded Thea.

Rachel was in the middle of the story of Lancelot and Elaine when they saw a cab stop in the road and the cabman get down to open the gate.

"It's Aunt Bridget," said Thea, starting to her feet. "Let's go and tell mother she's come."

But Susan had seen the cab too, and when Thea and Rachel reached the front door the others were coming out to wait for it in a welcoming group.

Aunt Bridget got down from the cab and fell upon them, snatching up Jane and Peter to hug and tickle them.

"*How* they've grown! Thea's quite a young lady now, aren't you, darling? And little Susan, the pet! And Rachel, isn't she growing! Isn't it *lovely* to see you all again! We've got such *heaps* to tell each other, haven't we, pets? Now I must just go and take off my hat and coat, and then we'll all have a lovely time together, won't we?"

Aunt Bridget was pretty and charming, but the strange thing was that, after the first few moments, you always began to wonder if she was quite as pretty and charming as she'd seemed at first.

She swept upstairs with mother, still laughing and talking. They heard mother take her into her bedroom and close the door. They looked at each other in silence. Then Rachel said:

"She's nice, isn't she?"

She spoke uncertainly. She wasn't sure whether she liked Aunt Bridget, but she was quite sure that she ought to.

"I think she's rather patronising," said Thea.

Thea loved being treated as if she were grown-up, but she hated to be told that she was "quite a young lady" in a voice that meant that she was only a little girl. Still—it was rather exciting to have a visitor. Thea and Rachel did not go out into the garden with the others, but stayed in the hall waiting for Aunt Bridget to come down again.

She came down soon, her arm round mother, and kissed and hugged them once more.

"And is our little Rachel as shy as ever?" she said, giving her a squeeze.

Rachel's heart sank. You could pretend not to be shy only as long as people didn't actually call you shy, but once they had called you shy in so many words it was hopeless. It made you shy always afterwards when they were there.

They went into the drawing-room, where Thea's sketching block lay on the table, and Aunt Bridget at once began to exclaim enthusiastically over the sketches. She seemed to feel instinctively that Thea was a person to be propitiated. Most people felt that. But apart from any idea of propitiation, Thea's sketches were really good. Her talent for drawing, like her talent for music, was distinctly above the average. Rachel listened eagerly to Aunt Bridget's praise.

She was passionately proud of Thea's talent, and their reconciliation after that odd, un-comprehended quarrel had deepened the bond between them. Miriam also was listening proudly, her arm round Thea. Though she loved Peter the best, she was the proudest of Thea. Of all the children, Thea was most like what she had been. She, too, had had outstanding artistic facility. She had been ambitious, and had secretly planned a career for herself. Then—she had married a poor curate, and her talents had rusted for lack of use. Housework, parish work, children, had filled her life. But her secret ambition had not died. It had been diverted to Thea. Thea must do the things that once she had meant to do. There was an unsuspected something of vanity in her pride. She was proud of her own talents in the child. She wanted to see her own life justified in Thea's.

"And now I must run out to have a game with the babies before tea," said Aunt Bridget.

Rachel and Thea followed her slowly into the garden.

"She was awfully nice about your drawing, Thea," said Rachel. Thea shrugged.

"She's smarmy," she said. "I'd forgotten what she was like, but I remember now. I thought she was smarmy the last time she came."

Aunt Bridget was kneeling down with Susan in the orchard. Lena and Hetty and Grace and Louise and Victoria lay in a row under Susan's favourite apple tree. The lantern hung from a twig stuck in the ground in the middle of them.

"What are you playing at, darling?" said Aunt Bridget.

"Hospitals," replied Susan.

"It's a *lovely* hospital," said Aunt Bridget. "Now you be the matron, and I'll be the nurse. What's this doll called? Hetty? Well, we'll call her Mrs. Brown in the hospital, and she's got a broken leg, hasn't she? We'll put her to bed. I'll take her temperature."

"Yes," said Susan, but she said it rather sulkily.

It was her game, and Aunt Bridget was spoiling it. Hetty wasn't called Mrs. Brown, and she hadn't got a broken leg. She was a prince who'd been bitten by a dragon, but she wasn't going to tell Aunt Bridget that. And she didn't want Aunt Bridget to be the nurse. The nurse was Agnes, who had taken part in all Susan's games since her visit to the Hall. And while Agnes was giving medicine to the prince she would suddenly find the spell that would change her to a beautiful princess.

"I think she'd better be operated on, don't you?" said Aunt Bridget.

"Yes," said Susan, still sulkily.

After the operation Aunt Bridget said:

"Now I'll pretend to be going away for my holiday. You can manage all right for a week without me, can't you, matron?" She kissed all the dolls and went across the lawn to Jane, who was making a garden for Owly.

"Well, baby," said Aunt Bridget brightly, "and what are you doing?"

"Making a garden," said Jane.

She hated being called baby, but she knew that you must be polite to visitors.

"That's lovely," said Aunt Bridget. "Now let's have a little seat here, shall we, under this tree, and this little stone will do for a sundial, won't it?"

Jane watched resentfully. Owly didn't want a sundial in his garden, and he didn't want a seat under that tree, either. . . . She *knew* he didn't.

Miriam turned from the study window to her husband.

"She's out in the garden playing with them already. She really *is* so good with children."

Bridget had gone up to her room to unpack and change. Now that she was alone the vivacity had left her face, and she looked considerably older than she had looked downstairs. She put her underclothing away in the drawers and hung up her dresses in the wardrobe. She had taken a good deal of trouble over her preparations for this visit, as indeed she took a good deal of trouble over her preparations for all her visits. She had made herself three new cotton dresses, two new muslin ones, and had had a new silk one made at the dressmaker's. After all, anything might happen when you went away to a new place among strangers. She hung up the new silk dress very carefully in the wardrobe and took out the family photograph that always accompanied her on visits. It showed her mother and herself and her two sisters, and had been taken ten years ago when they all lived at home. They had had a very jolly time in those days. They had belonged to a set of young people who attended all the local parties and dances together and had a good deal of innocent, hilarious fun, teasing each other about their love affairs, giggling and whispering confidences to each other in corners. She had been one of the most popular members of the group, and everyone confided in her. She knew all about their love affairs, and she had plenty of her own to confide in return. That state of things had come to an end so gradually that she hardly realised it was coming to an end till it had actually ended. One by one the other girls had become engaged, one by one they had married. She had been bridesmaid at a succession of pretty weddings and had thoroughly enjoyed each one. Violet, her elder sister, had married, and then Enid, her younger sister. It was Enid's marriage that pulled her up sharply, that brought home to her the hateful, almost incredible fact that she was "getting left." She didn't know how it was. She was quite as pretty as Enid. She was prettier than a lot of her girl friends who had married, and she took a good deal more trouble to make herself pleasant to eligible men. There were, in Bridget's eyes, only two sorts of men in the world, the eligible and the ineligible—or rather there was only one sort, the eligible, for the others simply did not exist for her.

And yet—despite her many flirtations—she never actually had a proposal, while Enid had had three. She couldn't understand it. She felt helplessly bewildered by it. But, whatever the explanation, the fact remained that every member of her girlhood's set had married except herself. She wasn't the centre of the little group any longer. She was now a barely tolerated hanger-on. They didn't confide in her now. They were young wives and mothers, and the things they discussed among themselves were not considered suitable for her, as a spinster, to hear. When she approached a whispering group of them, they would begin to talk about the weather or clothes in voices that plainly showed they had been discussing something much more intimate before she joined them. They were quite kind to her, but girls who a few years ago had been proud to be noticed by her now patronised and obviously looked down on her.

She clung to the outer edge of the set of young matrons with a sort of desperate eagerness, afraid of being ousted from it altogether. She flattered them and made herself useful to them, posing as an ardent child-lover, and helping to look after their children on their nurse's "afternoon out." In return they asked her to their parties and occasionally invited her to meet some eligible man, though, of course, the society of a small country town is limited, and Bridget knew that she had already been weighed in the balance and found wanting by every eligible man for miles around. As she reached and passed thirty, her prettiness began to sharpen somewhat, but her vivacity increased.

She lived alone with her mother, and her mother, she knew, was as anxious for her to get married as she was herself. In public they made a great show of affection, but secretly they jarred on each other, and when alone snapped at each other continually. Enid, of course, had always been her mother's favourite. . . .

She went over to the dressing-table to tidy her hair. A large chestnut tree growing near the house shaded her window, and in the softened light she looked unusually young and pretty. As she gazed at her reflection, her spirits rose. How silly she was to get so depressed sometimes! Of course she'd marry. Thirty-five wasn't old. . . . Lots of girls married after thirty-five. It often happened, too, just when they'd begun to think that they were getting left. And it often happened on a holiday like this. Nina Merton had gone away on a visit, had met the Right Man there, and had come back engaged at the end of a fortnight. (Bridget always gave the Right Man capital letters in her thoughts.) There wasn't any reason why she shouldn't meet the Right Man here on this visit to Miriam and Timothy. Of course the Right Man wasn't always as you'd imagined him when you were younger. Betty Edwards had married an elderly widower, and Moyna Darenth's husband, though rich enough, was fat and greasy, not at all the sort of man Moyna used to say she'd marry when they were girls together. Bridget thought rather wistfully of the man she herself had meant to marry then . . . tall and dark and handsome with a kink in his hair and a cleft in his chin. Well, she'd long ago given up hope of that. . . .

She heard a man's voice—not Timothy's—downstairs, and automatically her face assumed its expression of strained, eager vivacity. It must be the organist's voice. Miriam had said that the organist was coming to supper to-night to arrange next Sunday's service. She'd asked Miriam quite casually if he were married, and Miriam had said that he was not. Organists were generally elderly and uninteresting, of course, but—oh, she was sick to death of being bright and cheerful and helpful, hanging on to the edge of her old set, fussing over their spoilt children. She felt sometimes—especially when mother had been snapping at her—that she'd be grateful to any man, whatever he was like, who would provide for her and enable her to hold her head up as a married woman among other married women. She put back the muslin dress that she had just taken down from the wardrobe, and took down instead the new blue silk one. It had a round yoke of lace threaded with innumerable rows of narrow, black velvet ribbon, each one tied in a little bow in front. A broad piece of black velvet formed the belt and the long train was heavily flounced. Having put it on, she examined her reflection again anxiously in the glass. The dress was perhaps a little elaborate for the occasion, but its colour intensified the blue of her eyes, and, of course, first impressions were so very important. It looked expensive, and nothing put a man off a girl so much at a first meeting as a suggestion of poverty in her appearance. Her neck was not quite as white and round as it used to be. . . . She took a piece of black velvet ribbon from a drawer and tied it high up under her chin, drew the soft, fluffy golden hair low over her forehead to hide the tiny lines that were beginning to form there, then, assuming her most vivacious expression, went downstairs.

Thea had gone to the drawing-room as soon as she heard Mr. Moyle's voice. He was just putting a roll of music on to the table.

"Here is the young lady," he said. "I've brought the book of exercises for you, Thea." Then he smiled at her and, pulling her curls, said to mother, "I've told her that she must give me one of these before she goes away."

Thea felt bewildered. Somehow it sounded quite different now. He hadn't pulled her curls like this in the organ lesson, and he hadn't smiled at her like this. It had been new and strange and exciting. But this—it was the way people treated Susan or even Jane. She felt hurt as well as bewildered. . . . She wasn't going to stay with him and be treated as if she were a baby. She put the roll of music away and went out into the garden to find Rachel.

Then Bridget entered the room, and as soon as she saw the visitor her heart leapt. This was the man she had dreamed of throughout her girlhood. Even his hair had the kink of her dreams, his chin the cleft. A flood of thanksgiving rushed over her. Here was her happiness—waiting for her all the years. How wrong she had been to grow despondent, to give up hope.

He saw the naïve admiration in her eyes, and the hunter in him sprang up hot upon the scent. He responded automatically, pressing her hand in his as Miriam introduced them, fixing his fine eyes meaningly upon hers.

"Now I'll leave you two to entertain each other," said Miriam. "I must go and see about supper. It's Cook's day out, and Maria's hopeless. You'll play to us after supper, won't you, Mr. Moyle?"

"If you really want me to."

"Of course we do. There are some cigarettes in that box if you'd like one."

She went out and closed the door. He took a cigarette from the box and lit it. Bridget sat watching him, trying to quiet the tumult of her heart. It wasn't only that she'd fallen in love with him, it was that he'd fallen in love with her. She'd seen it in his eyes as soon as he looked at her, she'd felt it in the clasp of his hand. It was all happening as it had happened in her most romantic girlhood's dreams. She saw herself on her return home, sitting with her sister and her friends—in the centre of the group this time, instead of on the outskirts—heard herself saying, "Yes, we fell in love with each other at first sight, and he proposed before the end of the week. Yes, he is rather nice-looking, isn't he? We shall be married quite soon, of course. There's nothing to wait for. Yes, white satin and arum lilies, I suppose." She'd have Thea and Rachel for bridesmaids, because she'd met him here. She saw herself in white satin with a train going up to the altar where a tall handsome figure awaited her. She felt strong masculine arms about her, heard his low thrilling voice say, "I fell in love with you at first sight, darling." And she'd say, "I did, too, only I tried to hide it from you." "You did only too well," he would reply. "I hardly dared to hope at first."

She pulled herself up sharply. It was immodest to imagine things like that.

Still—he was looking at her just as Enid's husband used to look at her when they were first engaged. It had made her want to scream then. She had hated Enid after she had got engaged, and was glad when she was married and couldn't flaunt herself and her trousseau about the house any longer. She still thought that Enid might have been less triumphant about it. After all, she was only two years older than Enid.

He was watching her through a cloud of cigarette smoke. His handsome face wore the expression of soulful admiration that it assumed almost mechanically when he was alone with any woman who wasn't over sixty or physically repulsive. Getting on, he decided, studying her critically. She'd been pretty enough a few years ago probably, but that fair, fluffy, delicate-looking type soon begins to look wizened. Not that she wasn't pretty now. Pretty enough, at any rate, to make a flirtation with her fairly entertaining.

His practised eye appraised her toilet. Dress over-elaborate and badly fitting. Made by a cheap dressmaker. The black velvet ribbon round her neck called attention loudly to her slightly sagging throat.

Bridget was trembling beneath his scrutiny. The very silence between them showed that they weren't just ordinary acquaintances, proved that he, too, felt this odd, breathless, bewildering ecstasy.

He came and sat down beside her on the sofa, leaning towards her. For one mad moment she thought that he was going to propose. In the same mad moment she decided to accept him if he did.

Chapter Eight

TIMOTHY had climbed the last lap of the hill from the valley and reached the open moors. They stretched, bare and windswept, before him, purple with heather, the grass tussocky and colourless except where here and there a patch of green showed a hidden bog. He swung along quickly, breathing in the pure moorland air with long deep breaths, his lips curved into a faint smile of pleasure. His forbears had been farmers, and the roots of his being went deep down into the soil. He felt at home in the quiet of the hills, with the open sky above him unshrouded by a veil of factory smoke. It was a real discipline of spirit for him to work in a slum parish in a manufacturing town.

He sat on a tumble-down stone wall and gazed around, still breathing in the air deeply. Down in the valley he could see the roofs of cottages and farm-houses among the trees. Little spirals of smoke arose into the sky, curling softly in the breeze. A cock crowed and a dog barked in a distant farm. Peace stole into his heart, deepening his faith, renewing his belief in the ultimate justice and goodness of things. And suddenly his mind turned to take stock of the year that had passed. Always this annual holiday in the country seemed to him like a rock on which he could rest for a moment after an exhausting passage through the tumult of the waves before he plunged into them again. He could look back and see how dangerous the passage had been, how he had acquitted himself in it. . . .

The worst times had been those moments when the sin and suffering among which he lived had seemed to form a dark cloud shutting him away from God. It never destroyed his faith, and for that he was thankful; but it brought to him a sickness of the soul that took all the joy from his work, all the comfort from his religion. These were times of black depression that he hid as well as he could from those around him. ... And connected somehow with them were the times when his nerves were so frayed and jarred that even his wife, whom he loved more dearly than life itself, irritated him by her every word and look. He saw both that and his periods of depression as a sort of tunnel. He had left the light, but he was travelling through the darkness towards it again. And always his faith was rewarded, and the tunnel came to an end suddenly and inexplicably. The sense of union with God would flood his soul again, and his joyful love of mankind would return as if strengthened by the period of alienation.

He looked back over the year, thinking with shame of the times when he had almost given up hope, of the times when he had allowed his irritation to escape his control. There were dark blots of failure, too, on his record—backsliders who might have been saved by a word from him had he known what word to say, a suicide who had once come to him for help and whom later he had lost sight of in the press of his work. These weighed heavily upon his conscience. He turned to the brighter side—children baptized and confirmed by him, living still in close union with God, sinners brought back into the church, saints untouched by the vice that surrounded them. In his slum parish, living in poverty and suffering, were some of the most radiant souls in God's kingdom. He sometimes thought that, if Christ came again, it would be in such places that He would find His disciples, as He had found them before among the fisher folk of Galilee.

He looked forward to the next year, buckling on his armour, renewing his vows, resolving to return to the battle with fresh hope and energy, feeling ashamed to have in any single case admitted defeat.

He took from his pocket his copy of *St. Julian of Norwich* and began to read it.

Its refrain rang through his heart like a paean of triumph. "All shall be well, and all shall be well, and all manner of thing shall be well."

In a blinding flash of revelation he seemed to see the purpose of God working itself out to its consummation, saw the sin and sorrow and suffering of the world vanish as the glory touched them. . . . "All shall be well, and all shall be well, and all manner of thing shall be well. . . ."

He put the book into his pocket and began to stride again over the moors. The love of God filled his soul as if it had been wine. Despite his occasional periods of depression, his religion had always been in its essence one of joy. It was indeed almost mediaeval both in its mysticism and exultation. He raised his voice and sang aloud as he swung along: "Praise, my soul, the King of Heaven, To His feet thy praises bring. . . ."

His voice rang out over the empty moor. His shabby clerical frock-coat fluttered about his thin, gaunt figure, his mild blue eyes held a blazing light in their depths.

He walked till he was out of breath, then stood looking around him, drinking in the bleak grandeur of the scene. Suddenly he noticed a figure hurrying after him along the moorland track. He waited. As it came nearer he saw that it was the small squat figure of Dr. Flemming, carrying his professional black bag. A fox terrier trotted beside him. Dr. Flemming had paid his formal call at the Vicarage on Monday, and Timothy had met him several times since in the village.

"You walk at a good pace," he said breathlessly. "I've been trying to catch you for about five minutes. I thought I was a good walker."

The light had faded from Timothy's eyes. He had resumed his ordinary manner—courteous, gentle, rather shy.

"I like to get all the fresh air and exercise I can on a holiday," he said in his old-fashioned, slightly stilted way. "It sets one up for the rest of the year."

They walked on side by side over the moor.

"I suppose you don't get much exercise when you're in harness?" said the doctor.

"There's a good deal of walking, of course, in the way of parish visiting, but walking on pavements in the town isn't the same thing as this."

"Of course not. I like a tramp over the moors too, whenever possible. I'm going over to Fletworth to see Dawson, the vicar, now. I can get there by road along the valley in half an hour—quarter of an hour in the trap—but, as I've got the afternoon before me, I thought I'd go there by way of the moors and stretch my legs. ... Have you met the Dawsons?"

"I believe we're going over there next week. My wife had a letter from Mrs. Dawson this morning."

"You'll like them. She's his second wife, you know. And he's her second husband. Both her father and her first husband were artists, and she'd lived most of her life in Paris till she met Dawson. Odd that they took to each other. They're the last two people in the world you'd have expected to take to each other. He adores her, and it's nothing to do with her money, though she's got plenty. His daughter loathes her. Only natural, of course. Lucy had run the house and parish entirely since her mother died, and, well, naturally, she doesn't cotton to a stepmother and two small stepsisters. Mrs. Dawson's a charming woman, but quite without tact. ... Excuse me a moment."

He darted off from the track to where the green grass showed a lurking bog a few feet away and carefully uprooted a plant with a small pink flower. He returned, examining it with interest.

"A bog pimpernel," he said. "I thought it might do for Miss Caroline's indoor garden. I want something that will grow by the pond there." He slipped it into his pocket. "It may not grow, of course, but one can only try. ... Have you seen her indoor garden?"

"The children have," smiled Timothy. "Susan was telling me about it."

"Wonderful woman, Miss Caroline. They lived at the Hall, you know, before the Lindsays."

"No, I didn't know that."

"They were born there. Then, when the father died, fifteen years ago, it turned out that he'd speculated rashly, and there was hardly anything left. They sold the Hall to the Lindsays, who'd just got married and were looking for a home, and went to live in Meadow Cottage."

"What a pity the elder sister is an invalid."

The brown eyes twinkled above the bushy brown beard.

"She's no more an invalid than you are, though you mustn't tell anyone that, of course. She had infantile paralysis when she was a girl, and it left her slightly lame, but no lamer than hundreds of women who do an active day's work. When her father died and his affairs were disclosed, Miss Bella found that the simplest way of dealing with the crisis was to become a chronic invalid. It relieved her of all responsibility and effort, and she'd always hated responsibility and effort. You see, they were left very badly off and have to be very careful. They keep one maid, but Miss Caroline does all the cooking and a good deal of the housework. Miss Bella's one of those people who are born to be invalids. Good health is completely wasted on her. She loves lying in bed and being waited on. For years she's done nothing but eat and sleep. She has an excellent appetite and eats far more than most people who are up and about all day. Of course, by now her muscles are probably so flabby that she couldn't walk a dozen yards if she tried to."

"It seems rather hard on Miss Caroline," said Timothy.

"Not at all. You see, Miss Caroline is one of those people who are born to be mothers. She'd have made a marvellous mother to a family of eight or nine children, but unfortunately no one wanted to marry her. Well, a fractious invalid sister is the next best thing to a family of eight or nine children. She enjoys waiting on her and humouring her, and," he chuckled, "it gives her an excuse for the scrap-books and garden. She's a child at heart like all really nice people—she *is* really nice, you know—and she thoroughly enjoys her scrap-books and garden. I go in every week on the pretence of visiting the invalid, but really to keep an eye on the garden. Miss Caroline's apt to get carried away. If I weren't very strict, she'd have the whole thing cluttered up with penny toys from Miss Thrupp's. She's no sense of proportion whatever. Women seldom have, of course. She'll put a china fish in the pond twice the size of the tin cow that's standing on the bank. I have to be very strict over it. She's full of amiable female weaknesses, is Miss Caroline. Dress, for instance. And she does it all on next to nothing, too, bless her!"

"Does she know that the sister isn't really an invalid?"

"Even I," twinkled Dr. Flemming, "have never been able to discover that."

Timothy smiled and took out his watch. "Well, I must be getting back, I'm afraid."

"I'm glad to have seen you. I'm a garrulous old woman, you know, and always enjoy a chat. Do you play chess? Drop in some evening and have a game with me. . . . Good-bye."

Timothy turned and retraced his steps, swinging back over the moor. His mood of ecstasy and exultation had left him. He was hurrying now to reach his home. Though his duties kept him frequently away from home, he was essentially a home-loving man, and always, when his work was over, he felt this glad eagerness to return to his wife and children. He would hurry till the house was in sight, then slacken his pace in a half-unconscious relief that, at any rate, the house that held them still stood there safely. It was a habit formed in the days when he was a young husband. His love for his wife was deep and unquenchable. Sometimes the thought of it troubled his conscience, so nearly did it approach in strength and devotion his love for God. There was an incalculable element in her that had always delighted him. He never knew in what mood he would find her on his return—sometimes she was as gay and radiant as a young girl, sometimes grave and withdrawn. Even when she was worried and on edge, as happened occasionally, she was in his eyes wholly adorable. He loved her best, perhaps, when she was gay and light-hearted, teasing him for his slowness of wit and absent-mindedness and bad taste, for it was a family joke that, when he had to make any purchase without her guidance, his choice was crude in colour and design. Though a student and a scholar, he was slow-witted and like a child in his penchant for the baroque. Only yesterday he had gone into Harborough with her to do some shopping and had bought a cap for the journey home while she was buying some things for the children. He was going home with them by train, and on a long train journey he always took off his round clerical hat and put on a cap in order to lean back in his seat more comfortably. He had chosen, with real pleasure, a cap of violent and multi-coloured check, at which Miriam had laughed delightedly. She had teased him about it all evening.

"You know, darling, you really have got the most atrocious taste of anyone I ever knew."

"But I chose you," he countered.

"Yes." She glanced into the mirror above the mantelpiece and sighed. "I was younger and prettier then."

He had put his hands on her shoulders.

" 'Age cannot wither her,' " he had quoted, " 'nor custom stale her infinite variety.' "

"Oh," she had laughed, "don't be quite so gloomy. It's not a question of 'age' and 'withering' yet."

The valley had come into view now. He could see the squat square tower of the little church and, through a gap in the trees, the roof of the Vicarage. Automatically he slackened his pace. . . .

At first he did not notice that someone was sitting on the low wall gazing out over the valley. Then the man turned his head suddenly, and Timothy saw that it was Mr. Lindsay. His face looked pale and lined in the bright sunshine.

"Hello, Cotteril," he said with unconvincing attempt at cheerfulness. "Taking a tramp for the good of your soul?"

"Yes," smiled Timothy, "it's wonderful air."

"Isn't it? I'm going away to-morrow, and I've come up to get the last breath of it before I go. . . . Sit down and join me in it."

Timothy sat down on the wall by him.

Beneath them the bracken-covered hill-side stretched down to the peaceful valley. The rays of the westering sun caught the trunk of a Scotch pine half-way down the slope, turning its red to gold.

Lindsay's eyes were fixed on the chimneys of the Hall that could be seen through the trees of the park.

"I always hate leaving it," he said.

In the silence that followed Timothy became dimly aware of the desperate unhappiness that underlay his companion's casual manner.

"Shall you be leaving it for long?" he said.

He spoke tentatively, as if equally ready to be treated as confidant or stranger. All his life he had striven without success to overcome his constitutional shyness and reserve. It was, he felt, a real hindrance to his work as a priest.

"I'm away a good deal," said the other man. "I meant to stay at home till the end of the summer, but I—find I can't."

There was a silence, then Timothy said, "It looks very beautiful from here."

Lindsay turned his head away. He seemed to speak with an effort, as if yielding against his will to Timothy's unspoken sympathy.

"My life at home is—impossible. You saw that, of course, the other day."

"It's the child?" said Timothy after a slight pause.

Lindsay nodded. His hands were clasped together so tightly that the knuckles showed like bare bones. "It's criminal that she should have to be kept in the world," he burst out jerkily. "How can one believe in God when such things happen? I could have loved a normal, healthy child as much as any man, but—this monstrosity!"

"She's not a monstrosity," said Timothy gently. "If you'd had a normal child whose body had been crippled by some accident, you would have loved her. This child's mind has been crippled somehow, somewhere—no one knows how or where. It's a far greater tragedy for her than if her body were crippled. She needs your love the more."

"Needs my love!" echoed the other man bitterly. "You saw my wife the other day. She looks fifty and she's only thirty-five. Since the child was born she's devoted herself to her day and night. She's sacrificed her whole life for the child. She has no friends, no pleasure, no interests of her own. She only lives in and for the child. She hasn't spent a day or a night away from her for twelve years."

"That's not wise, of course."

"Wise?" The man turned to him with a short laugh. "It's killing her. I've begged her to get someone to look after the child—even to send her away to some place where they'll care for her properly, but it's useless. The child frets if her mother leaves her for an instant. More than frets. She's got a violent temper when she's crossed, and now that she grows bigger it's—dangerous. She tyrannises over my wife. She makes a slave of her. . . . I—can't stay and watch it."

"Your wife won't take your advice?"

"No."

"Why is that?"

"The child's a—sort of—wall between us. We're strangers. She's slept in the child's room ever since she realised how things were with her. She won't have another child. . . . My home isn't a home to me. I came up here to decide whether I'd go away for good or not. I think it would be a relief to her if I did."

"Why does your wife feel as she does towards you?" said Timothy.

The other man looked away again. "She can't forgive me for—disliking the child, and being ashamed of her. I *am* ashamed of her, you know. I hate even to think of her. I can't endure to watch my wife waiting on her, humouring her, putting up with her tempers. I've begged her not to have the child down when people visit us, as your wife and children did the other day. That makes her angrier than anything—that I should want to hide her away. She won't go anywhere without her, so it means that she goes nowhere. You see, the child screams now if my wife leaves her for even a moment . . . it's killing her. . . ."

"Isn't that the very reason you should stay and help her?"

"I'm no help to her. She's happier when I'm not there."

"What has made her feel like this to you?"

"I've told you. Because I dislike the child."

Timothy made no answer or comment. Then Lindsay turned and looked at him.

"Why do you disbelieve me?" he said.

"I don't disbelieve you. Only there's something you haven't told me. I don't mean that I want you to tell me. I'd rather you didn't if you think you'll regret it afterwards." He rose from the wall. "Shall we go on towards home?"

The other man did not move.

"Sit down," he said curtly.

Timothy obeyed.

"How do you know that I'm not telling you everything?"

"I don't know how I know. But I do know. . . . And I don't want you to tell me unless you think I can help you."

"You can't help me. No one can help me. . . . But I want to tell you all the same. . . ." He stopped, then continued very slowly and deliberately, as if choosing his words: "Eight years ago I tried to kill the child. My wife has never forgiven me for it and never will forgive me. . . . No, don't speak. Listen. I'll tell you just what happened. The gas was always left low in the child's room when she was in bed. I went in and turned it out, then turned the tap on again. There was a gale and the window was shut, all except for the smallest chink. I'd thought that I could make people believe that the wind had blown it out."

"It would have been murder, you know."

"I know. I was prepared to take the guilt of that, if I could free my wife. She was bearing more than any woman should have been asked to bear."

"You were no judge of that."

"I thought I was. I still believe that if it had been successful we should have been living happily together to-day."

"No man with murder on his soul lives happily."

Lindsay gave a jangling laugh.

"How do you know? Well, I was saved from murder, at any rate. . . . My wife saw me coming out of the room, and she went in. I presume that she found the gas on and turned it off. We've never mentioned the incident to each other, but she's never spoken to me since then except when she had to. I still love her, but it has killed her love for me. I think it's made her hate me. She's afraid of leaving the child alone with me even now, though God knows that, as far as a man can resign himself to a life that's hell, I've resigned myself. Well," he turned a hard, defiant stare upon Timothy, "you're a parson. It's your duty to show me a way out of it."

"There's only one way out of it," said Timothy, "and that is for you to learn to love the child. God sent a maimed soul to you to care for, perhaps to cure. I don't mean, of course, that the child can be cured in the human sense, but—she needs your love and tenderness. She was sent into the world to receive it. We don't know where we come from into the world or where we go to when we leave it. Perhaps to other worlds. Certainly to further training. A human lifetime must be only an infinitesimal part of the training of a soul. For some reason it is essential for the training or healing of this particular soul that she should receive your love. Your act brought her into the world. You owe her your love. It's a sin to withhold it from her."

The other man again uttered the short unhappy laugh.

"Even if I wanted to love her, love doesn't come for wanting."

"It comes for prayer."

"I lost touch with that sort of thing years ago. . . ." He glanced wonderingly at Timothy. "How can you, who must see sin and suffering on all sides of you, still believe in God?"

"It isn't God who causes sin and suffering. It's man."

"Then why hasn't God put an end to it?"

"Because those whom He sends into the world to do it for Him forget their errand. . . . But the fight goes on, and evil will be conquered in the end."

Lindsay gazed over the peaceful valley, his face set flintily.

"You pray, of course," he said. "Will you pray for me?"

"Yes. . . ."

"I must be getting on now."

They rose and walked together in silence down the hill-side. At the gate of the Hall they stopped, and Lindsay held Timothy's hand in a tight grip.

"Good-bye. I'm glad I told you. You're the only man I've ever told, though I think that Flemming guessed."

Chapter Nine

THEA was having a lesson on music theory from Mr. Moyle in the vestry, and Rachel was sitting on her bed in the bedroom she shared with Thea, writing a poem in a small tattered note-book. She wore a clean white pinafore over her blue sailor suit, and the starched frill stood up round her neck, tickling her and occasionally obscuring her vision. She was writing a poem on Evening.

Dimmer and ever dimmer grows the daylight,

she wrote,

Lower and lower sinks the sun.

She put up an impatient hand to pull down the pinafore frill, then, thinking she heard a sound on the stairs, sat tense and rigid, listening, ready to slip the note-book under the counterpane if anyone came in. No one, not even Thea, knew that she wrote poems. She couldn't have told why it was so important that no one should know, but somehow it was. She felt that if anyone ever knew about it she couldn't bear to go on living. Connected with her poems, too, was that insistent longing that sometimes came to her to get right away from everybody, to be quite alone. And, of course, she hardly ever could be alone. Thea shared the bedroom with her, and the other children were always in the downstairs rooms. Sometimes she tried to go for a walk alone, but always Thea would say, "Wait for me, I'll come too," or mother would say, "If you're going out, dear, take Susan. She walks quite quickly, and it's so dull for her always going on walks with Peter and Jane."

Another trouble was that she had no place of her own to keep the book in which she wrote her poetry. She shared a play cupboard with Thea, and, though they had separate drawers in their bedroom, mother looked through them all regularly to see that they were tidy. Rachel kept the notebook under the paper lining of her handkerchief drawer, but she was always terrified of someone's finding it and reading her poems. If that happened, of course, she'd be miserable and ashamed for all the rest of her life. She'd much rather die at once.

She stared in front of her, nibbling her pencil and frowning, then tucked the starched frill of her pinafore firmly under her chin again and went on.

Its rosy rays touch moor and hill and woodland—

"Rachel!"

It was mother's voice. A sudden wave of anger, hot and suffocating, swept over Rachel at the interruption.

"Yes."

"Where are you, dear?"

"In the bedroom."

"What are you doing there? Come downstairs."

Rachel went slowly downstairs. Miriam, standing in the hall, looked at her anxiously. She liked the children to be together. She always felt uneasy if one of them was away from the others. She could imagine no reason for Rachel's staying upstairs alone in her bedroom, except that she was ill or unhappy.

"Are you feeling all right, darling?"

"Yes, thank you."

"You aren't upset about anything?"

"No."

She bent down and kissed her.

"Well, run into the garden with the others, there's a good girl ... and ask Aunt Bridget to come here and give me a hand."

She turned back towards the kitchen. Nurse had gone for her holiday, and Maria was still being difficult. She'd certainly give her notice as soon as they got home.

Rachel went slowly into the garden. The hot, suffocating feeling of anger was still with her. But suddenly she remembered the times—few enough but very terrible—when she had been in disgrace with mother, and mother had been cold and distant, not speaking to her except when she had to, not seeming to care what happened to her. They had been nightmare times of desolation and loneliness.

The anger left her.

One has to pay for things, she said to herself, making, as it seemed to her, a tremendous discovery. I want her to love me, so I mustn't mind when it sends my secret self away.

She went across the lawn to the orchard, where Aunt Bridget was teaching Susan the names of the flowers that grew in the grass.

"Now what's this one, darling?" she was saying brightly. "Have you forgotten?"

"Bird's-foot trefoil," said Susan obediently but without interest.

Rachel knew that Susan hated knowing the real names of things. She had made up names for all the wild flowers in the orchard, and it spoilt them for her to be taught the real ones. One Christmas, when Aunt Bridget had come to stay with them, Susan had cried because Aunt Bridget tried to teach her the names of the stars from the nursery window. No one knew why Susan was crying except Rachel, and Rachel knew that it was because Susan wanted to go on imagining an angel with a taper flying round the sky and lighting up the candles one by one.

Rachel gave Aunt Bridget mother's message, and Aunt Bridget said, "Never mind, Susie pet, I'll be back as soon as I can," and ran indoors. Aunt Bridget always spoke very brightly, and ran in and out of the house instead of walking like other people.

"I'm glad she's gone," said Susan. "She worries Lena. Make some poppy babies for me, Rachel, please."

There were some wild poppies growing in a little patch in the orchard, and Susan picked some for Rachel to make into poppy babies. To make a poppy baby you turned the petals down, leaving a little head with a circular tuft of hair. Then you tied a piece of grass round the middle of the petals for a sash, then stuck a piece of stalk through just above the sash for arms and made another leg with another piece of stalk. Then you pulled away the little tuft of hair from the front and drew a face with a piece of stick, and the poppy baby was made. Susan wanted six, because she wanted Lena to have six children.

"There!" said Rachel, finishing the last poppy baby.

Susan arranged them on Lena's knee.

"Now tell me a fairy story," she pleaded. "*Do*, Rachel, please!"

She loved to get Rachel to herself like this. Rachel could make up far better fairy stories than any of the ones in books. But generally Thea was there, and Rachel was never quite as nice when Thea was there. Just as Rachel was finishing the fairy story, Peter came across from the lawn and said:

"Susan, Owly's having a feast. Will you bring Lena?"

"I'll bring them all, and the poppy babies, shall I?" said Susan.

"No, not all," said Peter gently. "You see, Owly only wants Lena."

Peter despised dolls in general, but he loved Lena. He loved her for her hairless head and battered, almost indiscernible features. These gave her, in Peter's eyes, a distinction that Susan's other dolls lacked.

"Very well," said Susan in a grown-up, condescending voice. Secretly she was rather flattered by the invitation. She was, despite herself, impressed by the respect and deference paid to Owly by Peter, and would never have been in the least surprised had Owly suddenly spoken in a tiny but imperious voice and asked her to choose three wishes.

The feast was at the end of the lawn. Owly sat on a box surrounded by his escort of battered tin soldiers. Jane was anxiously preparing the feast—little piles of hawthorn berries on the plates of her dolls' tea-service and cups of water coloured with liquorice.

"And when they've etten that," said Jane, "there's some gooseberries for them."

"Eaten, Jane," Susan corrected her.

"Eaten," repeated Jane obediently.

The others laughed at Jane's funny words, but it worried Susan. She thought that Jane was quite big enough to talk properly now, and, when Jane said the words wrong, she always corrected her. Jane didn't mind being corrected, but she hated being laughed at. Yesterday at lunch there had been custard and plums, and Jane, who didn't like plums, had said, "May I have a little custard—lonely, please?" Everyone had burst out laughing, and Jane had cried bitterly.

After the feast Owly and Lena were to go for a ride in the cardboard box, to which Jane had fixed a string.

"He must have his soldiers with him," said Peter, "because he's a very high-up person, you know."

"Yes," said Jane, "but you've tooken the other box for your earwigs."

"Taken, Jane," said Susan.

But Jane looked doubtful.

"I think it's tooken," she said.

"Yes, of course it is," said Peter, who always said "tooken."

Susan wished that she had stayed in the orchard with Rachel, who might have told her another fairy story, instead of coming to play baby games with Jane and Peter. Rachel had followed them to the lawn, but she wasn't taking part in the feast. She was lying on her back with her hands over her eyes to keep the sun off.

While Jane and Peter prepared the cart, Susan began to play a game of her own. Agnes came shambling to the feast and sat down opposite Owly and Lena, and the liquorice water was a magic drink, and as soon as Agnes had drunk it, she turned into a beautiful princess and Owly into a prince and Lena into a fairy.

She left Peter and Jane and went to lie down on her back by Rachel, putting her hands over her eyes, partly in imitation of Rachel and partly in order to see the pictures more clearly. Princess Agnes and Prince Owly lived in a beautiful castle. Princess Agnes had four pages to carry her train wherever she went. She had golden porridge plates decorated with diamonds. She wore a dress of cloth of silver with a girdle of sapphires. Prince Owly wore armour and a helmet with feathers and rode on a white horse. They had five sons and six daughters.

Thea came round the house from the drive, carrying a roll of music under her arm. She wore her white voile dress, her leghorn hat, and a necklace of amber. Mother wouldn't let her wear the seed pearls, because she said they were unsuitable, but she had lent her the amber necklace to wear instead. Thea loved wearing the amber necklace. It was annoying that Rachel was almost as tall as she was, but the amber necklace, she felt, would show people how much older than Rachel she really was. She'd been afraid that mother wouldn't let her put on the white voile dress and best hat for her music lessons, but mother had been rather pleased about it. Thea had heard her say to Aunt Bridget:

"Thank heaven she's beginning to take a pride in her appearance. It's such a relief. I get so sick of telling them to go and wash and do their hair again."

The organ lessons were still exciting in that odd mysterious way. It wasn't that Mr. Moyle ever said or did anything that the music master at school (a small ugly man with a lisp) mightn't have said or done, but—it was his voice and the way he looked at her that were so exciting. She always felt transported by them to a strange, new, glamorous world—a grown-up world, where wonderful things might happen. And whenever he bent over her shoulder to turn a page of the music-book and leant against her by accident (as he very often did), a curious but quite pleasant thrill shot through her. He still teased her about the curl.

"When am I going to have it?" he would plead.

And she would toss her head and smile at him and say:

"Oh, I haven't made up my mind to give you one at all yet."

Father or one of her Uncles might have teased her in just the same way, but—somehow it wouldn't have been the same.

The funny thing was that when people were there he was quite different. His voice and the way he looked at her were different. They didn't make her feel grown-up and excited as they did when he was alone with her.

It was all very strange and ununderstandable and—thrilling.

It was the first secret she had ever had from Rachel. And yet it wasn't exactly a secret, because there wasn't anything to tell. Only—since the day when they had had that odd, inexplicable quarrel, the day of Aunt Bridget's arrival, she had never spoken to Rachel about Mr. Moyle. She thought about him a lot, and often she wanted to talk about him, but she was afraid of its making Rachel angry again. And that again was part of the mystery—why it should make Rachel angry, when so few things made her angry and there was no reason why it should make her angry. And yet the deepest part of the mystery was that something right down inside her knew why Rachel was angry, though she couldn't have explained it to herself or anyone.

She could see Rachel lying in the sun on the lawn with her hands over her eyes. She didn't want her to know that she had put on the white dress for her music lesson, so she slipped quietly in at the side door without speaking to her and went upstairs to her bedroom to change.

She opened the wardrobe and looked at her cotton frocks hanging there. She was tired of the blue sailor suit. There was a pink cotton frock that she had worn a good deal last summer. She had always liked it, because it had buttons down the front and a white collar and cuffs. She put it on and studied her reflection in the glass. It was too small. It pulled across her chest, outlining her breasts sharply. She looked with deepening interest at her reflection, noticing for the first time that her breasts were growing larger and rounder. They weren't flat as Rachel's were and as her own had been a year ago. She took off the pink frock and put on the blue sailor one and again studied her reflection. Yes, even in that she could see the outline of her breasts quite plainly. She felt half pleased, half ashamed.

She went downstairs to the drawing-room to practise.

Peter, who had grown tired of Owly's feast, came in from the garden at the sound of the piano and began to dance round the room. Peter loved dancing, and, whenever he heard the piano, came in to dance to it. He pirouetted round the room, his small face very solemn, waving his arms.

Jane followed him and stood in the doorway.

"Thea's the queen of the dragons, Jane," he said, "and I'm all the dragons dancing."

"I want to be a dragon dancing," said Jane.

"You can't be, Jane," said Peter breathlessly, still dancing lightly in and out of the furniture, "because, you see, I'm *all* the dragons."

"Let me be a dragon, Peter," pleaded Jane.

"You *can't* be, Jane. I'm *all* the dragons."

The corners of Jane's mouth turned down. Peter watched her, smiling. He hated anyone else to make Jane cry, but sometimes he enjoyed doing it himself. Thea swung round suddenly on the piano stool.

"Go away, both of you," she said severely. "You know perfectly well that you aren't allowed to come in here."

They went out obediently. Both of them stood in awe of Thea.

"You can be a dragon now, Jane," said Peter.

But Jane still wept. She had wanted to be a dragon dancing. . . .

Thea shut the piano and, going into the garden, sat down on the lawn by Rachel.

"Wake up, Rachel."

Rachel opened her eyes and sat up.

"I wasn't asleep."

"Let's go for a walk, shall we?"

"All right."

"Up on to the moors. I'll ask mother, and you get our hats."

They set off briskly together and were soon on the open moor. They did not talk much. Thea was hugging to her the odd exciting feeling that her music lesson with Mr. Moyle always left. Rachel was dreamily watching the colours of the moor—the browns and dull greys and the purple splashes of the opening heather. Above them the clouds were like large white sheep asleep in a blue field.

"Let's go on to Hinchley," said Thea suddenly; "we've never been there, and we'll have walked eight miles if we go there and back."

When Rachel, went for a walk she liked to wander slowly, stopping now and then to gaze about her, exploring side paths, examining the hedgerows, or else just to stroll along, lost in her dreams, seeing nothing around her. But Thea liked to walk quickly so as to cover a certain number of miles. Once when she was eight years old she had been for a ten-mile walk with father on the Holiday, and father had been proud of her, and everyone had praised her. Since then she had half unconsciously looked upon a walk as something to confer kudos upon the walker. One walked a certain number of miles in a certain time and told people about it, and they said, "Did you really? How splendid!" She hated Rachel's habit of mooning along.

They reached Hinchley—a small collection of grey stone cottages, a tiny church, and one or two farms—and sat down to rest for a moment on the low stone wall by the roadside.

"I think it's more than four miles here," said Thea. "Well, it's taken us an hour, and I'm sure we've been walking five miles an hour."

A woman was coming along the road wheeling a pram. They watched her idly and without interest till she was within a few yards of them, then both sprang to their feet.

"Elsie!" called Rachel, and ran to her with outstretched arms.

Thea followed. They clung to her, and she held them closely, her brown eyes full of tears.

"My lovies, my pretties!" she said, "how I've longed for a sight of you!"

Even Thea forgot her grown-upness and clung to her as if she had been Susan. Rachel, looking up into the girl's homely face, so placid and gentle and full of uncritical love, found it impossible to believe that the vague cloud of horror that loomed just beyond the brightness and happiness of life had once swallowed her up.

"Tell me all about the others," Elsie was saying. "How's Miss Janie? And your mother? What's the new nurse like? Better than me, I'll be bound. Your mother was very patient with me, but I've always been a feckless lass."

Rachel remembered that mother used to say that Elsie was stupid and dirty and careless and unmethodical. Looking back upon her regime, she could not help admitting that it was true. What mother had never understood, of course, was this gentle, radiant love, this unquestioning devotion. With other people—even with mother—you felt that their love was somehow dependent on the way you behaved. When you were naughty it was turned away from you, but Elsie loved you just the same, however naughty you were. She had never punished any of them and had tried always to shield them from punishment. When Peter flew into his tempers and kicked and threw things about, she used to say:

"Yes, that's it, laddie; kick as hard as you like and have a good old scream. You'll feel better after it."

The funny thing was that Peter came out of his temper more quickly with Elsie than with anyone. Thea was looking into the pram.

"What a nice baby, Elsie," she said. "Who are you nurse to now?"

"He's mine," said Elsie.

"Oh, Elsie!" said Thea excitedly. "Are you married?"

Elsie's soft brown eyes met Thea's unflinchingly.

"No, Miss Thea. I was wrong to have him."

Thea looked at her for a moment in silence, then said:

"It's not wrong to have babies, Elsie. How can it be?"

"It is when you aren't married," said Elsie.

Thea was silent, digesting this new and startling piece of information. But the baby had awakened and was beginning to cry. Elsie bent over the pram.

"There, there, my pet, my precious. Look who's come to see you. . . . Here's Miss Thea and Miss Rachel."

The baby stared at her, his cries soothed by her low sweet voice. Her eyes shone with love as she bent over him.

"Isn't he a bonny boy?" she said proudly to Thea. "I was wrong to have him, but I wouldn't give him up now for all the world. Yes, it's Miss Rachel, pet. Isn't she a nice little girl? I told you she was."

The baby smiled suddenly at Rachel.

"He knows you, bless him. And he ought to know you, too. I talk to him of nothing else. I suppose he can't really understand, but sometimes he seems to listen. I go on and on about Master Peter and Miss Jane and Miss Susie and you two. I missed you all something cruel at first; but then he came, the rascal, and he gives me little enough time to miss anything."

"Look!" said Thea excitedly. "He's smiling at me now."

"*His* heart's light enough," smiled Elsie, "bless him! Come along home, will you? It's only a few yards off. Have you walked all the way? You'd do with a glass of milk and a biscuit, I reckon. But you mustn't tell your mother you met me. It would fret her."

Suddenly it was one of the old lawless expeditions with Elsie—as if they were visiting the fair again or eating ice-cream from the ice-cream cart in the street. "Now you mustn't tell your mother. . . ."

A feeling of gay adventure possessed them. Thea wheeled the pram, and Rachel held Elsie's hand.

"You *must* sing 'Randall, my son,' before we go," pleaded Rachel. "Sometimes Thea and I sing it, but we can't remember it all."

"Doesn't the new nurse sing for you?"

"No," said Thea. "She's just an ordinary baby's nurse. None of us love her. She's—just ordinary, you know."

"It's wrong of, me," smiled Elsie, "but I'm proper glad to hear you say that."

They entered a tiny cottage kitchen, with a flagged floor and low rafters in the ceiling. A fire burnt in the old-fashioned range, and on the mantelpiece above was a cheap alarm clock flanked by gaily coloured biscuit tins and two old brass candlesticks. The walls were covered by a faded paper of a complicated and once colourful pattern, hung with texts, enlargements of photographs, funeral cards, and framed supplements from *Pears' Annual*, in which Highland cattle disported themselves in romantic glens, and picturesque children frolicked in park-like gardens. On the blue-and-white check tablecloth stood a jar of honeysuckle.

"I live here with my mother," explained Elsie. "I work at Flint Farm in the morning and she looks after baby, and she works there in the afternoon."

She was lifting the baby out of his pram. He had rosy cheeks and curly hair and blue eyes, but there was about him the faint suggestion of griminess that there had been about Jane and Peter when Elsie looked after them. His robe was crumpled and dingy, his face none too clean. Elsie, too, was as untidy as ever. The buttonholes of her blouse met the wrong buttons, leaving strange gaps, her collar was pinned together by a safety-pin, her hair was falling about her face as it had always fallen in the old days. Rachel remembered mother's looking at Elsie's hair, frowning and biting her lip, then saying in the voice that she used when she was trying not to sound as irritated as she felt, "I think that if you put on a hair-net, Elsie, your hair would keep up better."

So Elsie had bought a hair-net that was always half on and half off and made her look more untidy than ever.

Still holding the baby, she filled two glasses with milk and put out a plate of biscuits with highly coloured sugar on the top, the sort that she used to buy secretly for them in the old days instead of the Marie biscuits that mother provided for the nursery.

They sat at the little kitchen table, with its gay checked cloth and jar of honeysuckle, and drank glasses of milk and ate sugar biscuits, while Elsie, her soft brown eyes shining tenderly, her thick hair tailing untidily about her face, rocked the baby in her arms and sang "Randall, my son," for them in her sweet husky voice, and Thea and Rachel joined in loudly with "A rope to *hang* her, mother," as they had always done in the old days.

Suddenly Rachel saw a snapshot in a celluloid frame hanging on the wall among the engravings and enlarged photographs.

"Why, that's the gardener at the Vicarage," she said.

"Yes, he's my uncle," said Elsie. "He lives next door. I told him not to tell your mother or father that he was any kin to me. I thought it might vex them to know it. Every day I go in to ask him about you all. He says I worrit the life out of him the questions I ask. Miss Susie's searching for the fairies same as she always was. Every morning she goes to him first thing to ask if he's found a fairy feast—acorns and such-like spread on the tree-trunk. I tell him, why can't he make one to please the child, but he says he's no time for such rubbish. I've been longing to come down for a sight of you, but I didn't like to come in case your mother or father saw me. I didn't want to vex them."

"Would you like to see Susan and Jane and Peter?" said Rachel.

"Like?" said Elsie. "It'd make me that happy I can't say. I used to fair break my heart for Miss Janie when I first left you—dreaming she was in my arms again. I dream it now sometimes, even though I've got this rascal."

"We'll bring them to see you," said Thea.

Elsie shook her head.

"No, they wouldn't understand. They'd talk about it, and it would vex your mother to know they'd seen me. No, I'll manage to get a sight of them somehow before you go."

"Thea," said Rachel excitedly, "let's take them into the spinney to play, and Elsie can be in the road and watch through the hedge. Let's do it to-morrow just before their bedtime, shall we?"

"I don't want your mother to see me."

"She won't, Elsie. It'll be all right, won't it, Thea?"

"Yes, of course it will," said Thea. "Let me hold your baby, Elsie," she went on. "I'll be awfully careful."

They held him in turn, and he stared at them with solemn blue eyes. Once he smiled, and once he puckered up his little face as if to cry, then suddenly decided not to.

At last they handed him back reluctantly to Elsie.

"I suppose we must go now," said Thea, "or we shall be late home."

Elsie put the baby down in the clothes-basket that formed his cradle and hugged and kissed the two children in her old, loving, impetuous way. Then she filled their pockets with sugar biscuits, and hugged and kissed them again.

"You mustn't tell your mother you've seen me, will you?" she said, standing at the door to see them off.

"No," promised the children.

"And I'll be in the road to-morrow evening."

"We'll be there in the spinney," they promised.

They waved to her till they turned off the road on to the moorland path, then walked on, munching the sugar biscuits. Thea first broke the silence.

"She said it was wrong to have children when you aren't married," she said.

"But how can it be?" said Rachel. "God sends children."

"Perhaps He doesn't. Perhaps people do it themselves."

"But He must do," persisted Rachel. "Don't you remember that mother once said that Mrs. Mallot had always wanted children very badly and was very sad because God didn't send her any? Well, that *proves* it, doesn't it? If it was people, she could have had them. But it was God, and He didn't send her any."

Thea sighed. Always when she thought she was getting to the heart of the mystery it eluded her in this way.

There was another long silence, then Thea said, "I wonder if it's wrong not to tell mother we've seen Elsie."

"It would be wronger to tell her now we've promised Elsie that we won't. It would be breaking a promise."

"Yes, of course it would."

"Besides," said Rachel, "after all, we're persons of our own. I mean, it's not *wrong* just to have a secret."

Rachel was feeling light-hearted with relief as if some great load had dropped from her.

The vague unformulated horror that lurked at the heart of life had ceased suddenly to oppress and terrify her. Elsie had vanished into it, and yet there she was, still the old, loving, generous Elsie, unshadowed by the darkness that had swallowed her up.

Chapter Ten

"THEY'VE reached Cape Town," said Miss Caroline excitedly. 'Did you read about it in this morning's paper? And they've had a magnificent reception. I simply couldn't help crying when I read the description of it to my sister this morning. It was so touching. . . ."

Miss Caroline had come over to the Vicarage to bring Miriam a pot of her new strawberry jam. She had found Miriam doing her household mending in the garden under the shade of the copper beech and had been sitting with her chattering for about quarter of an hour. Miss Caroline's chatter was as spontaneous and irrepressible as a bird's song, but her elder sister did her best to repress it at home, so that, when there was anything particularly exciting in the morning's paper, Miss Caroline generally made some excuse to call upon a neighbour to discuss it. Her excitement over the Royal tour had been gathering momentum with each morning's news, till now it was almost more than she could contain. Her eyes filled with tears of emotion whenever it was mentioned.

"And we need some cheering news," she went on, "with this dreadful war. Whenever I take over a pair of socks to Lady Cynthia at Fletworth for her parcel of comforts for the troops, I say, 'Now, I'm *sure* that this will be the last, Lady Cynthia,' but it never is. . . . Did you see in Saturday's paper that Kitchener has said that all commanders who haven't surrendered by September 15th are to be permanently banished from South Africa? They need really *firm* treatment." Miss Caroline's face looked very severe for a moment, then softened into its usual lines of kindliness. "But we mustn't be impatient. I'm sure the dear troops and generals are doing all they can." She rose irresolutely. "Well, I suppose I must be getting back. My sister doesn't like to be left for long. . . . She's so brave and patient, but an invalid's life is very wearisome." She gathered up the train of her dress, then turned to Miriam, struck by a sudden memory. "Oh, my dear, did you see a *terrible* letter in yesterday's *Times?* I simply daren't read it to my sister, and I didn't paste it into our news record at all. In fact, I destroyed it at once. . . . It was from someone in Dieppe saying that long skirts aren't being worn at all there, in fact that women are wearing skirts that only just touch the tops of their boots, and that the fashion will soon be spreading to England. Can you imagine anything more horrible? I'm sure that English women—*gentlewomen*, at any rate—would have too much good sense to adopt such a fashion. Well, I really *must* be going now. You'll let the children come in to-morrow to play with the garden again, won't you? My sister does so enjoy their visits. Oh, I was forgetting my other piece of news. We had a letter this morning from an Australian cousin we've never seen and didn't know existed, saying that he's over in England and is going to come and see us some day this month."

"But how exciting!" exclaimed Miriam.

"Yes, isn't it? I was quite moved when I read the letter, then the reception at Cape Town simply drove everything else out of my head. . . . Well, *good*-bye, Mrs. Cotteril, and don't forget to tell the children to come in any time."

She hurried down the drive, turning as usual at frequent intervals to smile and wave.

Miriam returned to her mending. She had a headache and felt unusually tired that morning. Peter had had nightmare, and she had been up with him several times in the night and had been unable to sleep afterwards. Moreover, Maria had been going about weeping unashamedly, saying that she'd dreamed of breaking eggs and it was a sure sign that she was going to die in this heathenish place and never see George again.

She missed Nurse more than she had thought she would. The children were somehow not at their best with Bridget. She couldn't understand why, because Bridget was a real child-lover and took a lot of trouble to entertain them. Of course, Bridget did rather get on one's nerves after a few days. Perhaps even the children found that. ... She was wearisomely bright one minute, and depressingly gloomy the next. She was very fussy, too, about her personal appearance, which was ridiculous in a country village like this. When Miriam invited her she had laid particular stress on the fact that the place was right in the country and it didn't matter what one wore. Therefore it irritated her slightly that the girl should spend hours in her bedroom, trying different styles of hair-dressing and retrimming her hats and changing her dress. She could never even take the children out into the village without first doing her hair again and trying her hat at a dozen different angles. It was absurd. ...

Timothy came striding round the house from his walk, very long and lank and loose-jointed. She always hoped that the holiday would make him a little fatter, a little less worn-looking, but it never did, chiefly because he never gave it a chance. He couldn't rest. He was never happy unless he was working.

He went in at the side door without noticing her, and a moment later she saw him seated at the writing-table at the window of his study.

She knew that his mind was full of his work, that he was quite unconscious of his surroundings, but she felt unreasonably hurt that he had not seen her and come to speak to her before he went in to work.

She caught a whiff of paraffin and screwed up her face in a grimace of disgust. She'd had to clean the lamps—a thing she hated doing, but Maria was hopeless at it—and the smell of paraffin still hung about her, though she had scrubbed her hands and rubbed eau-de Cologne on to them.

Somehow the Holiday wasn't turning out as enjoyable as she had thought it would. But then holidays seldom did. She had hoped—as she always hoped—that, when Timothy left his parish behind, they would have a holiday together, as other married couples did. But wherever Timothy went his work seemed to absorb him. It wasn't only his book. ... Already, though it had been agreed that he need do no parish visiting, he was calling regularly on all the invalids in the parish. He was calling, too, on the reprobates and paupers. Only yesterday he had given some money—she didn't know how much—to a farm labourer who was out of work. He was tender-hearted and easily deceived. The few real quarrels they had had in their married life had been about that. She resented his giving money away, suspecting that any scoundrel could melt his heart and open his purse by a tale of suffering.

"It's all we can do to manage with five children," she would say, "and I think it's wrong of you to give money away when your own children need it."

That made him angry, and, as neither of them could understand the other's point of view, she had learnt to avoid discussing the subject. She showed her displeasure now, when he told her that he had given money away, only by silence and a tightening of her lips.

She felt resentfully that his attitude put her unfairly in the wrong. It wasn't that she was mean or hard-hearted, but—he was so dreamy and impractical. He had no idea what a struggle it was for her to make both ends meet on his stipend, how often she had to go without things that she really needed, and even deprive the children of what her parents had regarded as necessities for her in her own childhood. He spent nothing upon himself, of course, living sparely and austerely, wearing his clothes till she had to insist upon his renewing them . . .

She glanced down at the piles of underclothing in her mending basket—stout little undergarments of calico made by her and Nurse. Her mind went back to her own childhood. She had had dainty, expensive clothes, she had regarded treats and presents as part of the ordinary day's routine. She remembered once hearing someone say of her father's house that it was the sort of house through which "money flows like water." Her girlhood had been very different from the girlhood her own daughters would know. It had been a continual round of gaieties—parties, dances, expeditions. And yet, through it all, she had found time to develop her talents, passing her L.R.A.M., working hard at her singing and drawing. Her beauty and charm, combined with her talents, had made it inevitable that she should have innumerable admirers, and her father, a genial, good-tempered, generous man, who spent every penny of his income as he earned, it, making no provision for the future, had been anxious for her to marry Frank Winfield, the most handsome, wealthy, and persistent of them all. He had been bitterly displeased and disappointed when she accepted Timothy Cotteril, a poor curate who had no footing in her circle, and who had only met her because it was considered the proper thing in those days for a young lady to dabble in church work, and Miriam had taken a Sunday school class when she happened to get up in time. The memory of Frank came back to her now, softened and idealised by distance. She saw his tall, well-proportioned figure, his handsome, regular-featured face, his fine brown eyes. If she had married Frank, she wouldn't have had to scheme and plan and darn children's socks till they could scarcely hold together. Frank had no work, no other interests, to stand between them, leaving her to bear the brunt of things alone. She pulled herself up with a hot flush of shame. . . . It was horrible to harbour such thoughts. . . . Still—she didn't really harbour them, she assured herself. It was just that she was tired by her sleepless night. She remembered the part of *Pilgrim's Progress* where "One of the wicked ones stepped softly up to Christian and whisperingly suggested many grievous blasphemies to him, which he verily thought had proceeded from his own mind. . . ." She knew that if she could have had her life over again she would still have refused Frank and married Timothy. She had never really faltered or looked back since the night she accepted him, and he had taken her into his arms and kissed her—the first time that he had ever kissed a woman or that she had ever been kissed by a man. Beneath her surface irritation and resentments, her love for him was the strongest, most enduring thing in her life.

She took up a cotton frock of Susan's, stitched on fresh buttons, and mended a small three-cornered tear. It was really too short for Susan—it came right up to her knees—but it might do for Jane next summer.

Just beneath it in the mending basket was a small much-darned vest. Jane couldn't possibly go on wearing it any longer. She'd give it to Mrs. Talbot, whose children were the most badly dressed in the parish, though she would probably pawn it for a few pence to buy a glass of beer. She folded up the vest and put it to one side. She hated to think of Jane's growing out of her baby garments, her baby ways and speech. She wouldn't have another baby now, of course. . . . She would like to have had more children, and she resented the economic necessity that forbade it. She looked back with regret to the years when Timothy had been her lover. The austerity of his religion made self-control easier to him than it would have been to many men, but he had been a passionate lover, and she sometimes thought that he missed her love more than he realised. Often behind his gentleness there was a suspicion of strain, and she on her side was, she knew, often nervy and irritable. Yet in spite of all this there had come an added tenderness to their love for each other from the very fact that it now lacked physical expression.

She heard the sound of the children's returning from their walk, and suddenly Peter came running across the lawn and flung himself upon her. Jane followed breathlessly, trying to climb on to her knee, pushing Peter away.

She held them both together on her lap, but Peter soon wriggled away and sat on the grass by her feet. He was boasting about his nightmare, though he had cried with terror of it in the night.

"It was a great big elephant, Jane, with a head like a lion's. You've never seen a great big elephant with a head like a lion's."

"You were frightened of it, Peter," Jane reminded him gently. "You cried."

"Cried?" repeated Peter, in amused contempt. "I never cry."

"I heard you. It woke me up."

"What you heard was me *laughing*, Jane, not crying."

Susan suddenly appeared, her sunbonnet hanging down her back. As soon as she saw the group she came to join it, leaning over the back of Miriam's chair and kissing her ears and hair and neck.

Then came Thea and Bridget, walking together. Miriam's eyes were fixed expectantly on the corner of the house. She always felt ill at ease when one of her flock was absent. She loved to have them all about her. She loved to think that they belonged to her wholly, that she knew their every thought and feeling. Then Rachel—always the last—came slowly and dreamily round the corner. At the same moment Timothy appeared in the front doorway. Jane scrambled down from Miriam's knee and ran to him. He crouched down so that she could take a firm hold of his shoulders, then hoisted her up pick-a-back and came across the lawn to the others.

Rachel and Susan struggled for the empty place on Miriam's knee, and Rachel won it.

Clasped in Miriam's arms, Rachel felt sheltered and happy and encircled by protective love. She forgot that sometimes it chafed and irked her and that she longed to be independent of it, to be "a person of her own."

Timothy was sitting down on the grass with Jane on his knee. He glanced up at his wife and said:

"You look very nice, my dear. That's a new dress, isn't it?"

They all laughed delightedly. She smiled down at him.

"I've worn it nearly every day for more than a year," she said.

It was a family joke that Timothy never noticed when Miriam wore a new dress, but frequently complimented her on a new dress when she was wearing a particularly old one.

Susan jumped up suddenly. "There's the baker's cart," she said. "Let's go and see if he's got any cookie boys."

They all ran across the lawn, through the paddock, down to the gate where the baker's cart had drawn up.

Jane's short fat legs plodded a long way behind the others. "Wait for me, Peter," she called. "Peter, *please* wait for me."

"I must go in and see to the dinner," said Miriam, but without stirring from her chair.

Timothy took her hand in his.

"I'm afraid that this holiday isn't all I'd like it to be for you, darling. . . . I'm afraid it's meaning a lot of extra work and worry."

And immediately all the vague discontent of a few moments ago left her, and it seemed to her that this was the ideal holiday, the holiday she had always longed for.

She laughed and dropped a kiss upon his head. "Nonsense!" she said. "I'm loving it."

Chapter Eleven

IT was three miles to Fletworth Vicarage, where the Dawsons lived. Timothy, who was walking, had already set off, and Mrs. Dawson was sending the dog-cart for the others. The children loved drives of any sort and were ready long before it was due, standing at the front door eagerly watching out for it. It drew up with a flourish, and the groom helped them to climb into the back seat. There was a strap that could be fastened round them, but Thea said, "We don't want the strap, thank you. We can manage quite well without it." Susan, tucked between Thea and Rachel, and feeling a long way from the ground, would have rather liked to be safely strapped in, but dared not say so. Miriam, wearing the green silk dress, was in front next the groom.

They wheeled along the white dusty road. The horses' hooves made a pleasant clop-clop sound that cut sharply through the sleepy air. Yarrow, campion, and tall, pink field thistles grew by the roadside, and the hedges changed from green to russet as hawthorn, beech, and sycamore succeeded each other in patches. Where they grew highest, wisps of hay still hung upon them, and once where the road narrowed Rachel put out her hand to try to catch some, but Thea, who was being very grown-up, said, "Don't do that, Rachel," and Rachel felt ashamed of her childishness.

Susan was holding on to the seat with both hands, hoping that neither of the other two would notice. Villagers, walking along the road, looked with kindly interest at the three little girls in white muslin frocks and white frilled sun-hats sitting together on the back seat of the dog-cart. Thea stretched up her neck to make herself look as tall as possible and hoped that they noticed the amber necklace. She felt quite disappointed when the dog-cart turned in at the gate of Fletworth Vicarage.

Fletworth Vicarage was built of stone like most of the houses in the neighbourhood, and had the same pointed, ecclesiastical-looking front door and mullioned windows as Barwick Vicarage. But the garden was larger and much better kept. Neat beds of begonias and dahlias dotted the immaculate lawn, and next to the house was a large conservatory full of flowering plants.

Mrs. Dawson appeared at the front door as the trap drew up. She was a rather plain woman with a long horse-like face, dressed in a vaguely "arty" dress of red velvet, confined loosely at the waist by a girdle and without the fashionable train. Her thick straight hair, of a dull brown shade, was parted in the middle, looped back on each side of her long face, and twisted into a thick coil in the nape of her neck. She greeted Miriam warmly, and helped the children down from the back seat, smoothing the crumpled white muslin dresses. Then she went into the house, holding Susan and Rachel by the hand.

"Anthea! Diane!" she called.

Two little girls of about five and six came running into the hall, and greeted Miriam with ceremonial politeness in French.

"*Ah, Anglais!*" laughed the lady.

"How-do-you-do?" said the children slowly and carefully and with a marked French accent.

"They have had a French nurse," explained Mrs. Dawson, "and they still have a French mademoiselle, but we are trying very hard now to talk English, *n'est-ce pas, mes enfants?*"

"*Oui, maman,*" said Anthea. "I remember to speek English now nearly always, but I steel theenk in French."

"Sometimes I theenk in English," said Diane proudly.

Anthea was plain, with a long large-featured face like her mother; but Diane was radiantly pretty, with small features, a pink-and-white complexion, and golden curls.

"Where's Lucy?" Mrs. Dawson was saying. "Oh, here she is."

A dark, sullen-looking girl of about twenty was coming downstairs.

"This is Mrs. Cotteril, darling," said Mrs. Dawson, "and Thea and Rachel and Susan. . . . This is my stepdaughter."

She slipped an arm affectionately round the girl as she spoke, but the girl stiffened and drew away.

Mrs. Dawson flushed at the rebuff. "Let's go into the drawing-room, shall we?" she said.

The drawing-room was gay with brightly coloured chintzes and fresh white paint. Several occasional tables were covered with literary and artistic reviews. Embroidered lace curtains swayed at the open window, and on every side were vases of roses and sweet-peas. A clavichord stood by the door. There was about the house none of that shabbiness that the little Cotterils had come to associate with clergymen's houses.

Toys were strewn about the floor, and a woman, introduced as "Mademoiselle," moved a pile of picture-books from her knees as she rose from the sofa to greet the visitors. Her blue-black hair was drawn tightly back from her forehead, and she wore her plain black satin dress with a French-woman's chic. She shook hands with them, said "How-do-you-do?" slowly and carefully, and then turned with a torrent of French to her charges.

"*Ramassez vos joujoux, mes enfants. Vite! Vite!*"

The little girls answered volubly.

"*Ce n'est pas à moi. C'est à Diane. . . .*"

"*Ah non, c'est à toi, Anthea.*"

"*Taisez-vous, mes enfants,*" said Mrs. Dawson. "*Allez-vous-en.* Take your visitors upstairs and show them your toys."

The little Cotterils were taken upstairs to the nursery, where again the young hostesses began to talk in shrill excited French to each other and to Mademoiselle. "*Parlez Anglais, parlez Anglais,*" she commanded. "*Votre maman vous a dit qu'il faut parler Anglais.*"

The little girls' volubility died away as they began to wrestle with the unfamiliar tongue.

"Theese-doll-beelongs-to-Anthea. Her name ees Clothilde. She is eel. She was—*qu'est-ce que c'est l'Anglais, Mademoiselle?*—run down."

"*Ah, je ne sais pas,*" said Mademoiselle impatiently, "*il faut demander à Maman. . . .*"

"*C'est* knocked," suggested Anthea.

"*Ce n'est pas,*" contradicted Diane. "*Ce n'est pas* 'knocked.'"

Mademoiselle appeared to be as excitable as her charges, and on any disputed point (such as whether the doll's armchair belonged to Anthea or Diane) would join in the argument as vehemently as the children, not remembering to say "*Parlez Anglais, mes enfants,*" till the point was finally settled.

Susan was frankly contemptuous of the three of them. It seemed to her silly and affected to talk a foreign language instead of English, and she wasn't going to encourage them by taking any notice of them. She busied herself with the doll's house. It had pillars at the front door and tiny lace curtains at all the windows. The little Cotterils' doll's house at home (only Susan and Jane played with it now) wasn't a real doll's house at all. It was a collection of wooden boxes that father had covered inside with wall-paper to form rooms. There was no front to it. It had this advantage over a real doll's house, however, that extra rooms could always be added as one acquired more furniture. It had begun with four boxes, and now there were eight.

Susan was playing a game of her own with the doll's house. The doll in the bed was Princess Agnes, asleep till a spell could be found to awake her. . . . The prince would come to the front door with the little pillars, walk up the tiny carpeted stair, bend over the princess, and—the spell would be broken.

Rachel watched her young hostesses with interest. The situation thrilled her by its very novelty. She was trying to fix the scene into her mind so that she could always remember it—the sunny nursery with its white-painted furniture, the large doll's house, the expensive toys, the two little girls, the rather exciting-looking Mademoiselle with her shining hair and tight black dress . . . the shrill, excited voices, arguing, contradicting. . . . The experience somehow made life seem more complete than it had been before.

Thea, beneath her nonchalant exterior, was secretly impressed. She tried to look as if she could easily have joined in the conversation if she had wanted to. To herself she practised saying, "*La maison des poupées est très jolie*," and tried hard to say it aloud just to show them that she could talk French too. But she was afraid that she wouldn't understand what they said in reply. Also she knew that it wouldn't sound a bit like the French they talked. They talked so quickly and pronounced the words quite differently from the way Miss Baltimore, the French mistress at school, pronounced them. When she grew up and was married to a rich husband and had lots of children, she'd have them all taught to talk French like this. They would have a Mademoiselle with black shiny hair and a black dress, and a beautiful nursery with white-painted furniture and lots of toys. Rachel would be poor, and her children would be very dull and rather plain, but Thea would always be very, very nice to them. . . .

A gong sounded in the hall, and they all went downstairs, Mademoiselle still calling out instructions and reproofs in her high-pitched voice.

Mr. Dawson was now in the drawing-room. He was a small, ordinary-looking man with a kind, rather wistful expression.

"*Où es-tu allé, Papa?*" said Anthea as she kissed him.

"*F' ai-été-à-l'Église*," he said in laboured French.

They corrected his accent, laughing affectionately.

The girl who had been introduced as Lucy sat by her father. She still looked sulky and did not join at all in the conversation. On the wall hung an enlarged photograph of a woman who was evidently her mother—handsome, heavy-featured, plainly dressed, belonging obviously to the provincial middle class.

Mrs. Dawson was discussing an exhibition of Post-impressionist art that she had attended in London the month before.

"We knew Cézanne in Paris," she said. "I've always admired his work. I can't understand the prejudice against it. After all, emotion should be the primary consideration of art. . . ."

"Do you go up to London often?" said Miriam.

"She can't keep away from an art exhibition or a concert," said her husband, smiling at her.

She laughed.

"Oh, I'm not quite as bad as that," she said. "I do hope to go up at the end of this month, though. I want to see the view of Meissonier's etchings and go to one of the Newman Promenade Concerts at the Queen's Hall. Madame von Stosch is playing there on the 24th. And there's a Wagner Concert on the 26th. I think I'll try to get up for those. I've been trying to persuade Lucy to come with me."

The girl did not speak or look at her. The father's wistful gaze went from one to the other. He laid his hand on his daughter's arm.

"I wish you'd go, my dear."

"Do come, darling," pleaded Mrs. Dawson again.

"I've told you I don't want to," said the girl shortly.

Again the woman flushed. She was evidently acutely sensitive, but lacked the perception to see that her persistent overtures of friendship only increased the girl's hostility.

"Do you play?" said Miriam, trying to cover up the awkward moment.

"I play the clavichord a little," said Mrs. Dawson. "I love the clavichord. Beethoven preferred it to all keyed instruments, you know, and Mozart used to play it. . . ."

"Do play for us."

Mrs. Dawson went across to the clavichord and, sitting down, began to play at once without a trace of self-consciousness.

As she played, her heavy face lost the slight suggestion of stupidity that it wore normally and seemed to lighten, suffused, as it were, by something ethereal. Under cover of the playing Lucy put out her hand with furtive swiftness and laid it on her father's arm, as if to apologise for her curtness. His hand closed over it.

Suddenly Anthea and Diane ran across the room to him and climbed upon his knee. There was evidently a very real affection between the vicar and his little stepchildren. Immediately Lucy withdrew again, going over to the farther corner of the room and pretending to be absorbed in a book she took down from the shelves.

Mrs. Dawson's hands still wandered over the keys. Her long,

slender, nervous fingers lacked the clumsiness that characterised the rest of her body. There was silence in the room. Her husband watched her tenderly over the little girls' heads. Miriam listened enthralled. Looking suddenly at the older girl, she saw her shoot a glance of hatred at the figure seated at the clavichord, then lower her eyes at once to her book.

Mrs. Dawson stopped playing and, turning abruptly to Miriam, the glow still illuminating her heavy features, said: "I never tire of Mozart, do you? I shall never forget the first time I heard his Symphony in G Minor. I could listen to it over and over again. Do you remember Schubert said, 'You can hear the angels singing in it'? The finale is such a masterpiece with those wonderful figures of counterpoint."

The woman's eagerness was waking Miriam's old enthusiasms from their long sleep. They discussed music, and Miriam watched her hostess covertly. Her neighbours, she knew, made fun of her—Miriam had heard her odd fashion of dress and her artistic proclivities mocked pitilessly in most of the local drawing-rooms—but one could not be with the woman for five minutes without becoming aware of something generous and large-hearted about her. She was without a trace of malice or littleness. She lacked even the adroitness to assume a surface likeness to the people among whom she lived, and this, of course, was the real cause of her unpopularity.

Once Miriam turned to Mr. Dawson to ask his opinion on a disputed point, and he smiled deprecatingly.

"I don't know one tune from another," he said, "and as to pictures—I like a picture to tell a story, which I understand is quite wrong."

Mademoiselle brought some books down for the two little girls to show to their guests.

"English!" said Diane in a tone of faint disgust, as she opened one. "Eet is such a deeficult language."

Rachel was only pretending to look at the picture-book. Lucy had gone out, mother was talking to Mrs. Dawson, and father to

Mr. Dawson. Father and Mr. Dawson were just behind her, and she could hear what they said. Mr. Dawson was saying:

"Yes, you have to go very slowly with them. They're very conservative, and once they've got their backs up it's impossible to do anything with them. I didn't dare to wear a surplice till I'd been here three years. . . . There were two old family pews in the chancel, and I wanted to have them taken away and choir stalls put there instead, but when I suggested it—two years ago—the people were so indignant that I had to let the matter drop. Then last week they came to me, quite aggrieved, to ask why they shouldn't have the choir in the chancel and too suggest that we take away the old pews and put choir stalls there instead."

Father laughed, and Mr. Dawson went on:

"That's the best way for it to happen, and it's the way it most often happens. You suggest a thing, and they refuse even to consider it, and two or three years later they come and suggest it to you, quite honestly believing that it's their own idea. . . . Except young Borrows at Tarryvale. He's rushed them along like a house on fire. Their last man preached in a black gown, and Borrows had lighted candles on the altar by the end of the first month. I believe they'd do anything for him. . . . It's the personal touch that counts, of course. I said one day to old Hobbs, who lives at Tarryvale: 'I hear you're all turning High Church up at Tarryvale,' and he said indulgently, 'Oh aye, 'e antics a bit, but we like 'un so well we antics wi' 'un.' "

Rachel looked at mother, who was still talking to Mrs. Dawson on the sofa. And suddenly for the first time in her life she seemed to be detached from her, to be looking at her from the outside as if she were someone she had never seen before. She was a stranger, the lady in the green silk dress with the hat that tilted forward to throw a soft shadow over the blue eyes. But how pretty she looked, how charming, how soft and gentle her voice, and how clever she was to be able to talk about these strange things called "technique" and "impressionism." It was obvious that Mrs. Dawson enjoyed talking to her. Then suddenly she ceased to be a stranger and became mother again, and a warm rush of pride swept over Rachel's heart.

But it was time to go home now. Mr. Dawson, who had to take Evensong, said that he would walk with father as far as the church.

"Now, do be careful, darling, and don't go and do a lot of visiting afterwards," his wife pleaded. "You know that Dr. Flemming said you weren't to get overtired." She turned to Miriam: "He's had a wretched cold all this summer, and it's pulled him down so. . . ."

The dog-cart drove up to the front door, and the children were packed again into the back seat. Anthea and Diane stood with their mother, calling "*Au revoir*" and blowing kisses. As the dog-cart turned into the road, Rachel looked up and saw Lucy at an upstairs window, standing behind the curtain and watching them. She waved on an impulse, but Lucy did not wave back.

Bridget had taken Peter and Jane to Southwood Farm for the afternoon. The farm was just opposite the Vicarage, and the farmer and his wife, Mr. and Mrs. Comfort, who had no children of their own, had taken a great fancy to the little Cotterils and encouraged them to visit the farm whenever they liked.

Peter and Jane had much enjoyed the afternoon. They had stroked the calves, held the baby kittens in their arms, played with the puppies, and fed the chickens. Then they had had tea in the farm kitchen—mugs of creamy milk, home-made strawberry jam, cream, and oatcakes. They both loved the large cool kitchen, with its stone floor and great old-fashioned fireplace flanked by deep ingle-nooks. Polished copper pots gleamed on the walls, and the air was aromatic with the scent of the drying herbs that hung from the blackened oak-beamed ceiling among the oatcakes and hams. The oatcakes fascinated Jane, bending over their strings, looking like pieces of flannel and tasting like porridge but much nicer. . . . Everything, in fact, went beautifully till their farewell visit to the farmyard. The pigs were being fed, and Jane, her round face pink with excitement, asked:

"Are they called pigs because they eat like that?"

All the farm hands standing by had laughed uproariously, and Jane had burst into tears. She was still crying when they reached home. They tried in vain to comfort her. She could hear nothing but those raucous roars of laughter, see nothing but those mouths stretched wide in grins of amusement.

"Jane," said Thea, "where we've been to tea to-day, there were two little girls who could talk French when they were as little as you."

"I don't care," sobbed Jane.

Chapter Twelve

IT was arranged that Peter and Jane should picnic in the wood with Bridget. The others had gone into Harborough by the market bus. Peter would have liked to go with them. He loved the old brown horse that drew the bus, and the stuffy, dusty smell of the inside, where the two rows of passengers sat facing each other with market baskets on their knees. But, even better than the inside, he loved the seat outside next to Truman, the driver. Truman occasionally gave the brown horse a friendly flick with his whip, and the brown horse returned the greeting with a friendly jingle of his harness, but never increased his pace, keeping up a steady, sleepy trot all the way to Harborough. As the bus jolted in leisurely fashion down the road, leaving a cloud of dust behind it, the massive hind quarters of the brown horse moved sideways to and fro. When he stopped and they let you get down and stroke him, his coat had a fascinating sticky feeling, and there was a funny smell about him that was somehow thrilling.

But mother had said that Peter and Jane would find the day in Harborough too tiring, and so Bridget had offered to take them for a picnic instead.

"We'll have a lovely time—we three," she had said in that very bright voice that made Peter and Jane suspect at once that they were being cheated of something, and that really the others were going to have a far better time.

They stood at the gate and watched Truman swing Thea and Rachel up into the seat beside him in front, while mother climbed up the steps into the bus. Then they waved till it turned the corner of the road.

"Now," said Bridget brightly, "we'll go back for the picnic basket, and then—*off* we go!"

They ran back to the Vicarage, and Bridget went upstairs to put on her hat before they started.

She was wearing a dress of pink muslin, the bodice made in the popular sailor shape, its front and sailor collar and short tie trimmed with rows of imitation Valenciennes lace. She tried on a white straw hat with a straight brim, the crown swathed with black velvet and large pink roses, then discarded it in favour of a hat whose brim was turned up sharply all the way round, the under-side plentifully trimmed with flowers and ribbons. This hat was officially her Best, but she had an uneasy suspicion that the other one was more becoming. She tried each of them several times, deciding finally in favour of the upturned brim. It was certainly smart, and she liked the effect of the bunches of flowers and knots of ribbon nestling against her hair.

She felt certain—absolutely certain—that she was going to meet him to-day. He had been to the Vicarage several times since their first meeting, and always the clasp of his hand and the meaning look of his fine dark eyes had sent a knife-like thrill through her whole body. She loved him, and he—oh, he wouldn't look at her like that unless he loved her too. It was the Real Thing at last. It had come to her after all these years. A sharp ecstasy swept over her whenever she thought of him, and yet—there was a faint, unacknowledged anxiety behind it. More than a fortnight of the Holiday had passed, and things were, after all, much as they had been at that first meeting. Surely it was time that the affair progressed a little. Surely it was time he Spoke. It was his place to make the opportunities, of course. As a woman—a nice woman—her hands were tied. ("Once a girl makes herself cheap to a man he never thinks anything of her again," her mother had frequently told her.) She was willing enough to be pursued, but the pursuing must be done by him.

Perhaps he was waiting for some sign from her that his attentions would be welcome. Perhaps he felt diffident about Speaking, fearing that she would not care to live in a small way in the country. She must try to let him know somehow that she would like it. In her pocket was a letter from Violet, asking her to come and stay with her and help with the children for the fortnight that Nurse took her annual holiday. She was sick of children—other people's children, that is. One's own would be quite different. She would love her own children, of course. She saw an idealised picture of herself sitting in the firelight, with a blue-eyed curly-headed baby on her knee and other blue-eyed curly-headed children clustered about her. The door opened quietly behind her, and a tall handsome man with crisp dark curls came in and, bending over her, pressed his lips upon hers. She caught herself up with a flush. One oughtn't to think things like that. It wasn't quite nice. Instead she imagined herself sitting at a charming little writing-desk and writing to ask—whom could she ask? . . . Oh, that dull little creature Maggie Wayland, who was absolutely *certain* never to get married—if she would come and stay with her and help with the children for the fortnight that Nurse went away for her holiday. She'd give Maggie a good time, too. She'd introduce her to nice men and give her a Chance. Really, Miriam was terribly self-centred. Any other woman would have seen that Mr. Moyle was attracted by her and would have—well, asked him to the house more and left them together occasionally. Women ought to help each other. If she'd been in Miriam's place and Miriam in hers, she'd have done all she could to give Miriam a Chance. Miriam was beautiful, of course, but hard and selfish, utterly wrapped up in herself and her husband and children. While as for Timothy—well, one couldn't dislike Timothy, because there really was something rather sweet about him, but he was so absent-minded and impractical that he didn't seem to count as a man at all. He never noticed anything around him. No, she wouldn't like Timothy for a husband. As a matter of fact, she quite frequently passed in review all her friends' husbands and decided that she would not have married any of them even if they had asked her.

It was funny that when she got Miriam's letter she'd had a sort of premonition that here at last she would find the Real Thing. She forgot for the moment that she invariably had that same premonition on receiving an invitation. She heard herself saying, "Yes, somehow I knew all the time that I was going to meet him. Yes, the first moment we met we fell in love with each other. . . ."

"Come *along*, Aunt Bridget," called Peter impatiently from the hall.

"Coming, darling," she called, and, setting her hat at what she considered its most becoming angle, ran downstairs to where Peter and Jane were waiting for her with the picnic basket.

She answered their chatter absently as they walked through the village. She was still wrapped in languorous day-dreams.

Just beyond the village they met Lucy Dawson on her cycle. She nodded curtly without smiling as she passed. She wore a small, neat sailor hat tilted over her brow, a plain navy-blue serge coat and skirt, and a white blouse with a stiff collar and tie. A horrible doubt about her own costume invaded Bridget's mind. Was it too elaborate for a country walk? She stood irresolute in the middle of the road, wondering whether to go home and change into her blue cotton dress and plain garden hat, but the children were growing impatient, so she hurried on with them to the wood.

The shade of the wood was grateful after the hot, dusty road. They followed the little path that wound between the trees and crossed a tiny stream that gurgled over its stones, half hidden by ferns. There was an undergrowth of bracken where the trees were thin, with purple drifts of willow herb in the clearings. She found an open space beneath a large oak tree and put down the picnic basket.

"Shall we have a game before tea?" she said.

"No, thanks," said Peter.

"Shall I read you a fairy story?"

"No, thanks," said Peter.

"What *do* you want to do?" she said, a faint note of irritation invading her brightness.

"I want to explore with Jane," said Peter.

"Well, keep where I can see you," said Bridget, settling herself down comfortably against the trunk of the oak tree. The Cotteril children were very unresponsive, she decided. One couldn't get really fond of them. Her own children wouldn't be unresponsive, of course. She saw the blue-eyed, golden-haired children running to her with outstretched arms: "Mummy, darling. . . . Oh, mummy, do come and play with us."

She half pulled herself up . . . was it quite nice to imagine things like that? Before she could make up her mind, Peter returned, followed by Jane.

"Look what I've found," he shouted.

It was a small stick with the end bent to form a handle. It made a little walking-stick just the right size for him. He considered it thoughtfully.

"No," he said at last with the air of one coming to an important decision. "If anything nice happens to me this afternoon, I want it to be finding a bird's nest, not a walking-stick. I'll give it to you, Jane."

Jane took it with delight and began to strut to and fro along the path with it.

Bridget returned to her thoughts, reviewing the fortnight that had passed. Those few meetings with Mr. Moyle were the only real things in it. The rest was shadowy and dream-like. There was that dreadful half-witted child at the Hall. They'd asked Miriam to go there and take the children again, but she had made an excuse not to go. Thea had rather wanted to go again, but Miriam had been quite firm. Then there was that clergyman's wife with the two little girls who'd come over from Fletworth to tea yesterday. The woman was so queerly dressed that it was all one could do not to giggle whenever one looked at her, and the little girls were affected and ill-bred. They talked French, and, when one answered them in French, pretended that they couldn't understand what one said, which was, of course, extremely rude. And then there was that dreadful Mrs. Seacome who lived at The Moorings and drank. She seemed to have taken a fancy to the children, and was always giving Susan little bits of ribbon and silk to make dresses for her dolls. The blue-eyed, golden-haired children wouldn't have been allowed to have anything to do with a woman like that. But Timothy had always had extraordinary ideas. He didn't seem to mind his children mixing with horrible people, even with the filthy children of his slum parish.

"They'll get more good than harm from them," he would say when Miriam objected.

The village people weren't much better. That Miss Thrupp who kept the shop was a raving madwoman, of course, or she wouldn't be nursing that doll all the time. There was something almost indecent in the sight of her standing with it at her shop door. It gave one the creeps, and one simply never felt safe until one had passed the door.

She glanced at her watch and began to unpack the tea basket. Peter was still looking for a bird's nest, and Jane had stopped strutting to and fro with the walking-stick to help him.

"Come to tea, children," called Bridget sweetly.

But she wasn't really calling Peter and Jane. She was calling the blue-eyed, golden – haired children, who flitted like little ghosts about the wood. And she wasn't sitting alone under the oak tree. A man with dark, deep-set eyes and crisp, curling hair sat with her, his arm around her. The blue-eyed, golden haired children ran to her eagerly. Peter and Jane came draggingly, reluctantly.

"I don't *want* any silly ole tea," said Peter. "I want to find a bird's nest."

"Look, Peter," said Jane, showing him a beechnut. "I've found a little tree seed. I'm going to put it in the earth, an' a long time ago it will be a big tree."

"A long time ago!" jeered Peter, but Jane only smiled at him. She never minded Peter's laughing at her.

"You mean 'one day,' " he said.

She considered this in silence for a moment, then said:

"No, I don't. I mean a long time ago. Trees take a long time to grow. Not like flowers. I know, because Susan told me."

"Isn't she silly?" he said to Bridget, " 'Ago' 's not right, is it?"

But his laughter was kindly. Jane's mistakes made him feel grown-up and superior and important. Once he'd been little like Jane and couldn't say words right, but now he was five years old and a Big Boy.

Bridget unwrapped the jam sandwiches, uncorked the bottle of milk, and took out the tin of sponge-cakes.

"Silly ole jam sandwiches," said Peter scornfully. (The blue-eyed, golden-haired children were saying, "Oh, mummy, how *lovely!*").

"I'm going to pick some flowers for mummy after tea," said Jane.

She laid the little walking-stick carefully beside her. Peter looked at it again thoughtfully.

"I'm *sure* to find a bird's nest after tea," he said.

"It's cruel to take birds' nests, Peter," said Bridget. "Think of the poor birds when they find their homes gone."

He looked at her coldly.

"They don't live in their nests now," he said. "They've all hatched out, and they don't lay any more eggs till next spring."

She hardly heard him, for the blue-eyed, golden-haired children were saying, "Oh, mummy, we never thought of that. We'll *never* take birds' nests again. . . ."

She wiped their crumby mouths and hands and put away the tea things, then took a book from the picnic basket.

"Who'd like to look at a picture-book with me?" she said with her hard, conscientious brightness.

The blue-eyed, golden – haired children, of course, crowded round her. Peter and Jane edged away. Then—quite suddenly she glanced up and saw him through the trees in the distance coming towards her. Her heart leapt, and the blood flamed into her cheeks. There was a loud roaring in her ears. She opened the book quickly and, holding the two reluctant children closely to her, one on each side, began to describe the pictures in a high-pitched, unsteady voice.

"And Goldilocks knocked at the cottage door, and nobody answered, so she went in."

Though her head was bent down, every nerve in her body was strained to catch the signs of his approach. He was coming nearer . . . nearer. Peter began to wriggle, but she held him tightly. This must be the scene that met his eyes as he came round the bend in the path—the two children nestling against her, their three heads bent together over the book, her clear voice telling them the story. She saw the picture through his eyes and said to herself reverently, "What a wonderful mother she'd make."

"I *know* that silly ole tale," protested Peter.

"But listen, Peter. I'm going to tell you quite a new part of it—a part you've never heard before. Listen," she said in desperate appeal, her clasp tightening about his wriggling form, and raised her voice again, investing it with a silvery sweetness.

"Well, there was a table in the kitchen and round the table were———"

He was almost upon them now. Her heart was hammering wildly in her thin breast. Her voice was escaping her control and becoming high-pitched and hysterical.

"And in front of each were three plates . . ."

He was upon them now.

"Here's Mr. Moyle!" called Peter.

She looked up with a badly simulated start.

"Well, this *is* a surprise," she said gaily. "Fancy meeting you here!"

Peter used the diversion to escape from her arm.

"I'm going to look for a bird's nest," he said. "Come on, Jane."

Jane picked up her little walking-stick and trotted after him.

Mr. Moyle sat down by Bridget beneath the oak tree and fixed his magnificent dark eyes upon her.

"May I?" he said.

He put such meaning into tone and look that for a second Bridget almost felt that he had Spoken. She gave an unsteady giggle.

"Why, of course," she said. "Of course you may. The wood's free, isn't it?"

Her naïvety made him feel half scornful, half amused. How absurd she had looked, her face bent over the book, red to the tips of her ears, pretending not to see him!

"I'm in luck's way to-day," he went on. "How is it I've never met you on your walks before?"

He had realised from the beginning that there was no need of subtlety with her.

Her flush deepened, and she tossed her head with a crude affectation of coquettishness.

"That must *be your* fault," she said. "We come out every afternoon."

"I've been busy lately," he said, "but now I know you come here. . . . You do generally come here, don't you?"

She tossed her head again and tried to look arch.

"*Sometimes* we come here."

Her archness consorted oddly with her heightened colour and the obvious trembling of her frame. She put her hands to her burning cheeks and giggled again.

"I've got so dreadfully sunburnt with this heat," she said.

As she dropped her hands he took one of them in his and fixed his eyes on her again.

"Sunburn's very becoming to you," he said. "I suppose you know that?"

She drew her hand away. She mustn't let him take liberties. No nice girl did that. But she must give him encouragement. In a nice way, of course.

"You know," she said, "I simply love the country . . . *this* sort of country. I'd love to live here."

Her strained, metallic brightness cut sharply through the sleepy summer air.

He looked down at her face, weak, amiable, stupid, its fading and slightly common prettiness marred by lines of discontent and anxiety. He could read her like an open book, and the reading did not displease him. Her unveiled admiration flattered his insatiable vanity. After all, he would rather flirt with a woman like this than with a woman who was sure of herself, fastidious, exacting. His conceit could not bear the faintest shadow of criticism. He was not likely to meet it here. Most people were away for August, and this silly, adoring little creature, who could still look quite pretty sometimes, would help to pass the time.

"That's good news," he said.

The words were meaningless enough, but his head was bent

towards her, and his deep-set eyes were fixed ardently upon hers. Her heart began to beat again with loud, suffocating strokes.

"I like housework, too," she went on breathlessly. "I like everything very simple. I'm not one of those girls who spend a lot of money on dress and that sort of thing. We've always been poor, and I've had to learn to manage."

Her voice was still gay and arch and shrill, but something about her was pleading with him so shamelessly that for a moment he felt embarrassed and even slightly ashamed.

He was relieved to see Peter and Jane coming towards them again. Jane was walking with her little walking-stick and carried a bunch of willow herb that she had found in a clearing in the wood.

"Look! I've got some flowers for mummy," she said.

"They're not real flowers, Jane," said Peter with his air of tolerant amusement. "They're weeds. She'll throw them away."

"She won't," said Jane. "She'll put them in a vase."

But her face had clouded over anxiously.

"She *will* put them in a vase," she said loudly in order to reassure herself. "They *are* flowers."

"I've not found a bird's nest yet," said Peter to Bridget. "Will you help me look for one?"

"Not just *now*, darling," said Bridget effusively. "We'll come again to-morrow and start looking in good time. I'm *sure* we'll find one to-morrow."

She tried to gather Jane into her arms with a graceful maternal gesture, but Jane eluded her adroitly.

"Come along, Peter," called Jane. "We'll look for a bird's nest again."

She put her little bunch of willow herb by the picnic basket and trotted off once more with Peter.

"I simply *adore* children, don't you?" said Bridget.

"Rather!" he replied, with automatic enthusiasm, though he disliked boys at all times and only liked girls when they were women in miniature. Thea, now. ... She was a little beauty, and already well aware of her charms. She knew instinctively how to draw a man on and how to put him in his place. She could certainly have given points to this girl beside him.

The mother was a beauty too, of course, but she was rather stand-offish and on her dignity. She made you feel instinctively that you had to mind your p's and q's with her. She was the type of woman with whom he never felt quite at his ease. Still, he admired her and felt genuinely sorry to see such a woman tied to a nincompoop of a parson, and a poor one at that. What a mess some women made of their lives!

"Well," he said, rising, "I must be moving on."

Bridget looked around with that anxious, flurried glance that was already beginning to irritate him.

"Oh, but we must go too," she said, "we must really."

"I'll have to run," he said. "I've stayed much longer than I meant to. It's been *delightful* meeting you like this. Good-bye."

A firm pressure of his hand, a deep meaning glance from his dark blue eyes, and he was off, striding quickly away from her through the undergrowth.

At once Peter and Jane returned, Jane walking with the little walking-stick. They were hot and tired and rather cross.

"I've not found a bird's nest, so I want the walking-stick back," said Peter.

"You gave it me," said Jane stormily.

"I only gave it to you because I wanted a bird's nest instead," he retorted. "I said, 'If something nice is going to happen to me to-day, I want it to be a bird's nest, not a walking-stick.' That's why I gave it you. Now I've not found a bird's nest, I want it back. I found it."

"But you gave it me," persisted Jane. "You gave it me."

Her eyes had filled with tears, and she clasped the little stick closely to her.

"You gave it me," she wailed.

Bridget still sat leaning against the trunk of the tree, her pale blue eyes fixed unseeingly on the distance. Her cheeks were still flushed, her eyes bright.

"I'm in luck's way to-day," he had said, and, "It's been *delightful* meeting you like this."

Now that he knew she often came to the wood with the children, he would surely come to meet her there.

She was glad that she had told him she liked the country and didn't mind being poor. There was nearly a fortnight left of the Holiday. A fortnight was a long time. Nina's husband had Spoken at the end of a week. Again she looked forward to that triumphant moment when she should tell her mother and sisters the news of her engagement. She saw the interested group listening to her intently, admiringly. "Well ... then he came upon us one afternoon when I was in the wood with the children and stayed so long that he was late for his practice. He tried to take hold of my hand that day but I wouldn't let him, and he asked me if I generally came into the wood. ..." So often she had been an unimportant member of the group that listened to similar confidences from her sisters or her friends. She wouldn't be an unimportant member of *this* group. And mother would be nice to her again. It was only because she hadn't married that mother had begun to be so snappy with her.

She was roused by the sound of the children quarrelling about the little walking-stick.

"It's mine, I found it," shouted Peter.

"It's mine, you gave it me," sobbed Jane.

Bridget, reasoning simply that Peter would make himself more objectionable than Jane if the decision went against him, decided in favour of Peter.

"Of course it's Peter's, Jane," she said sharply. "Don't be so selfish."

She took the stick from Jane, gave it to Peter, packed up the picnic basket, and they set off homeward. Peter was justifying himself at great length and in an unnecessarily loud voice.

"If I'd found the bird's nest I'd have let you keep the walking-stick, Jane," he shouted. "But I only gave it you if I didn't find a bird's nest, didn't I, Aunt Bridget?"

Bridget didn't answer. She wished she hadn't had the children with her. Perhaps if she hadn't had the children she could have walked back to the village with him. He naturally didn't want to trail about with a couple of children. And they looked so dirty and hot and untidy. And Jane was still crying. She must stop Jane crying, now that they had reached the road. It looked bad—as if she weren't good with children.

"If you stop crying, Jane, I'll give you both a penny to spend at the shop on the way home," she said brightly.

"All right," said Jane, who was tired of crying in any case and was keeping it up with rather an effort.

"Let me tidy you a bit, darling," went on Bridget, "and throw those nasty weeds away. They're quite dead."

"They're not weeds," said Jane indignantly; "they're flowers, and they're for mummy."

They called at Miss Thrupp's to spend their pennies, and Miss Thrupp served them smilingly without laying down her doll. Peter bought a pennyworth of bull's-eyes, and Jane a penny bar of chocolate wrapped in coloured tinfoil. Bridget, who had regretted her promise to let them call at Miss Thrupp's as soon as she made it, stood in the doorway, nodding nervously at Miss Thrupp with a vague idea of humouring her.

Jane ate the chocolate as they went along the road, then smoothed out the tinfoil.

"Isn't it nice, Peter?" she said.

Peter looked at it covetously.

"Give it to me, Jane," he pleaded, "to make a crown for Owly."

"No, Peter, no. I want it . . . it's mine."

He began deliberately to cajole her.

"I thought you loved me, Janie. I'm a poor little boy, Janie. . . . You've got lots of nice things. I haven't got anything."

"You've got the walking-stick, Peter. I'll give it you if you'll give me the walking-stick."

"No, I *need* the walking-stick for walking. My poor legs ache so. Janie, I'm a poor little boy, and if you don't give me that coloured paper I'll lie down and die."

She gazed at him, aghast, but still hugging the piece of coloured paper to her.

"No, it's *mine*, Peter."

"Very well. Now, I'll lie down and die, and it's all your fault."

He laid himself carefully down on the grass by the roadside and stayed there, a small limp figure, with his eyes closed. Jane began to sob desolately. She knew that he wasn't really dead, but somehow the sight of him lying there distressed her almost as much as if he were.

She trailed along with Bridget, sobbing and clasping the drooping weeds and bit of crumpled paper tightly to her.

At the bend of the road they turned to look back.

The small figure of Peter still lay motionless on the grass by the roadside.

"Come on, Peter," called Bridget.

It did not stir.

They turned the bend in the road, Jane's sobs increasing in volume as they lost sight of Peter.

"*Do* stop crying, Jane," said Bridget irritably.

Her rapture had vanished, leaving a heavy depression. Perhaps she'd been rather silly to snatch away her hand like that. Perhaps he'd been just going to Speak, and her snatching her hand away was the same as telling him that she didn't want him to.

It was so difficult. One had always been told that one mustn't make oneself cheap, and yet—well, of course, unless one was very beautiful and charming, which she knew she wasn't, one couldn't afford to seem stand-offish.

She turned round. Yes, Peter was coming slowly along behind them in the distance. He looked very crumpled and dirty and hot. Jane looked worse, her face streaked with tears, and black where her dirty fingers had rubbed it. She stopped crying when she saw Peter walking behind them, but she dragged at Bridget's hand so that it was almost as tiring as carrying her.

"Shall I tell you a story, Jane?" said Bridget with rather bedraggled brightness.

"No," said Jane ungraciously.

The blue-eyed, golden-haired children weren't like this when they came home from a picnic. She could see them, fresh and dainty, dancing around her on the road ("Hasn't it been lovely, mummy?" ... "Do tell us a story, mummy").

She tried to recapture the feeling of exaltation that had possessed her in the wood, tried to summon again the memory of his deep, meaning glance, his smile. But her depression remained like a heavy black cloud enveloping her.

"I'm tired," wailed Jane, dragging more heavily at her hand.

It was hopeless—going about everywhere with the children like this. Miriam really ought to see that she needed some time to herself. She'd tell her to-night that she'd like to go for some walks by herself. If she met him then, there'd be more chance. The choir practice was on Friday evening. She might easily happen to meet him on his way from that—quite by accident, of course, and without making herself cheap.

"Why don't you answer when I say I'm tired?" said Jane aggrievedly.

Peter was behaving abominably, shouting:

"Wait for me! *Wait* for me, you horrid woman!" from a hundred yards or so down the road.

Other people's children were hateful, decided Bridget for the thousandth time.

But they were nearing the Vicarage gates now. She threw off her depression with an effort and assumed her cheerful, brisk, good-with-children manner.

"Come along, you little silly," she called brightly to Peter, and to Jane:

"*Here* we are, Janie! Now we can have a nice rest and *then* you won't be tired."

The others didn't come till she had got Peter and Jane washed and tidy.

Peter had discovered that he had left the little walking-stick where he had lain down to die, and Jane, feeling sorry for him, gave him half her paper. He made a crown for Owly with his half, and Jane, not knowing what to do with hers, made another. They decided that Peter's should be his Sunday one and Jane's his everyday one.

As soon as the others appeared, Jane snatched up her bunch of drooping weeds and ran with it to Miriam.

"They're for you, mummy," she said. "I picked them at the picnic."

"They're lovely," said Miriam. "Thank you so much, darling. I must get a vase for them at once."

She put them in a vase on the bureau in the drawing-room where she always sat to write her letters.

"They're *lovely*," she said again. "Thank you so much."

When Jane saw them standing in a vase on the bureau her heart was so full of pride and joy that she could hardly speak.

"Did you have a nice picnic?" said Miriam.

Jane's thoughts went back over the afternoon. She forgot the quarrel about the walking-stick and coloured paper and how tired she had been on the way home.

She only remembered looking for birds' nests with Peter and having tea in the wood.

"Oo, *yes!*" she said enthusiastically.

Chapter Thirteen

"ANYONE coming to church with me?" called Timothy from the front door.

Rachel ran downstairs, slipping the elastic of her hat under her chin.

"I'm coming. . . ."

Rachel liked the morning walk across the fields and the short service in the little church, where the sunshine poured in through the open door and you could see the grass and trees and blue sky and hear the sound of the birds blending with Miss Caroline's clear voice as she made the responses.

She put her hand into father's, and they set off across the garden. August was nearing its close. The days were still hot, but there was a touch of frost in the air now at night and in the early morning; and in the early morning, too, an opaline mist that vanished as the sun gained strength. Their footsteps made vivid green marks on the film of dew over the lawn. Gossamer cobwebs gleamed everywhere—outstretched on the grass, entangled in the hedges, silver grey in the shadows, sparkling bright where the sun caught them.

The air was fresh and sharp, faintly acrid with the smell of the fire that the gardener had already lit in a corner of the kitchen garden.

At the church porch Timothy left her to go round to the vestry, and she slipped into a seat at the back of the church. The church seemed very dark after the brightness outside—dark and cool and mysterious.

Mrs. Carew was there as usual in her seat, deeply engrossed in a book of private devotions. Rachel watched her with an almost passionate interest. Her large pale face was bent over the book. Her lips moved silently, the jet ornaments in her bonnet nodded softly to and fro, her large black silk cape, plentifully trimmed with black beads, gave her a mysteriously pontifical air.

Miss Caroline had not come yet. Rachel looked at the altar. A shaft of sunshine from the chancel window fell upon the cross, making it shine like gold. Mother had given it a good clean yesterday, because the person whose turn it was to clean it was away from home, and, anyway, mother said that it couldn't have been done properly for months. She'd cleaned the vases, too, and filled them with big white daisies. Their round pale blossoms looked like angels' faces, thought Rachel, watching them dreamily.

Her thoughts went back over the Holiday. The days of it were slipping by like brightly coloured beads sliding down a string, days golden with sunshine, fragrant with the smell of roses and honey-suckle, of sweet-peas and scented stocks, of garden fires and mown grass and freshly cut corn.

She and Thea had got up early that morning to gather mushrooms in the fields. It was thrilling to hunt for the little grey buttons shining in the dewy grass. The sheep had watched them sleepily as they ran from one to the other, hardly stirring even when they came quite close to them in their search.

Southwood Farm had gradually become the background of the Holiday. They were in and out of the farm all day, helping to feed the animals, riding on the farm horses, collecting the eggs, or watching the milking. Susan liked feeding the chickens, throwing the corn well away from her feet, because, despite her delight in the operation, she had a secret fear of the sharp, pecking beaks. Thea and Rachel fed the calves every day. They were friendly creatures, and the little girls loved to put their fingers in their mouths to be sucked with soft long pulls. Jane was afraid of the bigger animals, but Peter was afraid of none of them. He rode to the fields on the cart horses, shouting "Gee up, gee up!" Jane watched him with pride and delight, but refused to be lifted up too. "I will when I'm a big girl," she temporised.

Last week Rachel and Thea had gone to watch the corn-cutting, but when they saw the boys standing round with sticks, ready to throw them at the terror-stricken rabbits that darted from the small, dwindling square of standing corn in the middle of the field, they had suddenly decided to go home.

When the corn was cut, however, they helped to tie it into sheaves and stack them up together in stooks, so that the air and sun could get to the middle of them, and later they gleaned with the women, leisurely gathering the golden armfuls of harvest. They took the affairs of the farm very seriously, coming home to tell Timothy and Miriam that the mangel crop was good but beginning to "run," that there was black-fly on the beans, but that Mr. Comfort's turnips were all right, though most farms had turnip fly.

They had been to tea several times with Dr. Flemming in his little cottage. He had a cocoanut in its husk that for some reason fascinated them, and a tame jackdaw who lived on terms of perfect amity with his other pets—an enormous ginger cat and a small fox terrier. Dr. Flemming always stopped his dog-cart to speak to them when he met them in the village. He would say to Jane, "Let me see, this is Peter, isn't it?" and to Peter, "Let me see, now, isn't this Jane?"—a joke that never failed to make both children laugh heartily.

Father was coming out of the vestry in his surplice now. Suddenly Rachel realised that Miss Caroline was not in her seat. Her heart began to beat unevenly. Mrs. Carew was deaf and never joined in the service. She put up a quick, desperate prayer: "Please, God, let Miss Caroline come in now ... now ... now, quickly." But Miss Caroline didn't come. Father was beginning the service, "Dearly beloved brethren." She looked at her prayer-book. The first thing she'd have to say alone was, "And our mouth shall show forth thy praise." She practised saying it to herself. ("Please let her come in before I have to say it. God, please let her come in now.") But still Miss Caroline didn't come.

"O Lord, open thou our lips," said father.

Small and tremulous and high-pitched came Rachel's answering:

"And our mouth shall show forth thy praise."

Miss Caroline wasn't coming now. She'd never come in as late as this.

"O Lord, make haste to help us," said Rachel.

She couldn't, *couldn't* go right on through the psalms. Her eyes fell upon the mountainous black silk back of Mrs. Carew, and a gleam of hope shot into her soul. ("Please, God, cure her deafness," she prayed earnestly. "Please work a miracle on her now and cure her deafness so that she can say the psalm.") But Mrs. Carew's large pale face continued to be bent over her book of private devotions, her lips continued to move silently.

"Let us come before his presence with thanks-giving," recited Rachel in a voice that grew more and more unsteady and high-pitched.

It seemed somehow terrible—almost blasphemous—to be speaking alone in church like this. Her eyes leapt on to the next verse. She'd have to say "provocation." She could never say a word like that. She stopped before it, gathering breath, said "prov" and stopped despairingly. "Provocation," said father for her, and the white daisy faces from the altar seemed to look at her in sorrowful disapproval. A big girl of eleven and couldn't say "provocation."

It was the 23rd morning.

"The Lord said unto my Lord," said father, "Sit thou on my right hand, until I make thine enemies thy footstool."

"The Lord shall send the rod of thy power out of Sion," stammered Rachel, abandoning herself to despair (quite evidently Miss Caroline was not coming, and God was not going to restore Mrs. Carew's hearing): "be thou ruler, even in the midst among thine enemies."

A horrible sense of loneliness swept over her. Mrs. Carew, in her large black cape, didn't seem human at all. She was a rock, a mountain, a prehistoric monster. She wasn't even trying to follow the service.

And father in his surplice never seemed to be really father. He seemed remote, majestic, like Moses or Abraham. Mother and the others—Thea and Susan and Peter and Jane—seemed so far away that she could hardly believe she would ever see them again. It was like a nightmare from which you know that you're never going to wake.

It was father's turn now, and she could read her verse through to herself to make sure that she could say the words. But her turn came again long before she'd got to the end.

"The Lord sware, and will not repent," she read: "Thou art a Priest for ever after the order of——"

She gasped and stumbled. It was the most terrible word she'd ever seen in her life. She couldn't even attempt it.

"Melchisedech," said father, and went on with his verse.

But the dreadful word had upset her so much that when he stopped she couldn't go on. Shame and terror swept over her. A lump rose in her throat. She was going to cry. What would happen if she cried? ("Please, God, let me die now, at once.")

But father had shot her a quick glance and had begun to say the verse with her, in a voice that made him her father again, not Moses or Abraham. The lump went down, and she stopped trembling. He said all her verses with her after that, and she began to feel rather proud and important. Thea pretended to be grown-up, but she'd never been a whole congregation all by herself as Rachel was being. Because old Mrs. Carew didn't count. And she'd done the "O come let us sing unto the Lord" without being helped at all. Well, except for "provocation." And she was sure that Thea didn't know how to pronounce Melchisedech, though, of course, she'd pretend she did.

When the service was over, she waited for father in the sunny porch. Old Mrs. Carew came out slowly and majestically. Little spikes of black beads danced in her bonnet, little strings of black beads dangled from her cape. She smiled at Rachel—a large, pale, meaningless smile—and passed on, secure and placid behind the defences of her deafness.

Then father joined her, and she slipped her hand into his to walk back over the fields.

"You managed very well," he said, "very well indeed."

She felt so proud that for a moment she could hardly speak. She hoped that he didn't know she had nearly cried.

The others were all ready for lessons when they reached home.

There was a tense, strained look on Susan's face as she sat down to do her copy. Rachel knew why that was. Susan had told her as a secret, and, though Rachel had laughed and said "It *won't*, Susie," she, too, watched it every morning with secret expectancy, because, as Susan had said, it would be nothing to some of the miracles in the Bible, and she was praying very hard both night and morning, and often in the daytime as well. Her small face relaxed into disappointment, however, as she proceeded with the copy the pen remained in her hand.

Peter was doing his letters quite nicely, but Jane's strokes were still very wobbly, and father always guided her, fat little hand so that some of them at any rate should look straight and even, otherwise the sight of them made her cry.

After lessons Rachel and Thea went for a walk with father. They met Miss Caroline in the village, who explained that she had not been able to come to Matins because her sister had had a bilious attack. She looked rather pale and tired, but brightened as she informed them the bog pimpernel really seemed to have taken root. She was keeping it very damp, so as to make it feel at home, and it certainly looked quite healthy.

They passed The Moorings, and Mrs. Seacome waved and smiled to them eagerly from an upstairs window. It always threw a cloud over Rachel's spirits to meet Mrs. Seacome. She was invariably bright and smiling, and yet her eyes made you feel so unhappy that you couldn't bear it.

They walked up on to the moors through Hinchley and passed Elsie's cottage but saw no signs of her.

They had told no one of their meeting with her and seldom mentioned it even to each other, but to both of them it was an exciting secret. Elsie, warm, placid, and loving, nursing her rosy-cheeked baby, living so near them, and no one knowing of it but themselves. They had taken Susan and Peter and Jane to play at the bottom of the spinney the day after meeting her, and had seen her standing in the road watching them through the hedge, a shawl drawn over her head so as to hide her face.

When they reached home, mother said that Mrs. Rothwell, who had returned from her holiday the day before, had called to ask them to go to tea that afternoon.

"Won't you come too, Bridget?" mother was saying. "Maria can look after Peter and Jane."

But it turned out that Bridget had arranged to go out alone that afternoon and had already asked Maria to look after Peter and Jane.

Chapter Fourteen

THEY had, of course, often passed Balmoral, the house where the Rothwells lived, on their walks. It was a new house just beyond the village, built of brick and stone not very harmoniously combined. Little gables and balconies broke out over its whole surface like a gigantic rash, and the front elevation was crowned by a row of turrets that had an air of being rather abashed by the company in which they found themselves. Susan thought that it was a beautiful house, but Rachel and Thea were not quite sure.

Mrs. Rothwell received them in a drawing-room that amply fulfilled the promise of the outside of the house. A wall-paper of brilliantly contrasted colours and intricate design was almost hidden by serried banks of enormous oil paintings in gilt frames, the interstices between them being filled by Oriental plates and mother-of-pearl shells. Heavily fringed plush draperies festooned the doorway, the windows, the fireplace, and the back of the piano. On the mantelpiece was a large brass clock in a glass case flanked by a closely packed array of Goss china; the top of the piano was covered by photographs in silver frames, while Oriental screens and tall Oriental jars of gilded bulrushes and pampas grass were placed haphazard about the floor.

Mrs. Rothwell was short and extremely stout. You realised at once that she had to be stout in order to provide space for the innumerable brooches and necklaces that covered her bosom. Diamond bracelets glittered on each of her wrists and her fat little fingers were half hidden by rings. Her fair hair was waved and dressed high over enormous pads. Her small pink-and-white face wore an expression of complacent insipidity.

With her were a boy and girl—the boy about fourteen, and the girl about twelve. They were strikingly alike, with pale expressionless faces, short-sighted eyes, and small, sneering mouths. The girl's hair—of a lustreless straw colour—was cut in a fringe just above her eyes and hung down in long lank ringlets over her shoulders. She wore spectacles and a purple dress with collar and cuffs of heavy lace.

Mrs. Rothwell introduced them with obvious pride as Rosamund and Percival.

"Now, pets, take your little guests out into the garden and entertain them nicely."

Thea and Rachel and Susan followed the young host and hostess through a side door and out on to a lawn.

"Let's go to the summer-house, shall we?" said Rosamund to Percival after subjecting her guests to a long silent scrutiny.

Percival agreed, and they went to a large pagoda-like erection at the farther end of the lawn. There the five of them took their seats round a table.

Percival began the conversation.

"Gosh!" he said. "What a scarecrow your father looks! Patches on his boots! And that hat! My father wouldn't be seen dead in——"

It was Thea who sprang at him like a small tigress, her face white with anger, hitting out furiously. In a minute she had him on the floor and. was kneeling on him, punching his head savagely.

"Stop it!" he yelled. "*Stop* it!"

"Take that back about my father," blazed Thea.

"All right. I take it back."

"Say you're sorry."

"Sorry."

He rose slowly, gasping for breath.

His sister had watched the short inglorious struggle dispassionately.

"I'd have helped you," she said to her brother, "if you hadn't pinched me when we were going into the drawing-room."

Percival was still rubbing his bruises and watching Thea with unwilling admiration.

"Do you have porridge for breakfast?" he said.

"Yes."

"That's why you beat me, then. Porridge doesn't suit me. I can't eat it. It gives me flatulence."

They had taken their seats again and sat in silence for some moments. Then Rosamund said:

"I've got a squint without my glasses. If you give me a halfpenny each, I'll take them off and let you see it. I charge a penny at school."

"I thought you charged twopence," said Percival.

"I did," said Rosamund, "before Sarah Perkins had her hair shaved off." She turned to the others. "Sarah Perkins wears a wig, and her head's quite bald underneath, and she charges twopence to take her wig off, so I've had to come down to a penny for my squint, because naturally a bald head's worth more than a squint. Well, will you pay me a halfpenny each? It's half-price."

"No," said Thea firmly, "we'll pay you a halfpenny for all of us."

"That simply doesn't pay me for the trouble of taking them off," said Rosamund indignantly.

"All right," said Thea, "don't do it, then. I can make myself squint if I want to."

"But I squint all the time without my glasses," said Rosamund, stung by this implied depreciation of her charms.

"We'll pay a halfpenny for all of us to see it," said Thea firmly, "and no more."

"All right," said Rosamund bitterly. "You're the meanest lot I ever came across."

With that she took off her glasses. It was certainly rather thrilling to see the prominent pale eyes swivel together as the glasses were removed.

Thea paid her the halfpenny, and she replaced her glasses.

"If you want to see it again you'll have to pay another halfpenny," she said firmly.

"We don't want to see it again," retorted Thea. Percival turned to Thea.

"Adam and Eve and Pinchme——" he began.

"We know that one," said Thea.

He turned to Rachel.

"There was a donkey tied by a rope two yards long, and three yards away there was a stack of hay. What did it do?"

"Give it up," said Rachel.

"So did the other donkey," said Percival, bursting into peals of high-pitched, jeering laughter in which his sister joined.

"Fine day for the race, isn't it?" said Rosamund politely to Rachel when she had recovered her breath.

"What race?" said Rachel innocently.

"The human race," said Rosamund, and again the two of them screamed in shrill delight.

Thea rose.

"We've heard all those silly things before," she said coldly. "Let's go into the garden."

They followed her. It was obvious that Percival was impressed by Thea, despite her onslaught upon him. He ogled her and smirked at her as he accompanied her on to the lawn, fetched a deck-chair for her, and even picked her a rose, which she pinned carelessly into her white dress. She accepted his attentions with an easy disdain that roused Rachel's deepest admiration.

"What's the difference between an elephant and an apple?" said Rosamund.

"Oh, shut up," said her brother, gazing at Thea's scornful profile.

But the full flood of Rosamund's repertoire could not be stemmed.

"I can make you say black," she said, turning to Susan.

"No, you can't," said Susan solemnly, "not if I don't want to."

"All right, see if I can." Rosamund winked at the others. "What are the colours of the Union Jack?"

"Red, white, and blue."

"There, you've said it!" exclaimed Rosamund.

"I didn't say black."

"Well, you have now," screamed Rosamund, rolling over on to the grass in an ecstasy of mirth.

"Oh, shut up," said Percival again, giving her arm a sharp nip.

"Now I'll tell mama you've pinched me," she said. "You know she said you'd not to."

He pinched her again, and she took a piece of his hair between thumb and forefinger, tweaking it violently.

"And I'll tell mama you pulled my hair," he said triumphantly. "I'll go and tell her now."

He set off towards the house,

Susan, who was feeling bored, got up too and wandered down to an old tree that stood at the end of the lawn. It had little holes in its trunk . . . just the sort of places where you might find a fairy asleep if you went very, very quietly. She tiptoed round it, peeping cautiously into each hole. If you went very, *very* quietly you might find a fairy asleep. . . .

Rosamund and Rachel and Thea were left alone on the lawn outside the summer-house. Thea still looked disdainful and aloof—a long way removed from the little girl who romped in the orchard and played hide-and-seek in the spinney. Rosamund was half resentful at, half impressed by, her attitude.

"I bet I can tell you some things you don't know," she said, "about people being married and babies and that sort of thing."

Thea turned her dark scornful gaze upon her.

"Thank you," she said coldly, "but we know *everything* about that."

Rachel at first felt surprised by this statement, then quickly understood.

Passionately as Thea longed for the forbidden knowledge, she would not owe it to the furtive-eyed Rosamund.

Miriam moved restively in her chair in the drawing-room. The woman was most offensively patronising. That was the worst of being a poor clergyman's wife. You had to put up with the patronage of insufferable people like this. She glanced across at Timothy. His face wore its gentle remote smile. He was listening with sympathy—yes, with real sympathy, that was the maddening part—to this dreadful woman's recital of the history of her rheumatism and the immense sums she had spent upon it. He didn't see that she was merely parading her wealth before him, saying in effect, "People like *you* couldn't afford to spend so much on your rheumatism."

Looking at him, a wave of passionate, indignant love swept over Miriam. He was so infinitely finer than the people with whom he had to deal. People . . . how she hated them. They surrounded him like a barrier, shutting him away from her. Before he'd been a day in this place, people had begun to establish their claims on him. That man from the Hall with the imbecile child had been to see him several times. What claim had he on Timothy that he should worry him with his domestic problems? Timothy had enough of that sort of thing at home. Couldn't they give him a rest here? Twice a girl had come for him because her father was drunk and was beating her mother. There had been a dreadful affair of an assault on a child at one of the outlying farms. Timothy had been sent for early in the morning and had not come home till night.

People, people, people, clinging to him, exhausting him, surrounding him on all sides, keeping him from her.

She glanced out of the window. She could just see the three little girls sitting on the lawn, Thea in a deck-chair, Rachel and Rosamund on the grass. Susan and the boy had disappeared. Rosamund's face was turned to the window. There was something sly and unhealthy in its expression. A stab of anxiety shot through Miriam's heart. What were they talking about? She knew what children with that expression liked to talk about. Suppose she were talking about *that* to Thea and Rachel. Her anxiety deepened almost to panic. Her children, she was sure, suspected nothing of what was generally referred to as the "facts of life." They were as innocent as babies. She loved that innocence. As long as they retained it they were wholly hers. Rachel turned her face towards the house, and Miriam felt a quick pang of relief. Rachel's small sweet face would not look so unconcerned if the girl were making undesirable confidences.

The husband had come into the drawing-room now. He was

very much like the two children, with a pale expressionless face, small shifty eyes, and a complacent little mouth.

"I'm glad you were able to come," he greeted them heartily. "I said to my wife, 'If we get back in time, we must have the locum's kids over and give them a blow-out.' "

Her hostess came over to sit by Miriam with a rustle of satin petticoats and a jingle of jewellery. Together they looked out at the children on the lawn.

"It's such a pity," Mrs. Rothwell said. "Only last month I sent a parcel of clothes that Rosamund's outgrown to a cousin of mine who married a poor curate. If I'd realised you were coming, I'd have kept one or two for you. They'd just have fitted your second girl."

Miriam flushed hotly, but a diversion occurred in the entrance of a nurse holding a little boy by the hand. His face, too, was ludicrously like his father's. He wore a black velvet suit with a lace collar over which his hair fell in long lank ringlets. His mother introduced him proudly.

"My baby," she said, "my little treasure. Kiss the lady, Fauntleroy."

Fauntleroy offered his fat pallid cheek languidly to Miriam.

"Now run out to the others, my pet," went on his mother. "They're in the garden."

"When shall I say my piece?" enquired Fauntleroy.

"After tea, pet," said his mother, and added, turning to Miriam: "He recites so sweetly."

Fauntleroy had fixed Miriam with a glassy stare.

"I can say two pieces," he said.

"He's so wonderfully intelligent," said his mother. "Sometimes we feel quite afraid for him."

"Tell her what I said on Sunday, "said Fauntleroy.

Mrs. Rothwell smiled fondly.

"We were nearly late for church, and he said, 'Hurry up, mama, or God will have gone up again.' Wasn't it sweet?"

"Tell *him*," said Fauntleroy, jerking his head in the direction of Timothy.

"He's talking to papa just now, pet," said Mrs. Rothwell.

"Will you tell him afterwards?"

"Yes, my precious. Now run out to the others. Tea will be ready in a moment. Where's Miss Coates?"

"She's gone into the garden," said Fauntleroy, and added dispassionately, "She forgot to give me my mouth-wash after lunch."

"How careless!" said Mrs. Rothwell. "I'll speak to her about it. And now, run along, pet."

Fauntleroy walked out of the French windows to join the group on the lawn. Miss Coates, the governess, had already joined it. She was an elderly, dejected-looking woman, dressed in a dark serge skirt and flannel blouse with plain linen collar and cuffs. Her thin greying hair was drawn tightly back into a small neat bun. A pair of pince-nez hung from a gold brooch pinned on to her blouse. Her face was weak and amiable, her manner nervous.

"I told mama you forgot to give me my mouthwash after lunch," Fauntleroy greeted her.

She ignored the remark.

"Come and sit down, and I'll tell you a nice tale till tea-time, Fauntleroy," she said, with an odd mixture of authority and pleading in her voice.

"I don't want to listen to your silly old tales," replied Fauntleroy scornfully.

At that moment Percival came up.

"*You're* going to catch it," he said to Rosamund, "for pulling my hair like that. I've told mama."

Rosamund laughed shrilly.

"Oh, have you? Well, we can see the drawing-room from here, and I know you've not been into it at all, so there!"

"No, but I'm going to."

"Tell-tale!"

She pinched his arm, and he gave a tug at her long ringlets.

"Now I'm going to tell her. See if I don't."

They ran to the house together, pushing and pinching each other on the way.

Their voices were heard from the drawing-room, raised in shrill denunciation of each other. Mrs. Rothwell came down to the lawn, the small mouth set tightly.

"*Really*, Miss Coates, I wish you'd try to manage the children better. I can't be bothered by them incessantly like this when I've got visitors."

"I'm sorry, Mrs. Rothwell," said the governess meekly.

"Now, darlings, don't quarrel any more," went on the mother. "There's sixpence each if you'll be good. I can't *think* why you have so much trouble with them, Miss Coates. They're *so* reasonable if you treat them the right way. . . ." A gong sounded in the house. "There's tea. Now be good children. . . ."

She waddled back across the lawn to the house.

Percival made a sudden attack upon Rosamund, snatched her sixpence, and ran into the house. Rosamund followed him, screaming.

"Come in to tea, Fauntleroy," said Miss Coates, throwing an anxious glance after the other two.

"I will if you'll go round that tree on your hands and knees," said Fauntleroy.

"Of course I won't do anything so foolish, Fauntleroy," said Miss Coates with unconvincing severity.

"If you don't," said Fauntleroy, "I'll scream till mama comes out. And then you'll get into another row."

Miss Coates considered this threat and finally decided to yield with a good grace.

"Well, I'll just have this *one* little game with you before we go in."

She went round the tree on her hands and knees.

Fauntleroy watched her with an expressionless face. She rose from the ground, slightly flushed, and straightened her hair.

"*Now* you'll come in, darling, won't you?" she coaxed.

"I'll come in," he said, "if you'll go with me all the way to the nursery on your hands and knees."

She glanced around. The sight of a gardener working on a neighbouring border near seemed to settle the question for her.

"Of *course* not, Fauntleroy," she said. "Come along, like a good boy."

"If you don't, I'll scream," he said.

"Come along."

"Shan't."

She took hold of his hand and began to draw him along with her. Scream after piercing scream rent the air. Mr. Rothwell came out of the drawing-room French window and strutted across the lawn, stout and self-important.

"I really can't have my wife perpetually worried by the children, Miss Coates," he said. "What on earth are you doing to the child? Don't drag him about like that. Let go of his arm." Miss Coates obeyed. "What's the matter?"

"He wouldn't come in to tea, Mr. Rothwell," said Miss Coates, her thin cheeks now hotly flushed.

"Of course not, when he's dragged like that. You'll go nicely if Miss Coates asks you to, won't you, my boy?"

"Yes, papa," piped Fauntleroy smugly.

"Go along then," said Mr. Rothwell, "and don't let's have any more of this fuss. The child only wants proper treatment, Miss Coates."

He stood there watching them till they had entered the house.

A large tea—jelly, iced cakes, and chocolate biscuits—was laid on the nursery table. Rosamund and Percival had evidently composed their differences. They had been hanging out of the nursery window watching the scene on the lawn and were still giggling.

Fauntleroy, elated by his triumph, began to extend his tyranny to the rest of the table.

"No one must speak again till I say they can," he commanded. "If anyone speaks again before I say they can, I'll pull the tablecloth off."

"Now, Fauntleroy," admonished Miss Coates.

He leapt from his chair and pulled off the tablecloth with a crash. Broken crockery, cakes, and biscuits rolled all over the floor. Rivers of tea and milk and jam spread in all directions.

At this minute the door opened, and Mrs. Rothwell entered,

followed by Miriam. They had finished tea in the drawing-room and were coming to see how the children were getting on. The situation was explained. Mrs. Rothwell's first expression of horror changed to one of fond pride.

"He's *so* highly strung," she said to Miriam, "and so *spirited*. Have all this cleared away, Miss Coates. I'll order a new tea-service from the stores to-morrow. It was a very expensive tea-service. But there's others where it came from." She turned, still smiling, to Miriam: "I expect it seems funny to you," she said, "not having to consider expense."

After tea Rosamund took Thea upstairs to see her bedroom, and Percival hung about in the garden with Rachel, waiting for them to come back.

"Your sister's jolly pretty," he said.

"I know," said Rachel.

"Mama said it would be a real treat for you to come to a house and garden like this," he went on pleasantly. "Parsons haven't got much money, have they?"

Rachel laughed.

"A *treat*!" she said. "We've got a house and garden much larger than this at home."

"*What?*" he said incredulously.

The enormity of her lie horrified her, but something outside herself seemed to be driving her on.

"*Much* larger," she repeated emphatically.

"I bet you haven't," he said. "Why, we've got three gardeners."

"We've got six," said Rachel.

"We've got a carriage."

"We've got two carriages," said Rachel, and went on wildly, "and we've each got a pony."

"Not each of you?"

"Yes, each of us. We've got five ponies." He stared at her open-mouthed, still half impressed, half incredulous.

Thea and Rosamund returned, and Percival left Rachel to join them. But he kept looking at Rachel in a speculative manner that gradually changed to covert mockery. She had overshot the mark, of course. .... His admiration of Thea restrained him from openly taxing her with her lies, and he contented himself with making mocking grimaces at her behind Thea's back.

Thea, who was an excellent mimic, would have liked to imitate the Rothwell children and their parents on the way home, but with father there she couldn't. Father wouldn't let you mimic people or even criticise them. That was one of the things about him that was rather a nuisance.

"Anyway," she said suddenly, "it must be nice to have as much money as they've got."

Timothy smiled at her.

"A wise man once said, 'Riches are only valuable to those who would be contented without them.' "

Thea tossed her head.

"I don't think that's wise," she said. "I think it's silly. I only mean that it would be nice to have as much money as one *needs*."

"*Semper avarus eget*," quoted Timothy, but Thea said: "Oh, Latin!" and, afraid that he would make her translate it, ran on in front to join Rachel and Susan.

Timothy was going to visit a sick cow-man at one of the farms and left them before they reached the village, taking the path that led up to the moors.

The children fell back to walk with Miriam, and Thea imitated Mr. and Mrs. Rothwell and Rosamund and Percival for the rest of the way home.

Though Rachel laughed with the others, she felt secretly aghast and conscience-stricken. She had told lies, not only one, but lies innumerable. Six gardeners, two carriages, five ponies. ...

When they reached the field that bordered the wood, she noticed half unconsciously that Aunt Bridget was coming out of the wood with Mr. Moyle.

At home her sense of apprehension grew heavier, and she felt sure that some terrible punishment for her untruthfulness awaited her. She wandered alone into the kitchen garden, and there, tangled in the netting that covered the currant bushes, was a thrush, dead, and not only dead, but chewed and mangled. Its feet must have been caught in the netting, and then, when it was caught, the cat must have found it. An unbearable horror and desolation swept over Rachel. This was her punishment. She felt no doubt about it at all. This had happened because she had told lies.

Thea found her sobbing by the little mutilated body.

"Don't cry, Rachel," said Thea consolingly. "Let's bury it."

"It's all my fault," sobbed Rachel.

"How can it be your fault?" said Thea.

Rachel didn't reply. She couldn't possibly have explained to Thea or to anyone how it was her fault.

"It's no one's fault," said Thea. "Let's have a funeral."

Susan and Peter and Jane came to take part in the funeral, and they covered the little grave with moss and daisy chains.

But Rachel still felt desperately unhappy. She was certain that, if she hadn't told those lies, the thrush would be singing happily in the trees.

Then Bridget came in. She looked flushed and excited.

"Yes, I've had a splendid walk," she said. "A good long tramp does one good."

Rachel wondered why she didn't tell them that Mr. Moyle had been with her. Probably she'd forgotten. And Rachel herself felt too dejected to mention it.

Chapter Fifteen

TIMOTHY followed the path that wound up the hillside among the bracken and the silver birches. When he reached the tumble – down wall that bounded the moor and from which one could see the whole valley outspread like a picture before one, he sat down and took out a book from his pocket. It was his custom to sit here for a few minutes reading before he started on his walk. He was reading the Epistle to Diognetus.

"To sum up all in one word: what the soul is in the body, that are the Christians in the world. The soul dwells in the body, yet is not of the body; and the Christians dwell in the world, yet are not of the world. The invisible soul is guarded by the visible body; and the Christians are indeed known to be in the world, but their godliness remains invisible. The flesh hates the soul, and wars against it, though itself suffering no injury, because it is prevented from enjoying pleasures. The world, also, hates the Christians, though in no wise injured, because they abjure pleasures. The soul loves the flesh that hates it, and loves also the members; Christians likewise love those that hate them. The soul is imprisoned in the body, yet preserves that very body, and Christians are confined in the world as a prison, yet they are the preservers of the world. The immortal soul dwells in a mortal tabernacle; and Christians dwell as sojourners in corruptible bodies, looking for an incorruptible dwelling in the heaven. The soul, when but ill provided with food and drink, becomes better; in like manner, the Christians, though subjected day by day to punishment, increase the more in number. God has assigned to them this illustrious position, which it were unlawful for them to forsake."

He closed the book and set off with long strides over the moor. He soon reached the straggling road that was the main street of Hinchley and swung along through the bleak little village, his blue eyes fixed unseeingly in front of him.

He would not have noticed a woman with a baby coming from the opposite direction, if she had not stopped by him with a little gasp. Then he looked at her.

"Elsie!"

The colour flamed into her cheeks, and her placid brown eyes faltered.

"Oh, sir!" she said.

For a moment they stood silent. Then he said gently: "Is this your baby?"

"Yes, sir."

"Let me see him."

He took the baby into his arms. The girl stood by him, trembling slightly.

He moved the shawl that covered the sleeping child's face and looked down at it, smiling.

"He's a fine child," he said.

"Yes, sir."

He put the shawl back with a gentle movement, still holding the child in his arms.

"You live here?"

"Yes, sir."

"I didn't realise that. Did you know we were down at Barwick?"

"Yes, sir. I've seen Miss Thea and Miss Rachel, sir. I met them up here and showed them the baby."

"They'd like that. . . ."

"Yes, sir. . . . I told them not to tell the mistress they'd met me. I thought it might vex her."

The gentle brown eyes met his now unflinchingly. There was something humble and abased in them.

"Perhaps you were right," he agreed. "Are you working here?"

"Yes, sir. I work at Flint Farm. I go there mornings and my mother afternoons."

He nodded.

"I'm glad to have seen you," he said. He parted the shawl again and looked at the sleeping child. "He's like you, Elsie. . . ."

She too looked at the child, and her face glowed into an ecstasy of tenderness.

"So they say, sir," she said in her soft low voice.

He bent his head and kissed the child's fore-head. "I know you'll be a good mother to him. And I know he'll be a great joy and comfort to you. . . ."

The clock in the valley struck twelve, and he put the child back carefully into her arms.

"Good-bye," he said. "I'm very glad to have seen you again. . . ."

He walked on, past the grey stone cottages, the small inn and wind-swept farms, and on to the open moorland again.

A feeling of depression and failure possessed him. He ought to have talked to her about her sin—for it *was* a sin—to have made sure that she realised it and repented of it, but as usual his shyness had hindered him. He was inarticulate except when actually in the pulpit, and he found unofficial "preaching" the most difficult part of his work. . . . When with Elsie he had felt only an overwhelming tenderness and pity for both her and the child. He had wanted only to reassure and comfort, but he should have spoken out firmly. It was a missed opportunity. . . .

Elsie walked on slowly, holding the child closely to her. She was trying to remember what he had said to her, but she could remember nothing. Only, whatever it was he had said had washed away that sense of stain and guilt that she had had ever since—it happened. She felt that she could start again now as if it had never been—she and the child. His kiss on the child's forehead made him no longer a child of sin. As she walked, she held herself more upright, as if actually a weight had fallen from her.

Timothy was making his way down into the valley again. His thoughts had returned to the book upon which he was engaged. The library of the vicar of Barwick was a small one, and he was hampered by lack of reference books. He had decided to call that morning at Fletworth Vicarage to see if Mr. Dawson had Eusebius's *Ecclesiastical History* or Blunt's *History of the First Three Centuries*.

The door was opened to him by the trim housemaid, and he was shown into the drawing-room with its embroidered curtains, its chintzes and silver and masses of flowers.

Mrs. Dawson came in almost at once. Her face wore an appealing look of helpless dismay.

"Oh, Mr. Cotteril," she said, "he's ill. . . . He's very ill. It's pleurisy, and they're afraid of pneumonia."

"I'm so sorry. Is there anything I could do?"

"No, thank you. Mr. Borrows is arranging the Sunday services."

He explained his errand quickly.

"Yes, of course. Do go into his study and take what you want. Lucy knows the books better than I do. I'd fetch her, but she's nursing him. The doctor said we couldn't do better than let Lucy nurse him. She's a wonderful nurse, you know."

A look of pathetic distress flitted over her kindly, horse-like countenance. "I'm useless in a sickroom. Useless. . . . The study's across here."

He followed her into the hall. Lucy was coming downstairs. She too looked different. Her air of sullen aggressiveness had gone. She was calm and composed, and there was a hard bright radiance about her.

"How is he, dear?" said her stepmother anxiously.

"He's about the same. His temperature's no lower, but he's had a little sleep."

"Is he asleep now?"

"No. He's just awakened."

Mrs. Dawson started forward eagerly.

"Could I see him?"

Cool triumph gleamed in the girl's eyes.

"I think it's better not. He's best kept quite quiet."

The other woman's face fell.

"Of course, dear. . . ."

The girl passed on to the kitchen. Mrs. Dawson turned to Timothy, and he saw that there were tears in her eyes.

"If only I could do more for him," she said. "I'm so clumsy in a sick-room. I always have been since I was a child. . . . I do so long for just a word from him. But Lucy's right. . . . She knows what's best for him. . . . Here are the books. Take what you want."

He found the book he wanted and went into the hall again. Lucy was just going upstairs. Her dark eyes still wore that look of cold, hard triumph. He was ill, stricken, but she had ousted the claims that she had resented so fiercely and for so long. . . .

Timothy let himself out, the pile of books under his arm.

In the drive he met the two little girls and their governess.

"*Papa est très malade*," said Anthea.

"*Anglais! Anglais!*" remonstrated Mademoiselle.

Chapter Sixteen

JANE trotted happily and importantly down the road. She was going on an errand to the village shop all by herself. She had never been sent on an errand alone before. Thea and Rachel and Susan had gone for a walk with Aunt Bridget, and Peter had been making mud-pies with water from the rain-tub and had to be washed and changed. Mother had put her hat on ready to go down to the village, but when she saw Peter she took it off and said: "Oh, Peter, you *naughty* boy. ... Janie, darling, you're quite a big girl, aren't you? Will you go to the shop for me while I see to Peter? Just give them this money and say, 'Two ounces of pepper, please.' You can say that, can't you? Just say it, darling."

Jane said it.

"That's right. And you know the way to the shop. Give Miss Thrupp the money and say, 'Two ounces of pepper.' And then we'll tell the others what a clever little girl you are when they come in."

She put on Jane's sun-bonnet, and Jane trotted off down the road. She clutched the money firmly in her hand and said, "Two ounces of pepper ... two ounces of pepper ... two ounces of pepper ..." to herself. It made a sort of tune. Her feet kept time to it.

There were some red flowers growing on the roadside. She stopped to pick some to take back to mother. She wondered if Thea had ever been sent on an errand alone when she was four. She hoped she hadn't. It was funny to think that one day she'd be a big girl all the time like Thea. She was tired of being sometimes a big girl and sometimes a little one. When she cried, people said, "Fancy a big girl like you crying!" but when she wanted to do things with the others, they said, "Oh no, a little girl like you can't do that yet." She watched her legs walking along—first one, then the other. It was funny how they always knew which one's turn it was. But, of course, with only two it wasn't so difficult. It must be very hard for cows and horses to remember which one's turn it was with four. ... The road was dusty, and she dragged her shoes along it—on purpose, but pretending to herself that it was by accident—to watch the fine white dust settle on them, changing them from brown shoes to white shoes like the wave of a magician's wand. Then her conscience smote her, and she sat down by the roadside to wipe the dust off by rubbing them in the grass. She was going on an Errand all by herself, so she mustn't look untidy.

She trotted on again down the road. A dog came out of a cottage by the roadside and walked up to her. She stopped, her heart beating rapidly. Its tail was wagging, and they said it was always a kind dog if its tail was wagging, but you couldn't really tell. It might be a cross dog wagging its tail to pretend that it was a kind dog, so that you wouldn't run away and it could bite you better. A woman came to the cottage gate. "He won't hurt you, missie. ... Prince!"

The dog returned to the woman.

The woman smiled at Jane, and Jane smiled back, hoping that the woman hadn't thought that she was afraid of the dog. She hadn't been afraid ... not *really* afraid. Only just a very, *very* little bit afraid. Not enough to count. ...

The woman was still watching her and smiling. She wanted to tell the woman that she was going on an Errand all by herself, but was too shy. She'd nearly reached the shop now. She clasped the money more tightly in her hand. ... Her pride deepened till it was almost unbearable. ...

A cow suddenly looked over the hedge at her. She wasn't afraid of cows when there was a hedge between.

"I'm going on an Errand," she said to it importantly. It stared as if impressed. ...

She entered the shop. Miss Thrupp sat behind the counter nursing her doll. It had never seemed odd to Jane that Miss Thrupp should nurse a doll. It had seemed, on the contrary, entirely right and natural.

She stood on tiptoe, so that she could see over the edge of the counter. She was sorry that there was no one else in the shop. She would have liked everyone in the world to know that she'd been sent on an Errand all by herself.

Poised on the toes of her shoes, her bare brown legs planted well apart, her sun-bonnet hanging down her back, she pushed her money on to the counter.

"Yes, missie?" said Miss Thrupp with a friendly smile.

And suddenly the eagerness died away from Jane's face. She stood there for a moment on tiptoe, her hand stretched out on the counter, frozen into immobility by sheer horror. She'd forgotten it! She'd forgotten the Errand! For a moment she could hardly believe it. Then desolation and terror swept over her; she turned, and with a little gasp ran out of the shop. Sobs choked her as she ran along the white, dusty road back to the Vicarage. She fell down and, picking herself up, ran on, still sobbing. Up the long path through the paddock . . . through the garden. . . . Her sun-bonnet came off, and she did not stop to pick it up. . . . Mother was in the hall. She flung herself into her arms as if only there could she find refuge from the shame that pursued her.

"But, darling, what's the matter? . . . What is it? Tell mother. . . . Did you fall? Has someone frightened you?"

Strangled with sobs came the answer:

"I forgot. . . ."

"Forgot what, darling?"

"Forgot . . . the Errand."

"But, darling"—mother was laughing, kissing the hot, wet little face and wiping away the tears—"it doesn't matter. Sweetheart, don't cry like that. . . . Everyone forgets errands sometimes. Even grown-up people do. I've often forgotten errands myself. . . ."

Jane's sobs died away into little quivering sighs. Grown-up people sometimes forgot. Even mother had sometimes forgotten. The blackness of the shame that had engulfed her faded away.

"You little silly! It was two ounces of pepper. Let's go together

and get it, shall we? ... And we'll get some fruit-drops too. ...
And you shall ask Miss Thrupp for them."

They set off together. Jane walked happily, trustingly, by mother,
holding her hand. Grown-up people often forgot errands ... even
mother sometimes forgot. ... They were going to buy some
fruit-drops. ...

When they reached home again Peter was in the garden collecting
earwigs.

"You can help me if you like," he said to Jane.

But Jane had a momentous piece of news to communicate to
him, a piece of news that seemed somehow to revolutionise the
whole world. It was the first hint that had ever reached her of a
flaw in the perfection of the Grown-up.

"Peter," she said breathlessly, "did you know that grown-up
people sometimes forget errands?"

But Peter wasn't interested. He was gazing at an earwig that had
already succumbed to the rigours of imprisonment.

"Don't make such a noise, Jane," he said. "I think that one's
gone to sleep. ..."

Susan wandered slowly and disconsolately through the orchard,
carrying Lena in her arms. There was less than a week of the
Holiday left, and she still hadn't seen a fairy. She hadn't even found
a fairies' feast, though she'd got up every morning to look at the
cut-down trunk in the kitchen garden. It would be dreadful if she
had to go home again without finding a fairy or a fairies' feast.
The pen hadn't flown out of her hand, either, in spite of her prayers.
... She'd stopped praying about it now, and had instead written
a note to the fairies asking them to come and snatch it out of her
hand. She'd left the note in the hole in the trunk of the apple tree
that she was sure was a fairies' hiding-place.

Lena had been away for three days. Susan had left her on the
desk in the study, and father had kidnapped her. He said that he
kidnapped all dolls left in his study. So Susan, helped by Rachel,
had written a very stern lawyer's letter to him, and he had written
a lawyer's letter back in reply, and then they had written several

lawyer's letters to each other. He left his by the apple tree where she always played with her dolls, and she left his on his study desk. He began his "Dear Madam," and she began hers "Dear Sir." She and Rachel had enjoyed writing the letters. They'd decided to arrest him and try him, and Peter was to be the policeman, when suddenly Susan found Lena behind the books in one of the bookshelves.

She was really rather sorry to find her, because the trial would have been fun, and she was tempted for a moment to put her back and pretend she hadn't found her, but she felt that that would have been cheating.

She returned to the apple tree. There was a row of wooden Dutch dolls there, elaborately dressed in satin and lace. They were quite new. She had bought the dolls at the village shop and made the dresses from bits of stuff given her by Mrs. Seacome. Aunt Bridget had promised to help her make the dresses, but, when Susan reminded her, she'd been cross and snappy and said that she'd no time. Aunt Bridget wasn't a bit like she had been at the beginning of the Holiday. She seemed sometimes so cross that you hardly dared speak to her, and sometimes she was so excited that it made you feel ashamed and uncomfortable somehow, you didn't know why. . . .

She propped up Lena against the apple tree and arranged the Dutch dolls in their dresses of silk and lace around her. Lena was telling them about being kidnapped.

"And I was imprisoned in a dark cave," she was saying, "without any food at all. . . ."

The little dolls made exclamations of sympathetic horror.

Mother was coming across the lawn with Thea and Rachel.

"Thea and Rachel are going over to Fletworth to ask how Mr. Dawson is," she said. "Would you like to go part of the way with them, Susan?"

"Yes, please," said Susan.

It would really have been more pleasant to stay and play in the garden, but it was more grown-up to go out with Thea and Rachel.

"She'll only be a nuisance and drag behind," said Thea.

That made Susan the more determined to go.

"I won't! I won't!" she pleaded. "I won't drag behind. I'm a *good* walker. Father says I am."

"Oh, all right," said Thea.

They set off together down the road. Susan was walking quickly and importantly in order to show Thea that she was a good walker. Thea was sulky and silent because she hadn't wanted to take Susan. Rachel was lost in her thoughts.

Father had finished reading *Swiss Family Robinson* to them in the evenings and was reading *Pickwick Papers*. Rachel loved Mr. Pickwick and was imagining him walking with them along the white, dusty road—short, stout, spectacled, infinitely endearing. He had somehow become merged into her old friend the Man in the Moon. There had been a full moon again last night, and when she had looked up at it, with that odd feeling of pity and compunction it always stirred in her, she had seemed to see the round, wistful, spectacled face of Mr. Pickwick gazing down at her. . . .

They were passing The Moorings, and, glancing towards the dining-room window as they passed, they saw Mrs. Seacome smiling and nodding and beckoning to them. They stopped.

"I don't think we ought to go in," said Thea. "It may make us late, and we've got to go to Fletworth."

"Oh, *do* let's go in," pleaded Susan. "*Please*, Thea."

Mrs. Seacome might open her bag of "pieces" again and find some more bits of lace or satin for her. The Dutch dolls hadn't any cloaks. She'd love to make cloaks for the Dutch dolls. . . . Thea, too, really wanted to go in to see Mrs. Seacome. There was something very exciting about Mrs. Seacome. They had been to tea there last week, and she had let them dress up and act charades. She had innumerable boxes full of beautiful old dresses, some of which had belonged to her grandmother—crinolines and lace scarves and fans and jewellery, the sort of thing that most grown-ups were very fussy about and said, "Don't touch," or, "You may hold it just for a minute, if you're very careful."

Mrs. Seacome had not only thrown open the boxes, but had thrown open, too, all the cupboards and drawers of her bedroom, even her jewel-cases.

"Take anything you like," she had said eagerly, "*anything.*"

They had swept about in embroidered shawls with lovely old lace on their heads. They had flourished fans of lace and feathers. Thea had held up an old dress of yellowing satin.

"That's my mother's wedding dress," Mrs. Seacome had said. "Try it on, darling. Do try it on."

She had been anxious to please them in an odd, tremulous, excited way they had never met in a grown-up before. The tea had been a sort of feast, with trifle and jelly and fruit salad and iced cakes and pyramids of sugar biscuits. . . . She must have spent days preparing for it.

And as they were going she had said:

"You must act a play. . . . Rachel shall write a play for you, and you must act it here for me, dressing up in these clothes."

She was at the front door now, waiting for them. Her cheeks looked very flushed, her eyes bright, and her thick brown hair was coming down.

"Come in, come in," she said. "Delighted . . . delighted to see you. . . ."

She seemed to have some difficulty in enunciating her words, and she swayed slightly as she led them into the dining-room. The parrot's cage was covered by a green cloth. An odd sweet smell hung over the room.

"Sit down," she said. "There are some biscuits . . . biscuits in the biscuit-barrel on the sideboard. Thea . . . Thea, gift of God. . . . Rachel, mourning for her children . . . and Susan, black-eyed Susan. . . . That's right, Thea, hand the biscuits . . . I mean biscuits. . . ."

They each took a biscuit and sat down, munching, watching her guardedly. She had never been quite like this before, though often before they had noticed this odd sweet smell about the house. Susan had an uncomfortable feeling that she was trying to be funny in order to amuse them and that they ought to laugh. But it would be dreadful to laugh, of course, if she wasn't trying to be funny.

"Have you thought of anything for the play?" she said, and at the same time uttered a foolish high-pitched giggle.

"Do you think we could have it about Roundheads and Cavaliers?" said Rachel earnestly.

She had been thinking a lot about the play and had already dramatised in her mind some of the stories that she had told Thea. Thea, of course, must be the heroine.

"That would be splendid ... splendid," said Mrs. Seacome. She seemed not to be quite sure of the word, and repeated it several times. "And we'll—manage the clothes all right. I've got lots of clothes ... lots of clothes. ... We can cut them up and alter them. We used to act charades in the old days. ... My little——"

She stopped abruptly, rose, and steered an unsteady course to the sideboard. There was a bottle and a glass on it—the glass had evidently been used recently. She opened the cupboard door and, after several attempts, took out three more glasses. ... One strand of her thick brown hair fell loosely over her eyes as she did so, and she made no effort to put it back.

"You must have a drink with me," she said, still enunciating her words slowly and carefully. "It won't do you any harm ... any harm ... whatsoever ... whatsoever. ... It's pure juice of the grape—pure juice of the grape. ..."

She swayed suddenly and caught hold of the sideboard to steady herself. Susan leaned forward eagerly. She loved grapes and, when Jane was a baby and had spoonfuls of grape juice, had always pleaded for a taste.

But Thea was rising, her young face set and stern. She was the Eldest. Responsibility drew the corners of her mouth firmly downwards, carved a small but determined frown upon the smooth whiteness of her brow.

"Thank you very much," she said with cold politeness, "but we mustn't stay any longer. Good afternoon."

She marshalled them out, Susan pouting and reluctant, Rachel rather perplexed.

Mrs. Seacome followed them unsteadily into the hall, still holding the bottle in one hand, the long strand of hair still loose about her face.

"No harm whatsoever," she said again thickly. "Whatsoever. Pure juice of the grape. ..."

She stood at the door-way watching them till they were out of sight, a foolish, appealing, bewildered smile on her face.

Susan trailed dejectedly behind the other two. It was horrid of Thea to make them come away before they'd had a drink of grape juice. And Mrs. Seacome might have given her some "pieces" if they'd stayed longer. She'd always given her "pieces" when they called before.

"Why couldn't we stay, Thea?" she said sulkily. "She was going to give us some grape juice. ..."

Thea turned on her sternly.

"It was *wine*," she said. "Didn't you know wine was made of grape juice? It was a bottle of *wine*."

Living in a teetotal household in a slum for whose misery and squalor drunkenness was primarily responsible, the little Cotterils looked upon alcohol in any form with horror and shrinking. ... But still Susan pouted.

"She'd have given me some more pieces if you'd not made us come away like that," she said, "and it might have been just grape juice like she said."

Thea looked at Susan with dispassionate contempt.

"You're a silly baby, Susan," she said, "and you don't know what you're talking about."

Susan, deeply offended, glowered up at her through her thick lashes.

"I'm going home," she said.

"Yes, go home," said Thea. "We don't want you."

Susan turned and began to walk disconsolately homeward.

"I'm glad she's gone," said Thea, "she'd have been an awful nuisance. ... And, of course, it *was* wine. ... In a bottle like that. ... Wine *is* made from the juice of the grape."

Rachel felt ashamed of not having realised this. The episode removed Thea to immeasurable distance of worldly knowledge. The decision and self-confidence with which she had swept her charges out of danger made Rachel feel ineffably humbled and diffident. She could never have done it, even if she had been the eldest like Thea. She was terribly ashamed of having thought that Mrs. Seacome meant real grape juice.

"Yes, of course, I suppose it *was* wine," she said, speaking in her most grown-up voice.

"Of course," said Thea.

She still sounded stern and authoritative.

Percival was outside the gate of Balmoral when they passed. He advanced upon Thea with an ingratiating smirk.

"Good afternoon," he said. "Are you going for a walk?"

Thea flung him a scornful glance from her grey-blue eyes. "Yes."

He infused his smile with a nauseating sweetness.

"May I come with you?"

"No," said Thea. "We don't want you."

So deeply smitten was Percival that he braved these snubs every day, hanging about outside the Vicarage gates or the road that led to the village.

He followed them for some distance down the road, then, as neither of them turned round to look at him, fell back, making a loud clicking sound with his teeth that was evidently meant to remind Rachel of her boast about the ponies.

They were passing the gap in the hedge through which they could see the Hall, and across the lawn two figures were moving. One was Agnes's, shambling, unsteady; the other, half-supporting it as they walked, was Mrs. Lindsay's.

"I really think that they ought to send her away somewhere," said Thea, "or have someone properly trained to look after her. It's not fair on Mr. Lindsay."

She spoke in the rather self-conscious voice that she always used when she was repeating something that she had heard a grown-up say.

"Yes," said Rachel without much interest.

She was looking up at the sky, where the breeze was playing with the small white clouds, building them up into fantastic shapes, scattering them, building them up again quite differently. ... A sheep-dog ... a sofa ... a house ... a camel ... a Chinese girl with tiny feet. ... They made them tiny by bending them back underneath. Once she'd asked Thea to bend hers back to see what it felt like, and it had hurt terribly. She'd screamed to Thea to stop long before she'd got them properly bent back. The little Chinese girl disappeared—Rachel was glad to see her go—and in her place came a lighthouse, and then a man, and then a pig, and then a boat. By the time the boat came they had reached Fletworth Vicarage.

"Here we are," said Thea. "Suppose you go in and ask, and I'll wait for you outside."

Rachel was surprised for a minute by this. Thea generally liked to deliver messages herself. Then suddenly she understood. Thea didn't want to meet the two little girls who spoke French. ... She always avoided situations in which she felt herself at a disadvantage.

Rachel walked up the drive to the front door and knocked. The trim housemaid showed her into the drawing-room, and there Mrs. Dawson came to her, looking pale and anxious. Rachel delivered her message.

"It's so good of you to come, my dear," said Mrs. Dawson, "and so kind of your mother to send you, but—Well, he really isn't much better. He's very weak, and his temperature stays high. Oh, I nearly forgot. Your father brought back some books yesterday and he wanted another. ... I forget what it was. I couldn't find it, but Lucy found it after he'd gone. She wrapped it up ready to send to him. I think it's in her bedroom. ... Come upstairs with me, dear, and I'll see if I can find it."

She looked, as she was, desperately unhappy. She was one of those people in whom illness of any kind induces a sort of panic bordering on paralysis. In a sick-room she was as clumsy as the proverbial bull in a china shop. The thin white fingers that moved with easy grace over the clavichord trembled so uncontrollably in pouring out medicine that half of it was always spilt. Her obvious nervousness made everyone around her embarrassed and ill at ease, and had a bad effect upon the patient. Yet she longed to help, longed to overcome her nervousness and wait upon the ordinary, kindly little man she loved so dearly. ...

A bedroom door opened, and Lucy came out. She moved with an air of quiet confidence. For Lucy, so awkward and sulky in the drawing-room, was completely mistress of the situation in a sickroom. As soon as she entered it, a feeling of quiet power possessed her. She knew, by an unfailing instinct, what to do and how to do it.

"How is he, Lucy?"

"About the same," said Lucy. "A little better, perhaps."

"Lucy, may I see him? If I could just see him . . ."

"I think it's better not," said the girl. "He must be kept very quiet."

Even Rachel could feel the triumph in the voice. "He's mine now," it said. "Your claims count for nothing now. . . ."

"Has he—has he asked for me?" faltered the woman.

The girl's dark eyes exulted silently for a moment as if savouring beforehand the climax of the triumph. There was something cruel in the look she fixed on the woman as she said:

"No. . . . You see, he's delirious, and he thinks I'm my mother."

The woman flinched, but her expression of humble anxiety did not alter.

"I see. . . . It must be as you think best, my dear, of course."

The girl made a little gesture of half-angry surrender, as if abandoning the struggle against one who would not even admit that she was a foe.

"Oh, you can go in," she said in a flat, dull, lifeless voice. "He'll know you. . . . I think he'd like to see you."

The woman started forward impulsively as if to kiss her, but the girl turned aside.

"You'd better go in now. He's awake."

"Thank you, dear," said the woman, and went into the room, closing the door softly behind her. The girl turned to Rachel.

"What do you want?" she said curtly.

Rachel explained about the book.

"Oh yes. . . . I'll get it for you."

She gave her the book, and Rachel went out to Thea, who was still waiting at the gate. She hadn't escaped the little girls, after all.

They were there with their governess, talking to her. But Thea, as usual, had risen to the occasion. As Rachel approached, one of the little girls had asked her a question in French, and Thea was saying in her most grown-up manner:

"I'm not going to talk French to you because Mademoiselle wants you to talk English. Say it in English."

Meekly they repeated it to her in English. They were evidently much impressed by Thea.

Chapter Seventeen

"ACTUALLY had the impudence to send to tell me that his motor had broken down by the Grange gates and could I lend him a horse to tow it. Did you ever *hear* of such impertinence? I sent a message back that he could go to hell and take his beastly machine back where it belongs. I don't suppose Parker gave him the message. Parker's manners are so bourgeois. A butler ought to be able to be rude to the right people, but Parker won't learn. I don't know why I keep, him."

"I've never even seen one, you know," said Miss Caroline rather timidly.

Miriam had called at Meadow Cottage, and almost immediately Lady Cynthia Savary had arrived, collecting contributions for her monthly parcel of Comforts for the Troops. She was a stout, handsome, middle-aged woman with a weather-beaten face and an aquiline nose. Her well-fitting riding-habit showed to perfection the lines of her magnificent figure. She held herself as erect as a soldier, and displayed in her manner and bearing a freedom and unconventionality that would have been condemned as "unladylike" had her birth left her open to such a criticism. But even the most carping critic of the neighbourhood realised that, whatever else an earl's daughter may be, she cannot be unladylike.

Outside the window her groom could be seen walking a spirited chestnut mare up and down the road. Lady Cynthia was so devoted a horsewoman that she was seldom seen during the day in any costume but a riding-habit, and her hatred of the motor-car, which had now passed the experimental stage and was fast gaining popularity, was great in proportion.

"It's just a ridiculous craze," she went on, "fit only for fools and children. It ought to be forbidden by law. Noise and dust and horses bolting all over the countryside. Horses will *never* be broken in to them, and it's no use pretending they will. You can't have both horses and those hellish contrivances on the road together, and we certainly can't do without horses. My aunt was out in her carriage the other day, when one of the wretched things came along. Both her horses bolted, her coachman fell from the box and was badly hurt, and my aunt is still in bed with nervous shock. I have another friend whose horse bolted at sight of one, ran against a tree, and had to be shot. And it isn't as if they were of any use. They go for a short distance, poison the air, deafen everyone for miles around, terrify the horses so that they're never any good on main roads again—then break down. And *then* they have the damned impertinence to ask you to lend them a horse to tow the thing."

Miss Caroline coughed deprecatingly, and, fearing further displays of Lady Cynthia's colourful vocabulary, hastily changed the subject.

"I'm afraid I've only done three pairs of socks this time."

"I hope that's all we'll need," said Lady Cynthia. "This ought to be the last parcel. Lord Milner will knock some sense into them now he's gone out. It ought to be over in a week. Our people have been too soft. If I'd been at the head of things I'd have had every single Boer in the country lined up against a wall and shot, and the war would have been over months ago. They want teaching a lesson." She rose. "By the way, my husband's just got Hall Caine's new novel, *The Eternal City*. Shall I send it over when we've read it?"

"Thank you so much," said Miss Caroline nervously. "He's always so clever, isn't he, but a trifle—outspoken, don't you think?"

"Yes, and a damn good thing, too," said Lady Cynthia. "I get sick of namby-pambies. ... Well, good-bye. Good-bye, Mrs. Cotteril."

They watched her from the window as she mounted the chestnut mare with surprising lightness and grace, then cantered down the road, followed by the groom.

"Dear, dear," said Miss Caroline in a flustered voice—she always felt flustered after a visit from Lady Cynthia—"Dear, dear—she's such a charming woman, isn't she? So—so *spirited*! I'll just go and get my sister up, Mrs. Cotteril. She'd never forgive me if I let her miss you, especially now that there's so little of your visit left. I won't be a minute. Do look at the news record, will you, while I get her up. I've bought photographs of the Duke and Duchess to put at the beginning of the Royal tour. It was rather extravagant of me to buy them, but I got carried away, and I don't regret it, because it will be a joy and comfort to me for the rest of my life. . . ."

She drifted away, still talking, and Miriam waited, chiefly because she knew that it hurt Miss Caroline to dissipate the fiction that her sister enjoyed the visits of her friends.

Soon Miss Bella appeared, swathed in shawls and leaning on her sister's arm. Her small pig's eyes and button of a mouth looked more surly than ever. She sat down, heavily on an armchair and, ignoring Miriam, opened a fire of peevish complaints. Before Miss Caroline, soothing, reassuring, humouring, as though she were the mother and her elder sister a fractious child, had arranged the shawl and cushion and footstool and screen satisfactorily, Dr. Flemming was announced.

He fixed Miss Bella with a genial smile, behind which lurked something slightly sardonic.

"How's the invalid?" he said.

Miss Bella sniffed petulantly and made no reply.

"Well, well! . . ." He looked at Miss Caroline. "Bog pimpernel all right? I'll go and have a look at it."

He was turning towards the door, then swung round, his attention caught by something outside the window.

"Hello, hello, hello!" he said. "What's this? What's all this?"

The lumbering old four-wheeler from Harborough had stopped at the gate, and from it a stout elderly man was descending. He wore a suit of black broadcloth, a straw boater, and, despite the heat, a thick muffler wound tightly round his neck several times. He evidently gave directions to the cabman to wait, as both that individual and his horse seemed to sink at once into a sort of stupor, merging into the sleepy summer landscape. The elderly gentleman came up the short walk with a bustling, important step. The little maid opened the door to him, but was so amazed and terrified at the sight of a stranger that she merely flung open the drawing-room door and plunged back into the kitchen, without asking his name or announcing him. He stood in the open door-way, smiling and rubbing his hands, which were encased in thick woollen gloves. Then he took off his hat with a flourish, revealing bushy white hair encircling a bald crown. The four people in the room gazed at him in silent astonishment. Finally Miss Bella said peevishly:

"Come in and shut the door. I can't stand a draught."

This seemed to break the spell. Miss Caroline stepped forward.

"Do come in," she said nervously.

He held up a gloved finger playfully.

"Now you don't know who I am," he said. "Confess! You don't know who I am."

"You're——" she began uncertainly, then her face cleared. "Are you by any chance our cousin Job?"

He rubbed his hands together again delightedly.

"Right," he said. "Right first guess. Now introduce me to the folks, and then we'll have a chat."

Miss Caroline performed the introduction.

Cousin Job bowed jerkily and finally waved a gloved hand in the direction of Miss Bella.

"The invalid sister, I take it," he said. "Well, it's her I've come about."

"Won't you sit down?" said Miss Caroline.

He sat down on the very edge of a chair and rubbed his hands together again.

"Now I can't stay a minute," he said, glancing at the slumbering cab outside. "I've told that feller to wait, because I've got a train to catch at Harborough. I'm only in England a week or so, and I've got to get busy. Now, I'm a self-made man. It wasn't my father that made good. He went out as a ne'er-do-well and he died one. But he left me, and I got busy pretty quick. And now I'm a rich man. Not a millionaire," he added cautiously, "but—well, a rich man. And I'm a man to take a sudden whim now and then. I can afford to. Well, I got a whim to come over to the old country and look up my own folks and do something for each of them. Just a little present, I mean, not settin' 'em up for life or anything like that. Well, I've been lookin' round and I find there's precious few of 'em left. Howsoever, I wrote to what there was, an' as soon as I got your letter, I said to myself, 'Well, I know what present I'll give them,' and do you know what it was?"

"No," said Miss Caroline faintly.

"Well, I thought, 'I'll have the best specialist in England to overhaul that invalid sister and see if we can't put her on her feet again.' And that's what I've come over for to-day. To get things fixed up. I'll have a specialist down to-morrow. There's pretty few things they can't cure nowadays, if you get the right man on to it. . . . Well?"

There was a tense silence. Miriam turned to look at Miss Bella. The tiny eyes were bright with fear, the podgy hands clutched the arms of her chair convulsively, the small pink tongue crept to moisten the peevish button of a mouth, the whole fat body trembled with terror. In the look she turned upon her sister there was desperate, abject pleading.

Cousin Job gazed at the blank faces around him. Where was the hysterical gratitude for which he had come prepared?

"Well?" he said again.

Miss Caroline had gone very white. Her eyes met Dr. Flemming's, and something of appeal seemed to pass from her, of assurance from him, in the brief interchange of glances.

Cousin Job began to beat his fingers impatiently on his knee. He'd expected amazement, incredulity, but the news ought surely to have sunk into their country bumpkins' heads by now.

"Well?" he said again, this time rather sharply.

Dr. Flemming cleared his throat.

"I am Miss Pilkington's medical adviser, sir," he said pompously, "and I think a second opinion in the case is quite unnecessary."

Cousin Job's face reddened.

"And who the devil asked you what you thought?" he said.

"No one," said Dr. Flemming. "But I consider it only fair to my patient to tell her that, if she insists on calling in a second opinion, I shall refuse to treat her in the future in any circumstances."

With his short, stocky figure, his bushy beard, and weather-beaten face, Dr. Flemming at that moment looked to the life the dogmatic, self-assertive country doctor, hidebound by convention and prejudice, who treasures and encourages all invalids for the sake of their quarterly cheques, and whose vanity cannot brook the suggestion of a "second opinion." Cousin Job obviously made great efforts to contain his anger. He turned to Miss Caroline.

"And would you," he said, "let the ignorant prejudice of this fool stand between your sister and her recovery?"

Miss Caroline, painfully agitated, was twisting and untwisting her long thin fingers. The elder sister's small sunken eyes, still bright with fear, crept from one to another of the group. Dr. Flemming put up a hand as if to silence Miss Caroline.

"I am the only medical practitioner for ten miles this side of Harborough," he said, "and I repeat that if these ladies decide to call in a second opinion without my consent, I shall refuse to treat either of them again in any circumstance as long as they or I live here."

"Without your consent!" repeated Cousin Job, spitting the words out as if they were some poisonous draught. "But I understand that you refuse your consent?"

"Most certainly I refuse my consent."

Again Cousin Job turned to Miss Caroline.

"Surely," he said, "you have the courage to defy this jackanapes. You'll let me send the specialist to your sister, and be damned to him?"

Miss Caroline was trembling. She caught hold of the edge of a table to support her.

"Oh no, no," she gasped, "I couldn't."

Cousin Job swung round upon Dr. Flemming.

"It's quite plain what your motive is," he said angrily. "All you're thinking of is the cheques you get from these poor creatures. You don't care how much suffering they have to endure as long as you feather your nest and——"

"Don't, *don't*!" moaned Miss Caroline. "He's never had a penny from us . . . never. . . ."

But Cousin Job wasn't listening to her. He was past listening to anyone. His eyes beneath their shaggy white eyebrows were blazing with righteous indignation. He gesticulated furiously with his gloved hands in Dr. Flemming's face.

"I tell you, if I weren't leaving England immediately, I'd show you up, sir. I'd write to the papers about you. I'd get you crossed off the register. I'd make the blood of every decent man in England boil at the mention of your name. You—*scoundrel!*"

With that he flung the loose end of his muffler over his shoulder with as great an air as if it had been a military cloak, turned on his heel, and stalked out of the room without looking at the others. In paralysed silence they heard the front door bang, saw the old gentleman fling himself into the cab, waking it suddenly from its deep sleep, and drive off, his lips still moving angrily, his gloved hands still gesticulating inside the cab.' They stood in silence till it had vanished from sight, then Miss Caroline burst into tears and ran from the room. Miriam followed her to the little conservatory and put her arms about her.

"Oh dear, oh *dear*!" sobbed Miss Caroline.

Dr. Flemming entered.

"Oh, thank you," said Miss Caroline, raising her head from Miriam's shoulder and looking at him with swimming eyes. "Thank you."

His eyes were twinkling.

"Come, come!" he said. "What's all this about? You see, I know that nothing can be done for her and that she'd only suffer a lot of unnecessary pain once the specialists got going on her with their treatments, so I just played the curmudgeon to get rid of him."

"Oh, thank you," said Miss Caroline again, drawing herself up and drying her eyes. By preserving the fiction of her sister's illness he had somehow restored to her all the self-respect that the terrible interview had stripped from her. "You're so *good*," she said vaguely.

"Nonsense! Now let's have a look at the bog pimpernel. Yes, it's doing quite well. But," his face grew stern as he took up a small metal-painted stag from the shadow of the bog pimpernel, "what on earth's this?"

Miss Caroline blushed guiltily.

"Oh, that," she said. "It—it's been in our china cabinet for years. I—I thought it would just go nicely with the bog pimpernel."

"Well, it doesn't," said Dr. Flemming grimly. "Put it back in the china cabinet. Did you ever see a stag quarter the size of a bog pimpernel? You've no sense of proportion. Women never have. Besides, what's a stag doing in the place anyway? Just because I let, you have a cart and horse in the lane and a cow in the field, you want to turn the whole placed into a wild-beast show. A *stag* indeed!" Under his familiar, affectionate scolding Miss Caroline was gradually recovering her self-possession.

They returned to the drawing-room.

Miss Bella was watching the door. Her eyes were dull and sunken and peevish again. Her button of a mouth pouted sulkily.

"You might ring the bell for tea, Caroline," she said. "You know how I hate being kept waiting for meals. And the sun's coming right on to me through that window. I wish you'd take just a *little* trouble to make me comfortable."

Chapter Eighteen

MIRIAM sat in the morning room, sewing fresh braid into the hem of her everyday skirt. What a nuisance this eternal braiding of skirts was! And of course if you didn't do it as soon as the braid frayed, the bottom of the hem wore through, and the whole skirt was ruined. She didn't mind the endless household mending, but somehow she hated braiding skirts. She was glad of the diversion when Thea and Rachel came in from the farm, where they had been spending the morning. They flung themselves upon her and hugged her. The skirt and length of braid fell to the ground as she slipped an arm round each.

"And we found a broody hen in the hedge by the corn-field," said Rachel.

"And there were ten eggs under her," put in Thea.

"And we took them away——"

"And she pecked our fingers——"

"And Mr. Whitaker said we were very brave."

"He lives at Flint Farm in Hinchley. He'd come down to see Mr. Comfort about some pigs."

"Hinchley?" said Miriam. "Oh, of course. It's up on the moors, isn't it?"

"Yes, it's where Elsie——"

Thea stopped. There was an odd, tense silence. Miriam's arms fell to her sides, and the smile faded from her lips.

"Elsie?" she said.

Rachel's heart began to beat unevenly.

A look of sulky surrender came into Thea's face.

"Elsie lives up at Hinchley," she said.

"How do you know?"

"We've seen her."

"When?"

"The first week we were here."

"And never told me?"

"No."

Miriam felt dazed and stunned as though from a physical blow.

It was not the thought of their meeting Elsie, whom she looked upon quite simply as a fallen woman, that shocked her, but the fact that they had kept the meeting secret from her.

She tried to control her voice to ask steadily:

"How many times have you met her?"

"Once," said Thea.

"Why didn't you tell me?"

"She asked us not to. . . . She said it would worry you."

She looked at them in silence. They seemed suddenly to have become hostile, alien children, who didn't belong to her. A fierce angry resentment against them filled her heart. It was as if they had deliberately broken the bond that held them to her.

She rose and gathered her sewing together slowly.

"It was very wrong of you not to tell me," she said in cold, measured tones, then went from the room, closing the door behind her.

The two children stared at each other aghast.

"I *did* tell her," burst out Thea, searching for an excuse.

"But you told her by accident," said Rachel. "She knew it was by accident."

They felt frightened and desolate, aware that she had withdrawn her love from them and that without her love life would be unbearable.

They went to the spinney and sat down at the foot of the big oak tree.

"I wish we'd told her at first," said Thea.

"But we'd promised Elsie not to," said Rachel.

"It was wrong of us to promise not to."

"There can't be anything wrong in not telling someone about something that—that doesn't belong to them."

Upstairs in her bedroom Miriam mechanically washed her hands and tidied her hair for lunch. Her heart still seethed with anger and bitterness and misery.

Timothy came into the bedroom.

"Here you are," he said cheerfully. "It's about lunch-time, isn't it?"

He took up his hair-brush and began to brush his hair. Then suddenly he caught sight of her face and turned to her in alarm.

"What is it, my dear?" he said. "Aren't you well?"

She sat down on the bed and fixed her eyes on him.

"Timothy . . . Elsie's living up at Hinchley."

"I know. I've met her."

"Why didn't you tell me?" she said, but she felt no real resentment on that score. She had never claimed to be told Timothy's doings. As a priest, his dealings with people had something of the inviolability of the confessional about them. She had always refrained from questioning him, had always known he was told innumerable secrets that he could not share with her.

"It would only have worried you, wouldn't it? And it didn't seem of any importance."

"Thea and Rachel have met her."

"I know. She mentioned it to me."

"They never told me, Timothy. Did they tell you?"

"No. I never mentioned it to them. I never thought of it again, as a matter of fact, till this minute. In any case——"

"They ought to have told me," she burst out. "It was wrong, deceitful, of them not to. It's hurt me terribly."

He came and sat on the bed by her. Her unhappiness stirred his tenderness.

"I'm sorry, my dear," he said. "I don't suppose they meant any harm. I expect it was just thoughtlessness."

"It wasn't, Timothy. They deliberately kept it from me. She's a horrible woman, and she's had a bad influence on them all from the very first. It's spoilt—everything for me. I wouldn't have believed it if anyone had told me that this would happen. I can hardly believe it now."

He put his hand over hers.

"My dear," he said.

In his voice was love, sympathy, reassurance, and a faint remonstrance.

She turned her face away.

"You don't understand."

The luncheon bell rang, and they went downstairs.

During lunch she ignored the two children, speaking to them, when she had to speak, in a cold, hard voice that they had never heard from her before.

After lunch she went out for a walk by herself. She had never done this before on a Holiday, had never even wanted to do it, but to-day she felt that she must get away from all of them, to think out the strange and terrifying thing that had happened to her. She realised that to most people it would seem a ridiculously trivial affair, but it shook her world to its foundation.

She set off at a good pace along the road towards the woods. Anger blazed high in her heart—anger against Elsie and Thea and Rachel, as if all three had conspired against her. For she saw the children in a dual light—as innocent babies snatched from her and corrupted, and as the villains who had snatched those babies from her. They had met the girl in the first week of the Holiday. All the days since then had been a carefully planned deception. To her over-sensitive imagination every word they had said had been a calculated lie, every childish smile deliberate acting in order to deceive her. She entered the wood by the stile and set off down a path. Suddenly she caught sight of two figures in front of her—Bridget and Mr. Moyle. They had not seen her. She turned back and took another path that led in the opposite direction through the woods. So that was why Bridget wanted to go out alone so often nowadays. . . . It afforded her an obscure satisfaction to turn her anger against Bridget. A second-rate, empty-headed little flirt. It was the last time she'd ask her to come and help with the children. She was quite useless. Lately she had not even pretended to take an interest in them. She'd been moody or over-excited all the time, spending hours up in her bedroom curling her hair and changing her dress when she ought to have been amusing them, and insisting on having two hours to herself every day just when she was needed most at home. This was the explanation, of course. The flash of anger against Bridget had relieved her somewhat. She walked on, trying to fix her mind on the beauty around her, hoping that it would bring peace and comfort to her spirit.

Rounding a bend in the path, she came suddenly upon Miss Coates and Fauntleroy, seated beneath a tree. Fauntleroy was dangling a worm in his governess's face.

"Eat it," he was shouting in his shrill, unpleasant voice. "Go on, eat it."

"Now, Fauntleroy, don't be silly," said Miss Coates.

She saw Miriam and smiled constrainedly.

"Good afternoon, Mrs. Cotteril. Fauntleroy and I are having a little game. Now that's enough, Fauntleroy."

"We're not having a game," shrilled Fauntleroy. "You've got to *eat* it, I tell you. If you don't, I'll start screaming the minute we're inside the house, and then mama'll be cross with you."

Again Miss Coates made the pitiful pretence of authority over her small tormentor.

"That's quite enough of that game, Fauntleroy. Do sit down with us, Mrs. Cotteril. It's so pleasant in the wood, isn't it?"

Miriam sat down on a smooth moss-covered hillock.

Fauntleroy was still dangling the worm in Miss Coates's face and shouting, "Eat it, I tell you. Eat it."

Miss Coates took the small velvet-clad shoulder and pushed it away from her.

"Now I'll tell mama you shook me," said Fauntleroy, with quiet satisfaction.

"Don't be so ridiculous, Fauntleroy," said Miss Coates. "I can't think what Mrs. Cotteril will think of you. You're being a very silly little boy."

"I'm going to make you eat something nasty before we go home, anyway," he said with decision.

He turned his expressionless face to Miriam.

"I made her eat some wild crab-apples last week," he said, "and she had awful stomachache after it. I could see she had."

Miss Coates flushed.

"Fauntleroy and I have little games together," she said, "and sometimes he gets over-excited."

Fauntleroy made an ejaculation expressive of amused contempt, then, meeting Miriam's eye, decided that it would be impolitic to torment his victim further in her presence. He rose with a swagger and said:

"Well, now I'll go for a bit of a walk."

"Keep within sight, Fauntleroy," said Miss Coates anxiously. He turned and pulled a face at her.

"Fauntleroy! Fauntleroy!" she said, feebly reproachful.

"Why do you put up with it, Miss Coates?" said Miriam impulsively.

Miss Coates stared at her in surprise, assumed a smiling, deprecating expression, murmured: "He's high-spirited. He doesn't mean any harm ..." then suddenly burst into tears.

Miriam put an arm about her shoulder.

"Oh, my dear ..."

For a moment Miss Coates sobbed unrestrainedly, then she sat up, straightened her hat, and wiped away her tears with a large serviceable pocket-handkerchief.

"I'm sorry," she said unsteadily. "I don't know what came over me. I've not been sleeping well lately. He's only a child, of course. Thoughtless and high-spirited."

"He's a hateful little wretch," said Miriam. "They all bully you. Why don't you leave them?"

Miss Coates was still wiping her eyes with nervous, fluttering movements.

"I mightn't get another place," she said. "You've no idea how hard they are to get now that people are sending their girls to boarding-schools."

"But isn't it worth trying?"

Miss Coates's pale short-sighted eyes blinked dejectedly.

"I—I'm not very well qualified," she said. "It isn't as if I'd had any reference when I came here. A cousin of Mrs. Rothwell's knew my father and got the place for me. My father was a doctor, but he," the pale face flushed again, "well, he wasn't steady, and when he died there wasn't any money at all. My mother had died several years before. And you see," the flush deepened, "I've not been very well educated myself. I mean, I wouldn't do for anyone particular. In lots of ways Mrs. Rothwell's very good to me."

"How much does she pay you?" said Miriam.

Miss Coates's hands in their darned black cotton gloves moved uneasily in her lap.

"Fifteen pounds a year," she said, and added hastily: "Of course it's generous, because I've no expenses, living with them as I do."

"What about holidays?"

Miss Coates seemed to shrink from the idea in horror.

"Oh, I never have holidays. I mean, I've nowhere to go."

"You're not happy or well treated here," said Miriam firmly. "You ought to leave them."

"Oh, but I couldn't, I couldn't," said Miss Coates. "She'd never give me a reference if I went on my own accord. I'd never get another place."

Miriam considered the situation, frowning thoughtfully. Ordinarily she would have felt little interest in it, but to concentrate all her mental energies upon it made her forget for a time at any rate the angry hurt of her own spirit. Suddenly the frown vanished and she smiled.

"Miss Coates," she said, "I believe I could help you. It's a place where we once went for a locum, and the old lady who owned the big house there often writes to me still. I heard from her the other day, and she said she wants a housekeeper. She asked me if I knew of anyone. I never gave it another thought at the time, but it's an easy post—a beautiful old house, a comfortable little sitting-room of your own, and only a few country servants to supervise. The old lady herself is delightful. She'd take you, I know, if I asked her to. Will you let me?"

Miss Coates blinked and drew up her drooping figure.

"Oh no, I couldn't dream of anything like that. Not a *housekeeper.*"

"But, Miss Coates," persisted Miriam, "I *know* the old lady. You'd be so happy with her. There's very little actual work. She just wants someone conscientious, whom she can trust. And I know she pays very good wages. You'd have peace and a comfortable home."

"But a housekeeper!" repeated Miss Coates. "Oh no. I couldn't *consider* anything like that. It's a sort of *servant's* post. Here I'm treated as one of the family."

"They treat you shamefully," persisted Miriam.

"I have meals with them," said Miss Coates, "and I sit with them in church and that sort of thing. No, Mrs. Cotteril, it's very good of you, but you don't quite understand. This is a hard post, I know, but it's the sort of post a lady needn't be ashamed of taking. Not like a *housekeeper's.*"

Miriam looked at her—bullied, overworked, dispirited, clutching the shabby rags of her social position about her. The flush that lingered on her thin cheeks was one of outraged gentility.

"You see, my father was a professional gentleman," she went on, "and his father kept his carriage. Oh no, not a *housekeeper.*"

"I'm sorry," said Miriam.

At that moment Fauntleroy reappeared.

"A lot of care you're taking of me, aren't you?" he said. "Not even looked round to see where I was. *Anything* might have happened to me."

Miss Coates furtively dabbed her eyes with the serviceable pocket-handkerchief, then assumed her parody of an authoritative manner.

"Now, Fauntleroy," she said, "don't get so excited. Say good-bye to Mrs. Cotteril. It's time we went home."

Fauntleroy muttered "Good-bye" to Miriam and set off with Miss Coates. His shrill voice reached Miriam as their two forms disappeared through the trees.

"And I'm jolly well going to pay you out. I'm going to get covered with dirt and then go and show mama."

Miriam dismissed the thought of Miss Coates with a helpless little shrug, then turned to face her own problem. Meeting the girl ... talking to her ... keeping it a secret all these weeks ... deceiving her in every word they said to her. ... The angry bitterness flooded her heart again, and she strode on through the wood unseeingly, her lips set, her brow drawn into a frown.

Thea and Rachel got into bed silently. The heavy cloud of mother's anger still brooded over the house. She had been for a walk in the afternoon, but when she came back she had still ignored Thea and Rachel, speaking to them only when necessary, and then in that cold, distant voice that made them feel outcast for ever from her love and kindness. Even Thea had lost her poise and grownup air, becoming just a frightened, unhappy little girl. She fastened up her nightdress and turned to look at Rachel. Rachel knew what she was thinking. Always, when they were ready to get into bed, one of them called down to mother, and mother came to kiss them good-night and tuck them in. They had never yet in all their lives gone to sleep without her good-night kiss. It was unthinkable, impossible, that they should do so.

Why hadn't they both died, thought Rachel desperately, before this happened?

"I'm going to call down to her," said Thea with sudden decision in her voice.

She went to the head of the stairs and called "Mother!"

Then she went back to bed and sat there waiting, taut and motionless, her eyes fixed on the door. Perhaps she wouldn't come. Perhaps she'd pretend she hadn't heard. But she was coming. They heard the soft rustle of her dress on the stairs. She entered the room, and they both saw that she looked pale and unhappy.

"Mother," said Thea, making herself the spokesman, "we're *awfully* sorry. ..."

She sat down on Thea's bed. "Tell me about it, Thea," she said "How often did you meet her?"

"Only once ... that first week."

"Where did you meet her?"

"At Hinchley. We were going for a walk. She took us into her house and we saw her baby."

Miriam's lips set in a straight line of disgust, and Rachel, watching, felt a cold desolation sweep over her spirit. That sunny afternoon at Hinchley, Elsie's sweet placidity, the laughing baby, had seemed to lift the horror from life, but that look on mother's face brought it back again.

"What did she talk to you about?" said Miriam.

Her swift glance from one child to the other reassured her. There was no constraint, no embarrassment. The woman had evidently the decency not to—talk about things.

"Susan and Peter and Jane," said Thea, "and we played with her baby."

"Oh, Thea," burst out Miriam suddenly, "if only you'd told me! You don't know how you've hurt me. . . . It was so *wrong* of you not to tell me."

She put her arm about Thea, and Thea burst into tears.

"I'm sorry," she sobbed, "I'm sorry."

They clung to each other. Mother kissed her and stroked back her hair.

"Darling, you won't ever hurt me like this again, will you?"

"No, no. . . ."

"You do see how wrong it was, don't you?"

"Yes."

"And you'll always tell me *everything* in future, won't you?"

"Yes."

Rachel sat staring in front of her, the desolation in her heart growing bleaker, colder. She wanted to feel like Thea, but she couldn't.

"You see, darling, don't you?" mother was saying, "that your not telling me made everything you've said to me since a sort of lie?"

"Yes," sobbed Thea in luxurious penitence.

Why has it? Rachel asked herself. Why should you be *obliged* to tell people about things that didn't belong to them? She was trying her hardest to feel wicked, but she couldn't.

Thea was still revelling in her penitence.

"I've been so unhappy, mother. You have *really* forgiven me, haven't you?"

"Yes, darling. Quite. And we'll neither of us think of it again."

She lay for a moment on Thea's bed, straining her in a close embrace, then kissed her, and came to sit on Rachel's bed.

"You're sorry too, aren't you, darling?"

Rachel was silent. She couldn't bear to stay outside the warm bright circle of mother's love. She couldn't live another day with mother as she'd been to-day, but——

"But, mother,' she burst out, "I—I didn't think it was wrong just not to *tell* you."

"Oh, Rachel!"

It was like a cry of pain.

She saw suddenly that there were tears in mother's eyes. An agony of pity seized her—a pity she did not understand, but that tore at her very heart.

"Oh, mother," she said, "I'm sorry. I'm sorry."

They clung to each other, and, though it was Miriam who stroked back the child's hair and kissed and rocked her in her arms, yet Rachel had an odd idea that it was she who was comforting mother, not mother who was comforting her.

"I'm sorry," she said again. "I love you so. I love you so."

When Miriam had gone, the children lay silent for a few moments. Then Thea said:

"You see it *was* wrong, Rachel."

Rachel said "Yes."

They didn't speak again, but tossed and turned for a long time before they went to sleep.

Chapter Nineteen

THEY awoke next morning to hear that there had been a fire at the Hall during the night. Fresh and contradictory reports arrived at the Vicarage every minute. No harm had been done. ... The whole house had been destroyed. ... None of the occupants had been harmed Mrs. Lindsay had been badly burnt. ...

Timothy and Miriam set off after breakfast to see if they could do anything to help.

Neither of them knew exactly how Susan came to be included in the party. The truth was that the thought of Agnes still fascinated her and that she could not bear the thought of anyone's going to the Hall without her. She put on her hat and walked behind them till, at a bend in the road, Timothy suddenly turned and saw her.

"Hello," he said. "Where have you come from?"

"I wanted to come with you," she explained simply.

"She might as well," said Miriam. "We shan't be staying long, of course. We'll just call and see how things are."

Much relieved, Susan continued to trot at their heels along the road and up the drive to the big front door. The house looked the same as usual.

It's not been burnt at all, thought Susan, greatly-disappointed.

Then she thought: Perhaps it has, and Agnes has built it up again by magic. Lately she had been considering, the possibility of Agnes's being a witch, not a fairy princess.

Mr. Lindsay opened the door himself. His left arm was in a sling.

"It's awfully good of you to come round like this," he said. "Come straight into the garden. My wife's there. Yes, I know she'd like to see you."

"Susan and I won't stay," said Miriam. "We just came to see if we could do anything."

"Oh, but you can," said Mr. Lindsay. "You can come in and see my wife and hear our adventures."

He led them through the hall.

"It didn't reach this part of the house. It was all in the other wing. That's pretty badly burnt. My wife's out here."

Even Susan noticed something different about him, something eager and zestful and happy.

Mrs. Lindsay looked pale and exhausted, but there was about her, too, a new air of tremulous happiness. She no longer gave that strange impression of being lost in an unhappy dream. She was awake, alive, radiant.

Chairs were being brought out of the house for them, despite Miriam's protest.

"No, of course you must stay," Mrs. Lindsay was saying. She smiled at her husband. "They must, mustn't they, Roger?"

"Of course they must," he said. "We have no end of excitements to tell them."

"I hope that none of you are the worse for the experience," said Timothy in his precise, old-fashioned manner.

"My wife was overpowered by the fumes," said Mr. Lindsay, sitting down by the visitors, "but she's recovered wonderfully. A maid discovered it first and roused the house by screaming. I ran to the room where my wife and Agnes sleep. My wife was unconscious, so I carried her down first and then went back for Agnes. She was conscious, but very frightened. I took her down and——"

"And then he fainted," put in Mrs. Lindsay eagerly. "He was terribly brave, Mrs. Cotteril. The staircase was going, and the whole place was thick with smoke. He fought his way through it. His arm is quite badly burnt. He wrapped Agnes in the blanket and carried her down. *Everyone* says how brave he was."

"I hope she's none the worse," said Timothy.

Mrs. Lindsay's radiance clouded over slightly.

"She's not burnt at all, but, of course, it's been a shock. The doctor says that it's affected her heart a little. He advised us to keep her in bed to-day. If it's not better to-morrow, we'll get a trained nurse, but she's soundly asleep, and we hope that that's Nature's way of healing. . . ."

She spoke lightly, hopefully, without the old dragging anxiety.

"Would you care to come and see the damage?" said Mr. Lindsay to Timothy. "It's all on the other side of the house. The workmen are there already."

They walked across the lawn, leaving Miriam with Mrs. Lindsay. Susan sat on the grass by Miriam's chair, her eyes fixed upon the window behind which Agnes lay sleeping. It would be dreadful if she didn't wake up before they went and they had to go away without seeing her. But perhaps she'd wake up and come to the window, and Susan would see the well-remembered face, large, vague, fascinating, gazing down at the lawn. She thrilled at the thought.

"It's been a sort of miracle," Mr. Lindsay was saying to Timothy, as they walked slowly across the lawn. "I'd given up all hope of happiness in my married life. You knew that, didn't you?"

"Yes."

"And then this happens. Yesterday I shouldn't have believed it possible. . . ."

"But what has happened?" smiled Timothy.

"I'm trying to tell you. You see, as soon as I heard the alarm I ran to Frances's room, as I told you, and carried her down. Then I went back for the child and——"

He paused.

"Yes?" Timothy prompted gently.

"She was frightened. She clung to me and, as I felt her clinging to me like that—her arms tight about my neck—well, somehow I felt for the first time that she was my child. I loved her as if she were my child. All the old shrinking from her went as if it had never been. It's—changed everything between my wife and me, of course. She saw at once what had happened. Where the child is concerned there's nothing she can't see. It's like a mist clearing away between us. I feel as if I'd lost her all these years since the child was born and had suddenly found her again."

"I'm more glad than I can tell you," said Timothy.

"It wouldn't have happened but for you, of course. It was you who persuaded me to stay here."

He led Timothy into the house by a side door.

"This is where the damage was done."

Pools of water still lay in the passage. There was a pungent smell of burnt wood, charred paper hung down in strips from the walls, and the staircase that ran up from the passage was a ruin, the wood burnt completely half-way up, leaving a gaping hole of more than a yard. The blackened remains of an antique mahogany table lay at the foot of the stairs. Some workmen were taking up the charred planks of the floor.

"It began here," said Lindsay. "A wire fused evidently, and of course there's a lot of old wood about. It's a miracle they stopped it spreading to the rest of the house. Frances and Agnes sleep just up those stairs."

They stood and watched the workmen for a few minutes, then returned slowly to the garden.

"There's a good deal of damage done on the whole," said Lindsay, "but somehow I don't care two pins. In fact I'm grateful to the thing. I'm going to pull my weight with the child now. There's some new idea of treating this, I believe . . . something to do with glands. I'm going to find out, all about it. I feel like a man born again, Cotteril." He smiled. "I'm sorry to be so garrulous, but you knew what a hell my life has been for years."

They rejoined the others on the lawn, and he glanced up at the open bedroom window.

"She hasn't wakened?" he said.

"No," replied his wife. "We've been listening all the time."

"A long sleep is often the best means of recuperation," said Timothy.

Miriam made a movement to rise.

"We ought to go."

"No, *please* don't," said Mrs. Lindsay earnestly.

Miriam relaxed in her chair again.

Susan rose from the grass and quietly made her way towards the house. It would be dreadful if they had to go before they saw Agnes. She entered the side door and stood for a moment surveying the wreckage. . . . Now I know what it looks like after a fire, she thought, with satisfaction. Even Thea doesn't know that. I'll tell Lena when I get home. I won't tell anyone else, not even Thea or Rachel. It shall be my secret—what it looks like after a fire.

She wandered through two rooms and found herself suddenly in the hall from which the main staircase ran up. She looked at it longingly. Somewhere up there Agnes lay asleep. A spirit of adventure seized her, and very, very quietly, her small pink tongue protruding, her heart beating with excitement, she crept up the big staircase and began to walk along a passage. Behind one of those doors Agnes lay asleep. She opened one at random and entered it. It was a bedroom, but no one lay on the large brass bed with its elaborate lace coverlet. She went to the window and peeped out cautiously. The group on the lawn was just beneath her. It wasn't this window, but it must be the next. She crept along the passage, turned the handle of the next door, and entered. She stood for a moment on the threshold, her heart leaping in triumph. It was the room. There lay Agnes asleep, her eyes closed. Susan tiptoed to the bed and stood, watching the still form. Then her heart leapt again. . . . This was the real princess . . . the spell was broken . . . the prince must have come and kissed her. . . . Perhaps he had come in the fire last night. The pale face in its frame of golden hair was beautiful, the dark lashes swept the colourless cheeks, the mouth, no longer drooping open, was set in lines of happiness and peace. The others must see her like this, thought Susan excitedly. She must wake up now, and Susan would lead her down, beautiful, queenly, the ugly spell removed? One white hand hung over the coverlet. Perhaps if she kissed it, Agnes would wake. Very softly she touched it with her lips, then started back as if she had been stung. For a moment she thought the hand was burning hot, then, her eyes wide with fear, she touched it again. It was colder than ice. Terror clutched her by the throat, and she turned and fled down the passage, gasping and sobbing as she ran. She plunged headlong down the rotten staircase. A workman caught her, but she tore herself from his hands, almost before he had set her on her feet. Out into the garden, fighting off everyone who came in her way.

"Mother! Mother!"

Timothy stepped forward, but Susan pushed him aside.

"Mother!"

Mrs. Lindsay, rising from her chair, vainly tried to arrest her headlong flight.

"*Mother!*"

Miriam turned from the rose-bed she was inspecting and came forward, arms outstretched. Susan flung herself into them, and they closed round her protectively.

"Darling ... what is it?"

"Mother. ... Mother." The shrillness of the terror died away. Nothing would harm her in the shelter of those beloved arms.

"Agnes," she sobbed. "Agnes ..."

Mrs. Lindsay turned to her husband, her face white.

"Roger," she said, "go quickly! See what's happened. ..."

Chapter Twenty

BRIDGET walked quickly through the village towards the wood. It was the last evening of the Holiday. They were going home to-morrow. She had been so sure that he would Speak this afternoon, and a heavy load of despair had gradually fastened upon her heart as the moments of their meeting had sped by, and he had mentioned nothing more momentous than the anthem for next Sunday and the holiday that he had spent in Antwerp the previous spring. She had made the necessary comments: "Really?" . . . "How interesting!" . . . "Yes, I quite agree," in an odd, breathless voice, and once in the middle of saying "Really?" had given a sudden unexpected little sob that she had managed somehow to change into a cough. It couldn't—oh, it couldn't end like this. When they came to the point where the road branched off to the Vicarage and where they usually parted, she had said, "We're going tomorrow, you know." She tried to sound casual and unconcerned, but her voice broke again and trailed away uncertainly.

"To-morrow? As soon as that? I hadn't realised. Oh, but I can't say good-bye to you now like this. Shan't I see you again?"

"I could—I could—meet you this evening," she had gasped.

"Will you really?" he had agreed with mechanical eagerness. "Good! I must see you again. Let's meet in the wood, shall we? What time?"

"Nine o'clock. . . . The children will be in bed, and I can easily come then. . . ."

"I'll be there. You won't forget?"

"Of course not."

He had lifted her hand to his lips, and she had set off again towards the Vicarage, her heart singing a paean of thanksgiving. It was all right. He would Speak to-night. He had as good as told her that he would Speak to-night.

The road was in darkness, and where the shadows lay thickest she caught sight of a man and woman standing in the hedge, strained together in a close embrace. She hurried past with averted eyes, the blood naming into her cheeks, her heart hammering suddenly in her breast.

She glanced up at the unlighted window of The Moorings. It was empty now. Only yesterday Mrs. Seacome's housekeeper had wired for the distant cousin who was her only relative, and he had come to take her to what was euphemistically called a nursing home, but what everyone knew was a Home for Inebriates. She had been there before several times, people said, since the death of her husband and little girls.

The Hall looked black and ghostly in the fading light. That also would soon be shut up. The daughter had been buried yesterday, and the mother and father were going to sell the house and travel abroad for a year or two before they settled down again in England. It was dreadful, the child dying suddenly like that, but a blessing in a way, of course. Heart failure after the shock of the fire, the doctor said. She must have been dead about a quarter of an hour when Susan found her.

The Dawsons were going away too. Mr. Dawson was out of danger, and the doctor said that he must have a change of air, so Mrs. and Miss Dawson were going to Cornwall with him, leaving the two little girls at home in charge of the French governess.

But her thoughts only touched lightly on these things. Perhaps in an hour's time she would be coming back along this very road an engaged girl. Often in later years she would think of this night.

"Do you remember that night when we met in the wood," she would say, "the night you proposed to me?"

She would tell Miriam quite casually when she came in. She'd say, "Oh, by the way, Miriam, I'm engaged to Mr. Moyle." She would let Miriam think that she'd had an understanding with him for some time, but hadn't confided in her.

She climbed the stile and entered the wood. As soon as she had entered it, a strange excitement seized her, and she began to run along the dark path, stumbling over the roots, covered thinly in moss, that stretched from side to side. Yes, he was there. The relief was so great that she caught her breath with a little cry, yet until then she had not been conscious of the fear that he might not come. She did not know which of them made the first movement, but suddenly she was in his arms, clinging to him, laughing and crying at the same time, while he kissed her eyes and lips and cheeks. Her heart was a tumult of emotion. It had happened at last . . . at last. He loved her . . . she was engaged. What need was there of words? And yet he was saying words. He was speaking in his deep thrilling voice. He was saying:

"You'll never know, little girl, what your friendship has meant to me."

Tenderly spoken words, his arms still round her, his lips still seeking hers, and yet they turned all the warmth of her body to ice, and her heart that had been soaring like a bird dropped as though shot dead in mid-flight.

An impulse came to her to plead with him, wildly, frantically: "Oh, marry me, marry me. I'll be a good wife. You'll never regret it. I love you so. I love you so."

But she didn't say the words, didn't plead with him, for the sharpness of the anguish dispersed the mists of make-believe behind which she had been hiding. She did not love this man . . . he did not love her. All along she had known it in her most secret heart, but now she faced it for the first time. She had only pretended to be in love with him because she wanted to be married, wanted to escape from the life she found so wearisome, so utterly, unspeakably wearisome. She was tired of pretending to be happy. She had wanted to be happy really, and marriage seemed the obvious way, but—she had never really loved him, never really believed that he loved her. The knowledge brought to her a sense of utter despair, and she still clung to him, sobbing, finding an odd impersonal comfort in the pressure of his arms about her, the touch of his cheek against hers.

Then she freed herself with a quick convulsive movement.

"I must go."

"No, no," he pleaded. "Don't go . . . not yet."

She looked almost pretty in the half light. Her lips were unexpectedly soft. He had enjoyed the flirtation. She had seemed to grow younger, more attractive, under the excitement of it, losing that air of drab middle-age that had repelled him at first. Her adoration of him had gone to his head like wine. But—the urgency of his voice was unconvincing. He didn't want to get carried away. It had been perhaps foolish to arrange this meeting. He was usually so careful not to compromise himself.

"No," he said again. "You mustn't go yet."

She recognised the insincerity of his tone. Secretly he was ill at ease. He wanted to be rid of her. She broke from him abruptly, still crying, and began to run down the path. He pursued her for some distance, calling, "Bridget! Bridget, come back!" but even in her hysterical distress she was aware that he could have caught her up if he had really wanted to. He abandoned the half-hearted pursuit, and she ran on alone, her sobs now dry, convulsive gasps.

Fortunately no one was in the hall of the Vicarage. She went to her bedroom and began to pack her things ready for the journey to-morrow. Her lips were set in a straight unlovely line that made her look old and haggard. Tears coursed down her cheeks unheeded, splashing among the dresses that she had made with such high hopes and dreams of romance only a few weeks ago.

When she had finished packing, she undressed and got into bed. In bed, she drew the clothes over her head, buried her face into the pillow, and, letting go her control with a feeling of almost sensual relief, sobbed in an abandon of despair till she fell asleep despite herself towards dawn.

Chapter Twenty-One

THEY were in the train going home. The Holiday was over. They had chattered a good deal for the first hour, but now they were silent. Timothy, wearing the check tweed cap, sat in one corner reading. Peter leant against him, holding Owly in one hand, trying hard to keep awake, looking occasionally with conscious superiority at Jane, who was sleeping openly on Miriam's knee. Susan was nestling against Miriam, her eyes fixed on the telegraph poles that danced past the windows in an unending procession. The little lantern was in the pocket of her blue sailor suit. Occasionally she felt it to make sure that it was there.

Rachel and Thea had been playing paper games, but they had tired of them now and were idly scribbling meaningless figures on their papers.

Maria sat bolt upright, staring unseeingly at a photograph of Blackpool pier that adorned the opposite side of the carriage. Her hair was inordinately frizzed, and she wore her straw hat at a rakish angle.

Bridget (who was going with them as far as Manchester) sat in the corner opposite Miriam, her elbow on the window ledge, her head resting on her hand. Though the day was hot, she wore a thick veil. Her eyes were shut, and occasionally she swayed with the motion of the train as if she were asleep, but every now and then a tear escaped her closed lids and trickled down her cheeks.

Everyone was silent. They were all thinking of the Holiday.

Timothy was looking back over it, remembering the long walks, the quiet hours of reading and writing, the peace and stillness of the countryside, the companionship of his beloved wife and children.

But, dominating everything else, blazing with a light that dimmed their lights almost to darkness, was that moment on the hill-top during the first week when he had had that sudden illuminating certainty of the goodness of God and the ultimate consummation of His purpose. It had not been faith or pious speculation. It had been a revelation, complete and enduring.

Miriam shifted Jane very gently so as to relieve her weight from one arm. It was over for another year. It would be nice to get back to civilisation again—gas and water-pipes and shops within reasonable distance. She'd miss the garden. Yes, she'd enjoyed it on the whole more than she had thought at first that she was going to. And the change had done her good. Something of the peace of the countryside had entered her spirit, soothing its turbulence. She realised that she was looking forward almost with zest to taking up the work of house and parish of which she had felt so heartily weary when she came away. Maria had been trying, but she'd probably settle down quite well again once they reached home. She wouldn't give her notice, after all.

Her thoughts went back to the people they had met during the Holiday—the Lindsays, the Dawsons, the Rothwells, Mrs. Seacome, Dr. Flemming, the Miss Pilkingtons. She had been deeply interested in them all as lately as yesterday, but since the journey began they had gradually become unreal, dreamlike . . . people one would never meet again. It wasn't the death of Agnes Lindsay, or the illness of Mr. Dawson, or the removal of Mrs. Seacome to an Inebriates' Home, or the general hatefulness of the Rothwells that stood out as the most important feature of the Holiday. Those all meant nothing to her. What was momentous, vital, was her loss of Thea and Rachel. She saw it quite simply like that. She had lost them. They would never belong to her wholly again. She heard Rachel's wondering "But, mother, I didn't think it was wrong just not to *tell* you," and at the memory a sharp pang shot through her heart. She had frightened Thea into submission, but it was a meaningless submission. Rachel had not even submitted—or rather she had only pretended to submit out of pity.

She turned for comfort to the thought of Susan—Susan pushing aside everyone else to reach her, clinging to her, "Mother! Mother! *Mother!*" The memory was like balm, healing her pain. Susan still belonged to her—Susan and Peter and Jane. She thought of Jane running back from the forgotten errand, flinging herself into her arms. They were still hers, but for how long? Soon—cruelly soon—time would steal them from her, as it had stolen Thea and Rachel. She bent down and laid her cheek caressingly for a moment against Jane's soft curls.

Maria sat staring at the picture of Blackpool pier, but she didn't see it. She saw the face of George with his large quiff and little waxed moustache. She was thinking: I'll see him to-morrow night. We'll have a fish-and-chip supper and then go to the Hipp. Every minute makes it a bit nearer. I'll tell him all about this awful month. I wonder I've ever got out of it alive. I'll never go with them again. Why can't people have gas and water like Christians? And those awful cows looking at you so savage wherever you go. I was as near tossed as anyone could be once. It came right up to me, and I only just got away in time. I'll tell George about that, but I'll make out it was a bull. It sounds better. And that creepy churchyard where Cook said she'd seen a ghost as plain as plain moving about among the graves with white hair floating out behind. . . . Yes, she'd have some things to tell George and no mistake. She'd make out that the carrier's-cart man had been much better looking and much more attentive to her than he had really been. It didn't do to let a man think he was the only-pebble on the beach.

Bridget moved her head slightly, but did not open her eyes. Her wet cheeks were stiff and smarting. Well, it was over. She wasn't going home engaged. She wasn't going home to an atmosphere of congratulation and excitement, of rapturous preparation for her marriage. She was going home to that odd hostility that had grown up between her and her mother, to that ceaseless, futile snapping and nagging that filled all their solitary moments. She'd probably never marry now, or, if she did, she'd marry someone she disliked just to get away from mother. She summoned up the memory of Gilbert Moyle's handsome face, his brown curls and deep-set dark eyes, his well-formed smiling lips . . . but the familiar thrill failed to seize her. She saw him clearly as a sordid adventurer without even the courage to accomplish his adventures, she saw her glowing romance as a cheap flirtation. Time, she knew, would give it back its glamour, would make him again the perfect lover, would invent glib lies to account for their not having married. She would, she knew, persuade herself eventually that he had proposed and she had refused him. She would tell people about it, and they would pretend to be interested, but no one would really believe her. The moment for this, however, had not yet come. The affair lay before her—ignoble, shoddy, stripped of its trappings of romance. An utter desolation of misery possessed her, a misery without spirit of resistance, a dreary, heart-broken surrender to the ineffable futility of life.

Thea was drawing little pin men on her paper block, but she was drawing them mechanically, not thinking of what she was doing. Memories of the Holiday swam before her—some hazy and already distant, some real, vital, momentous. The episode of Elsie had already faded into unreality. It had been wrong of her not to tell mother about it, and mother had at first been cross and then forgiven her, and that was all there was to it. The most real part of all the Holiday was that new, thrilling feeling of being grown-up, that strange sensation of power that Mr. Moyle had brought to her. It wasn't really connected with him, although it was he who had roused the feeling in her. He was, as a matter of fact, rather a silly little man—it was strange how she always thought of him as a little man, though he was in actual stature quite tall—soppy and very annoying in the way he leant heavily over her to turn over the pages of her book or put his hand on her shoulder as she played. Her first admiration of him had soon turned to contempt, and yet she still thrilled to his admiration of her, still revelled in the feeling it gave her of being mature, powerful, desired. That was a secret part of her, of course, to be hidden from mother and Rachel and the others. Mother did not even guess it. Rachel had once guessed it, and it had nearly endangered their friendship. She longed to put that strange new feeling to the test again. Doreen Parker had asked her to go to tea when they returned from the Holiday, and Doreen had an elder brother who smiled admiringly at Thea when he met her in the street, and more than once had waited to come home with her from school. Thea had always felt shy and inadequate and rather frightened, but she knew now that she wouldn't feel like that any more. And she'd get Lily Beverly to tell her about—things. Nearly all other girls of her age knew, she was sure. She wasn't going to ask mother again and be told to wait till she was older.

Rachel was drawing spiders with long wriggly legs, but she too wasn't thinking of what she was drawing. The Holiday was reviewing itself before her eyes also. Southwood Farm, Mr. and Mrs. Comfort, the little girls who talked French, Lucy, Mrs. Seacome, Fauntleroy and Rosamund and Percival, Miss Caroline's "garden," Elsie. In Elsie the horror that lurked behind the pleasant life one knew had deepened, become lighter, then, at that look of disgust on mother's face, deepened again. But from it all had come a new consciousness—a consciousness of herself as a separate entity. She didn't belong to anyone else—even to mother. She belonged to herself alone. Somehow, before they came away, she had belonged to mother so completely that she had almost been part of her, but now suddenly they had become separate persons. And the new separate person she had become could look at mother dispassionately, critically, as she had done for the first time in the Dawson drawing-room. She's beautiful and kind and clever, she thought proudly, and she's my mother. She's just the sort of person I'd like to have for a friend. Perhaps one day she'll let me have her for a friend.

Her thoughts went back again over the memories of the Holiday. Far more real than the memory of the people she had met was the memory of the branches of the oak tree swaying against the sky, of sunshine falling slantwise through the beech leaves on to cushions of emerald-green moss, of cool, misty mornings with films of gossamer over lawn and hedge, of that hour after sunset when the light that had faded from the sky seemed to have entered the earth so that grass and trees shone with a strange radiance of their own through the twilight, of the deep violet sky at midnight (once she had awakened and gone to the window to watch it) spangled with stars above the sleeping trees.

These memories were real and significant. They would stay with her through the years.

Susan's eyes were still fixed on the fleeting telegraph poles. The train was quite still, and the telegraph poles were running past it, trying to catch each other. Right at the back of her mind was the memory of a bad dream that she'd had about Agnes—it was too dreadful to be real—but it was hidden away. She wasn't looking at it or thinking of it. It would creep out of its hiding-place, of course, sometimes, like other bad dreams, but just at present it was safely hidden. She was thinking of something quite different now. There was a dancing light in her eyes, an eager, triumphant smile on her lips. For she had found a fairy feast. This morning—the last morning of the Holiday, when she had almost given up hope—she'd gone into the garden very early before the others were up, and there on the trunk of the cut-down tree was the little circle of acorn cups, and between each a tiny leaf. She had run in to tell the others, and Thea had asked the gardener if he had done it, but his denial was convincing in its emphasis. He seemed indignant that anyone should suspect him of such a piece of folly. And certainly it could not have been anyone in the house. Susan, of course, had known from the first that it was a real fairies' feast. She didn't mind now if she never saw another all her life. She'd always think about it to herself, when people said that there weren't such things as fairies. She *knew* now. . . . The thought of it had wiped out the memory of the bad dream, had made the Holiday the most wonderful Holiday she had ever had in her life. She met Rachel's eyes, and Rachel smiled and looked away. There was something almost guilty in Rachel's smile, but Susan did not notice it.

Rachel had awakened early, when the garden lay cool and grey in the dawn, and, going to the window, she had seen Elsie creeping down the path to the gate of the kitchen garden, had seen her stop by the tree-trunk, arrange the little circle of acorn cups and leaves, then creep silently away. Rachel felt glad about it—she didn't quite know why—but she hadn't told anyone, not even Thea.

Ten of them, said Susan to herself, all sitting cross-legged on the tree-trunk, drinking dew out of the little acorn cups. If I'd been just a little earlier, perhaps, I'd have seen them. I think they'd only *just* gone.

Peter sat up.

"Aren't we nearly there?" he said impatiently.

"Hush, darling. Don't wake Jane," said mother, "she's asleep."

But Jane was only half asleep. The Holiday had come to an end, and everything now would be the same as before they went away. But not quite the same. She'd only been a little girl when they came away. Now she was a big girl and could do lessons, real lessons—strokes and pot-hooks. Well, she could do pot-hooks when father held her hand. She'd thought that it would be lovely doing strokes—straight and upright like soldiers—but they kept going crooked and dropping down and jumping up, and then it made you unhappy and you cried, and people said you were a baby. Nearly always things weren't as nice as you thought they were going to be.

"Manchester's the next stop," said Timothy.

All at once the Holiday became definitely a thing of the past. Even regret at its ending was over, and they were all filled with excitement at the thought of the home-coming.

Nurse would be there waiting for them. Cook would have an iced cake for tea, as she always did when they came home from the Holiday. Blackie would purr and run round them in excited little circles. People would meet them in the street tomorrow and say, "How brown you look! Have you had a nice holiday?"

It would be fun seeing people again, real people, home people.

The train slowed down.

Miriam and Maria began to bustle about, collecting bags and packages.

Bridget pretended to wake up, dabbed at her cheeks quickly with her handkerchief, and straightened her veil.

The children crowded eagerly to the window, anxious each to catch the first glimpse of the station.

Timothy rolled up his tweed cap and put on his round black clerical hat again.

The train drew to a stop.